# Catch of a Lifetime

## A CRICKET CREEK NOVEL

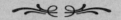

LuAnn McLane

A SIGNET ECLIPSE BOOK

SIGNET ECLIPSE
Published by New American Library, a division of
Penguin Group (USA) Inc., 375 Hudson Street,
New York, New York 10014, USA
Penguin Group (Canada), 90 Eglinton Avenue East, Suite 700, Toronto,
Ontario M4P 2Y3, Canada (a division of Pearson Penguin Canada Inc.)
Penguin Books Ltd., 80 Strand, London WC2R 0RL, England
Penguin Ireland, 25 St. Stephen's Green, Dublin 2,
Ireland (a division of Penguin Books Ltd.)
Penguin Group (Australia), 250 Camberwell Road, Camberwell, Victoria 3124,
Australia (a division of Pearson Australia Group Pty. Ltd.)
Penguin Books India Pvt. Ltd., 11 Community Centre, Panchsheel Park,
New Delhi - 110 017, India
Penguin Group (NZ), 67 Apollo Drive, Rosedale, Auckland 0632,
New Zealand (a division of Pearson New Zealand Ltd.)
Penguin Books (South Africa) (Pty.) Ltd., 24 Sturdee Avenue,
Rosebank, Johannesburg 2196, South Africa

Penguin Books Ltd., Registered Offices:
80 Strand, London WC2R 0RL, England

First published by Signet Eclipse, an imprint of New American Library,
a division of Penguin Group (USA) Inc.

First Printing, January 2012
10  9  8  7  6  5  4  3  2  1

This book is dedicated to my brothers, Bob and Jay. In all of the ups and downs in my life, your love and support has been a rock to cling to and has always been appreciated. I admire you as husbands and fathers and you both exemplify what real-life heroes are made of.

# Acknowledgments

I would like to thank Baltimore Orioles' catcher Jake Fox for showing me how tenacity and determination can lead to a professional baseball career. Following your rise to the major leagues has been an inspiration!

Thanks once again to the editorial staff at New American Library. The lovely e-mails that I receive from pleased readers are the result of a team effort and I can't thank you enough. I would like to extend a special thanks to my editor, Jesse Feldman. You have been a joy to work with and have made my writing stronger.

As always, thanks to my dear agent, Jenny Bent. In this ever-changing world of publishing, you continue to lead me in the right direction.

I would like to give a shout-out to my reader loop, VampsScampsandSpicyRomance@yahoogroups.com. Your encouragement and unending support over the years has been amazing. And a heartfelt thanks to my readers, not only for reading my stories but for the e-mails and reviews sent my way. It is my fondest wish to bring a smile to your faces and put joy in your hearts as you turn the pages of my novels.

# 1

## *Fighting Forty*

" *L* ORDY, LORDY, JESSICA ROBINSON IS FORTY!" MADISON AN-nounced in a singsong voice. "So, Mom, how does it feel to be turning the big four-oh?"

"It's just a number, Madison," Jessica answered evenly, giving her daughter a little flip of her hand for good measure. Of course, that was a big, fat lie.

"Well, you certainly don't look it. That's for sure." Madison plopped down on the sofa and patted her mother's leg.

"Thank you, sweetie." Jessica smiled but didn't look up, and continued to flip through the *Modern Bride* magazine, knowing that her eyes would give her away. Madison had an uncanny way of reading people, which was one of the reasons she was an amazing writer. Her sweet and poignant play *Just One Thing* was a smash hit at the Cricket Creek community theater last summer and had landed her a job teaching creative writing at Cooper College, a small but prestigious liberal arts school just outside of town.

"I just hope you've passed those good genes along to me," Madison added, making no mention of the father she never knew or the grandparents who were mortified when Jessica had become pregnant at sixteen. Jessica had felt so scared and so alone, but when she had shown up on Aunt Myra's doorstep in Cricket Creek, Kentucky, twenty-four years ago, her feisty, free-spirited aunt had welcomed her with open arms. When Jessica and Madison had returned last year to help with the struggling diner, they hadn't expected to stay, but, then again, Jessica's life never seemed to go as planned. "I want to be a cougar just like you."

"You can't be a cougar if you're married." Jessica flicked her daughter an amused glance. "Or at least you shouldn't be."

"A MILF, then."

"Madison!" Jessica shook her head so hard that her golden blond ponytail shook from side to side. "Wait, what is that?"

"A mother I'd like to f—"

"Okay, I get it. I swear you've got more of your outrageous aunt Myra's genes than mine!"

"That's because her outrageous genes overpowered your calm ones. Like little gene sword fights." She made swishing motions with her hand.

"You are truly crazy."

Madison lifted one shoulder and grinned. "I'm just sayin'. But really, Mom, I would never peg you as forty. You truly don't look it, but . . ." Madison swallowed and then nibbled on the inside of her lip.

Jessica inhaled a deep breath and prompted, "But what?"

"You need to get out more often."

Jessica drew her eyebrows together. "I *am* out." She sliced her hand through the air.

Madison tilted her head downward and rolled her eyes up. "Mom, coming over to my condo isn't going *out*. I mean going out . . . out."

Jessica tried not to squirm in her seat. "Madison, Monday is the only day Wine and Diner is closed. You know how demanding the restaurant business is, and the remodeling of the diner has added even more to my workload."

She didn't verbalize that the financial burden was causing sleepless nights, and, like the rest of the town, she was banking on the new baseball complex to bring in tourists' dollars. If that failed to happen, she would be sunk along with everyone else.

"Mom . . ."

"Sweetie, you know me. I like to kick back and relax during my time off."

"But—"

"Oh . . . did you see this dress?" Jessica tapped the glossy page with her fingertip in an attempt to change the subject. "I love the simple yet elegant design. Don't you?" she continued. "You should really say yes to a dress soon."

"Mom, Jason and I haven't even set a date yet."

"And you've been engaged for nearly nine months!"

Madison tilted her head and sighed. "With all of the riverfront construction going on, Jason barely has time to breathe, much less worry about a wedding. When things settle down with the new construction, we'll set a date. We're thinking next spring. But anyway, about going out . . ."

"Madison," Jessica warned in a low tone.

"Mom, it's your birthday!"

"Just another day, as far as I'm concerned, and I am so grateful that you didn't throw me one of those cheesy fortieth parties with droopy-boob gag gifts."

"You made your thoughts on the subject crystal clear." Madison leaned over and looked at the wedding dress. "But what do you say we head over to Sully's and grab a bite to eat and a martini? Celebrate just a little?" Madison held her thumb and index finger an inch apart.

Jessica scrunched up her nose. "I don't think so." She nonchalantly turned another page of the magazine, but had to swallow a stupid lump forming in her throat. Flipping through the bridal magazine reminded her of the fact that at forty, her chances of a fairy-tale wedding were getting slimmer and slimmer. She put out the vibe that she was happy as pie with her single status and treasured her independence, but lately, seeing her feisty aunt Myra blissfully in love and Madison happily engaged suddenly hit Jessica with bouts of loneliness. It sure didn't help that sexy-as-sin Ty McKenna, manager of the Cricket Creek Cougars, ate at Wine and Diner several times a week. And he didn't simply eat the food, but savored and appreciated her culinary efforts, carefully choosing the perfect wine to go with his meal. For Jessica, there wasn't a better turn-on, and she was growing way too accustomed to his visits. Ty McKenna had awakened a yearning she had thought was long gone, but she knew him from his pro-baseball days when he'd frequent Chicago Blue Bistro, where she had been head chef. She had never seen the hotshot athlete with the same woman twice. She might be physically attracted to him, but he was definitely not the type of man she should let herself get involved with. He could flirt until he turned blue in the face, but she wasn't about to let him see how it affected her.

"Earth to Mom. Are you getting hard of hearing in your old age?" Madison teased, and gave her arm a playful shove.

"What?" Jessica cupped her hand over her ear, but then mustered up a chuckle. "Sorry. I was thinking about the summer menu," she fibbed.

"Well, give yourself a break! It's your birthday!"

"So you keep reminding me."

"Because you seem to keep forgetting, old lady."

*Oh, I haven't forgotten.* "Madison, thanks so much for the lovely necklace. Nicolina Diamante makes such beautiful handmade jewelry. It was so sweet that you remembered how much I adore her creations." Jessica put the *Modern Bride* magazine on the glass coffee table and dusted her hands together. "Now, I really should get home and start working on the menu. Summer will be here before you know it," she added breezily, but it was true. She had invested so much time and money into revamping the diner and she was really starting to feel the heat. "I'm thinking about adding a mango salsa, cold corn, and black bean dip—"

"Come on, Mom!" Madison pleaded firmly, but her expression was soft and knowing. "The menu can wait until tomorrow. Let's go celebrate. You deserve it."

"Sweetie, I love my gift! And, look, I know I'm turning forty, but like I said, to me it's just another birthday. You know I don't want to make it a big deal."

Madison pressed her lips together, which was a sure sign she wasn't giving up. "Well, then, let's go out and celebrate my teaching position at Cooper. You promised we'd go out and clink glasses together, but we never did." Her chin came up in challenge.

*Damn* . . . Madison had her there.

"Besides, I'm hungry and I don't have anything in the fridge to fix."

"Imagine that." Jessica cocked one eyebrow. "You really need to learn your way around the kitchen, Madison. Jason is a small-town boy used to home-cooked meals."

"I can't believe my ultraindependent, modern mother just said that to me," Madison muttered.

"The boy's gotta eat . . . and so do you."

Madison bounced around on the sofa cushion to face her mother. "Okay, I'll make you a deal. Come with me to Sully's and I'll find some time soon to come over to the diner for some cooking lessons."

"Oh . . ." She really wasn't playing fair.

"Come on, Mom." Madison pounced on her slight wavering. "Jason is working more long hours at the baseball stadium. I'm bored. And hungry!"

Jessica rolled her eyes. "Girl, you want some cheese with that whine?" She kept her voice light, but she truly didn't want to celebrate. What she really wanted was to go home, get into her pajamas, and wallow with a bottle of merlot. The fact that this so-called milestone was hitting her hard took her by surprise! But deep down, Jessica knew the reason why.

Her birthday reminded her how many years she'd been living without any real romance in her life. It was something she thought she'd never missed, but now her heart kicked into high gear every time Tyler McKenna walked through the door of her restaurant. She wanted to box his ears for making her long for a hot kiss and strong arms wrapped around her.

"Yes! I do want some cheese. Mozzarella sticks will do nicely." With a laugh, Madison stood up and tugged on Jessica's hand. "Let's go. Pete Sully declared Monday as martini night in my honor."

Jessica gave her daughter a pointed look. "That might not be something you want to be proud of."

"But I am." In true Madison form, she gave her hips a sassy wiggle that had her blond curls brushing against her shoulders. Her blue eyes sparkled with mischief, and Jessica felt another wave of emotion wash over her as her own eyes misted. This unfortunate *mistake*—as her parents had called her teen pregnancy—had become a lovely, talented, vibrant young woman, and Jessica was abundantly proud of her daughter. Hot moisture gathered in her throat, but she swallowed hard. Tears were for the weak, and over the many years of working endless hours in the restaurant industry with temperamental men, she had developed a backbone made of steel that refused to bend beneath the constant pressure. On the toughest of long days, it had been Madison's golden curls and smiling face that had kept her from collapsing. And now her sweet baby girl was engaged to be married! She sniffed again. *Wow!* What in the world was coming over her?

Madison tilted her head to the side. "Mom, are you okay?" she asked softly.

"I'm fine," she assured her daughter with a quick, firm nod. "It's just stupid middle-aged hormones. It sucks."

"We don't have to go," Madison said uncertainly.

Jessica took a deep breath and shook her head. "No. Suddenly a cold, crisp martini sounds heavenly. And I did promise to celebrate your creative-writing position at Cooper. You know I'm so very proud of you, don't you, sweetie?"

"Yes, I do." Madison's smile wobbled at the corners, but she laughed as she tugged Jessica to her feet. "Happy birthday, Mom. I love you so much," she said, and sniffed hard. "Now, are you ready to have some fun? You do remember how, right? Look, I totally respect your dedication, but sometimes you work too damned hard."

Jessica clucked her tongue at her daughter. "For someone so petite and cute, you sure have a potty mouth. Learned it from your aunt Myra," she said with a chuckle, but Madison's teasing comment hit a little too close to home. Did she remember how to kick back and have a good time? How long had it been?

*Since Ty McKenna last summer* snuck into her brain, but she shoved it away. That magical night had scared the crap out of her. Losing her heart to a player like him would just be plain stupid.

She needed somebody solid and dependable. *What?* She didn't need anybody! She needed to concentrate on the success of Wine and Diner and not be distracted. While there was a buzz of excitement in the air, everyone in town knew what was riding on the success of the season. She was no exception.

"You didn't answer the question. Mom, are you *ready* to have some fun?"

"I'm ready!" she insisted with more conviction than she felt, and then gave Madison a quick hug.

"Okay, I'm going to freshen up just a bit," Madison announced with an excited grin.

"Oh. Am I dressed okay?" Jessica glanced down at her skinny jeans and billowy lemon yellow tunic cinched below her waist with a woven leather belt.

"Sure." Madison reached down and opened the long box containing the necklace. "Hey, why don't you put this on? It will glam you up a bit, even though we're only going to Sully's."

"Excellent idea." Jessica brushed her sleek ponytail to the side and tilted her neck forward so Madison could fasten the sterling silver and red coral strand offset by a bold turquoise pendant. "Why, thank you." While touching the smooth stone, she turned to her daughter with a smile. "What do you think?"

"Lovely, even at your ripe old age," Madison said with a wink, and then ducked out of the way of a shove. With a giggle, she gestured toward the kitchen. "Why don't you grab a glass of wine and relax on the balcony while I change out of these sweats? It's not too chilly out yet. It's been so unseasonably warm that I put the patio furniture out there already."

"I think I'll do that. I just adore the view of the river." Water always had a calming effect on her. "And it's great to see so many of the empty units in this building finally being sold or rented by the Cougar staff and baseball players. I'm sure you do a super job showing the model unit."

"Yeah, I was lucky to land that job. I love living here, so it's an easy sell. Oh, Mom, I'm so glad that Noah Falcon came back home last year to star in my play. None of this would have happened without him. The stadium is amazing, and I'm so proud of my Jason's hand in designing it. He has so much more talent than simply doing remodeling."

"Jason Craig is a fine young man, Madison. Just another reason I'm glad that we moved back to Cricket Creek."

"Me too. I miss some things about Chicago, but I truly enjoy this little town. And the baseball complex is going to be so much fun!"

"I can't believe it's almost finished. It's hard to imagine that just last year we were wondering how this little river town was going to survive the lack of tourism. Now we just need to fill the stands."

"Mom, stop worrying! Noah Falcon built it, and they will come! And eat at Wine and Diner. Positive thinking!" Madison tapped her head firmly. "The Cougars have already been practicing. Jason said that Ty and Noah should have the team picked by the end of the week." Madison cocked one eyebrow and then gave her a slow smile. "You should totally be like Annie Savoy in *Bull Durham*."

"Madison! For Pete's sake, were you watching a Kevin Costner marathon or something?"

"No . . . I'm just sayin'. There are some hot ballplayers trying out for the team."

"Yeah, and I'm old enough to be their mom. No, thank you."

"There's always Ty McKenna. You keep giving him the brush-off, but the man is so into you, it's not even funny."

"He's into my food at the diner," Jessica scoffed, and hoped her face wasn't beet red. She was not about to admit how she looked forward to seeing Ty walk through the door, or their conversations that were getting longer. "Plus, the man is an absolute player, and I'm not talking baseball."

"Then play with him."

"Madison! I can't believe the stuff that comes out of your mouth." She rolled her eyes and changed the subject. "But I'm looking forward to opening day. It really should bring much-needed tourism back to town and entertain the locals too. Cricket Creek has always loved baseball, and now we finally have a professional team," she said breezily, but Madison's comment brought a hot vision of Ty McKenna slamming into her brain. *Now,* he *sure as hell looks good for forty,* she thought with a little internal shiver. In fact, Ty could still be playing professional ball, but he had said that he wanted to quit while at the top of his game.

In spite of how she felt about his playboy shenanigans, she had to admire that he had walked away from millions to retain his integrity. Ty was one of the investors in the base-ball complex aimed at giving major-league hopefuls a sec-ond chance at the big show. Ex-pitcher and hometown hero Noah Falcon spearheaded the project, along with another silent partner. Jessica prayed it would bring back prosperity to the once-booming river town. And while business at the diner had improved since she had taken over last year, the renovations had been more extensive than Jessica had first projected. She inhaled deeply and realized that a glass of wine would hit the spot. "I'm going to head out on the bal-cony for some fresh air."

"You might see Owen laying down some mulch down by the stadium. Aunt Myra said he was going to be doing some landscaping over there today." Madison added over her shoulder, "If he looks up, give him a wave."

"Will do," Jessica said as she headed to the kitchen and uncorked a bottle of merlot. She had to smile when she thought of soft-spoken local landscaper Owen Law-son and her spunky aunt Myra falling in love. "Crazy love," she mumbled with a soft chuckle. After pouring a glass of wine, she opened the sliding door and stepped out onto the balcony overlooking the Ohio River. A cool breeze brought the musky scent of muddy water and a hint of fish, sweetened with the fresh fragrance of bud-ding trees. She closed her eyes and inhaled deeply before taking a sip of the smoky merlot. "Wow." Jessica looked over at the shiny new baseball stadium trimmed in fire-engine red and felt hope blossom in her chest. Opening day was already sold out, and season-ticket sales were go-ing strong. Local merchants were sprucing up their shops with glossy paint and stocking inventory where shelves had been bare. Spring pansies cheerfully spilled out of the planters lining Main Street. After several years of battling the sluggish economy, the sleepy little river town was rubbing its eyes and coming wide-awake. "Think positive like Madison said," she whispered. "Everything will fall into place."

Jessica leaned against the railing and smiled. When she had returned to Cricket Creek last year to help revive her aunt Myra's diner, she had fully intended to go back to Chicago. But the struggling town had gripped her heart, and instead she had sunk her life savings into the restaurant, using her culinary expertise to update down-home dishes and add modern flair. When they finally got their liquor license, Madison had laughingly called it Wine and Diner, and the new name had stuck. But no matter how amazing the food or how inventive the menu, they still needed customers in the seats, and locals weren't enough. Jessica inhaled another deep breath and tried to push the constant worry from her mind. Positive thinking wasn't always easy, but Madison was right about one thing: She needed to kick back and have some fun. Maybe it would ease her stress level back out of the red zone.

Jessica took another sip of wine and wondered what was taking Madison so long, but just when she turned to go inside, she spotted Ty McKenna walking out of the side door of the stadium. She watched his long, purposeful stride toward his Audi TT convertible. His hand was to his ear, so she guessed he must be talking on the phone, and unless he looked up, she could watch him unnoticed. Jessica had been floored when the superstar former center fielder had decided to settle down and manage the Cricket Creek Cougars, but she wondered how long it would be before the bright lights, big city called him back to party. Jessica supposed Ty was simply protecting his investment, but she doubted that he would last long in a small town. She watched him open the door of his sleek silver convertible, but he paused to laugh instead of folding his long frame into the small car. The rich sound of his sexy voice drifted upward and held her rooted to the spot.

Jessica sighed once more. The man was eleven floors down and across a parking lot and still managed to make her heart beat faster. "Damn him!" she whispered.

And just like that, he looked up.

# 2

## Dream On

THE BUILDING WAS FIFTEEN STORIES HIGH AND FIVE BAL-
conies across, and yet when Ty raised his gaze, he
immediately zoned in on the corner condo where Jessica
Robinson was standing. Even at this distance, he knew it
was the hot little chef who had been keeping him up at
night—unfortunately, only in his dreams and not in the
soft, silky flesh. The setting sun glinted off of her golden
hair, and in his imagination he could smell the subtle scent
of her vanilla and lily-of-the-valley perfume. He knew
what it was because he had asked her one night at the
restaurant. While she had answered in a clipped tone, the
blush in her cheeks had told Ty a different story. She wasn't
as immune to him as she pretended. He swallowed, unable to tear his gaze from where she stood, and the conversation he was having with Noah Falcon faded into the
background.

Jessica made no movement to acknowledge him. Ty
knew that although she might seem to be gazing out over
the river, she saw him standing there. He could feel it. He
thought about waving, but for some reason that felt dorky.
*Should I give her a little salute?* God, no, that was even
dorkier! *Incline my head?* Ty ground his teeth together,

gripped the phone tighter, and simply stood there, feeling like a love-struck fool.

"Ty? Hey, man, are you there?" Noah asked.

"Yeah," he answered absently. No other woman had ever gotten to him the way Jessica Robinson did. He tried to convince himself that it was all about the chase, but he knew better.

*Everything* about her sucked him right in.

For a moment he thought she waved to him, but he realized that she was lifting a glass to her lips. God . . . the thought of her lush mouth made his breath catch, but try as he might, she continued to keep him at arm's length. The only conversation he could get her to engage in was about cooking. Luckily, he was a total foodie, which was one of the reasons he had frequented Chicago Blue Bistro. Jessica's menu was inventive and delicious but without the pretence of chefs who went overboard with presentation at the expense of substance. He loved what she was doing with Wine and Diner and was truly fascinated with the process, but Ty knew that Jessica thought he was simply trying to get in her pants. He couldn't blame her. He had built quite a reputation for himself during his major-league days, and he had his reasons for keeping up that persona, even though now it was coming back to bite him in the ass. He wasn't exactly what he seemed, but he wondered if he could ever convince Jessica otherwise.

"Are you going to answer my question?" Noah's voice at the other end of the line again brought Ty out of his trance. "Dude, did you fall asleep on me?"

"Sorry." Ty dropped his gaze and turned away from the high-rise. "I was distracted. What did you ask?"

"I wondered what you thought of that young pitcher, Logan Lannigan."

Ty shrugged. "He used to throw some real heat, but an elbow injury screwed him up."

"He was probably overworked as a kid growing up,"

Noah grumbled. "My dad was careful not to let that happen to me. I hate when coaches and even parents care more about winning than the health of the kids. Pisses me the hell off."

"Oh, I know." Ty nodded in agreement and thought of his own overbearing father. "Damn, I hear ya on that one. I've seen it all too often myself. Lannigan is working on an effective slider and cutter so he doesn't have to rely on smokin' a fastball past the batter. If he can do that, he'll be a real asset and perhaps be able to claw his way back into the minor leagues, maybe as a middle reliever at first rather than a starter. But I want to make sure his arm is ready. He came back too soon from his Tommy John surgery."

"Do you think he's a bit of a head case?" Noah wanted to know.

"Oh yeah. Lannigan thinks he's God's gift to baseball and that playing for this league is beneath him, but it's his only chance to prove he's still got game, and he damned well knows it."

"So you're on board with adding him to the roster?"

Ty nodded again. "Yeah, I figured you could whip his ass into shape. Show him how to throw some breaking stuff. Throw with his head and not just his arm."

"All right, so we're on the same page. And, Ty. Look, I know you're all about that crazy catcher Tate Boone, but we've got to talk about that one."

"He's a bit of a nut job," Ty agreed with the lift of one shoulder. "But the kid has some talent. I think we should give him a shot."

"Okay . . . but he has to calm it down a bit."

Ty laughed. "You sure about that? He could be a real crowd pleaser. And local boy Reed Wilson is a helluva short-stop."

"Ty, come on. The boy can't hit in the clutch. And he's too damned small."

"I know he chokes, but we can work with that," Ty assured Noah. "Everyone told me I was too small, and I worked my ever-lovin' ass off to prove myself."

"Yeah, but you grew six inches after high school. Most kids don't."

"I want him on the team," Ty answered firmly. "Hustle goes a long way with me. He'll have plenty of local backing and keep asses in the seats." Plus, Reed reminded Ty of himself as a young player, and he wanted to give the kid a fair shot.

Noah sighed at the other end of the line. "Okay, I'll respect your judgment on this one. Hey, by the way, are you going over to Sully's for Jessica's surprise fortieth-birthday bash? I just got a call from Madison, and she finally got her stubborn mother to head on over there. Evidently, it took some doing."

*Imagine that,* Ty thought, but then frowned. "I didn't know anything about it." He felt a bit put out that he hadn't been invited. Of course, the way Jessica constantly pushed him away, he supposed he shouldn't be surprised. Even Noah had no idea how much he was into Jessica. He found his thoughts drifting to her throughout the day. And she could deny it all she wanted, but whenever they were in the same room, you could cut the sexual tension with a knife.

"Well, listen, man. I've got to get over to Sully's now to be there for the surprise, or Olivia will have my ass in a sling."

"You are so whipped," Ty commented with a low chuckle; in fact, the schoolteacher was a total sweetheart and he liked her a lot.

"Yeah, I am and I love it," Noah acknowledged without hesitation. "It makes me happy just to see Olivia smile."

"Dude, you've got to hand over your man card with that sappy statement. Come on . . . *really*? 'I just want to see her smile,'" Ty chided in a falsetto, but Noah simply laughed.

"Quit giving me a hard time."

"Where's the fun in that?"

"Right," Noah scoffed. "Karma is gonna get ya. You're gonna fall so damned hard, and I'm gonna laugh my fool ass off when you do."

"Ain't gonna happen," Ty said, but had to use extreme willpower not to glance back up at the balcony.

"Whatever. But seriously, you should come on over to the party. I'm surprised that Olivia hasn't told you about it. She still has it in her head that you and Jessica would make a cute couple."

"She tried that last summer, remember? Didn't work." Except for a hot kiss that haunted Ty still.

"Olivia's not one to give up easily. Come on over."

"I might pop in for a little while," Ty replied in a non-committal tone, but knew he wouldn't pass up the chance to get up close and personal with Jessica. He just might have to give the birthday girl another kiss. "Catch ya later." After ending the call, he couldn't help himself and glanced up at the balcony.

She was gone.

Ty raked his fingers through his damp hair. He'd showered in the locker room when tryouts ended and had been wondering what to do with his free evening. Now he knew, but he glanced down at his outfit and grimaced. The faded Lucky jeans were his favorite pair, but he didn't want to show up in a weathered T-shirt, and yet didn't feel like going all the way over to the extended-stay hotel to change. Ty was so glad that he was going to move into a condo in the high-rise as soon as the unit he chose was freshly painted. Walking to work was going to be damned sweet, and he loved the river view. In fact, he was seriously considering buying a boat.

Ty inhaled a deep breath and shook his head. When presented with the offer to invest in the stadium and to manage the Cougars, he had been worried that he would go stir-crazy here in Small Town, USA, but Cricket Creek, Kentucky, was already growing on him. In truth, he couldn't remember being this relaxed on a day-to-day basis. Time moved slower here. People waved and shouted greetings like "Hey, y'all" or "How y'all doin'?" And Ty had learned that the correct response was "Doin' all right."

Ty grinned and then shook his head slowly. Who would have thought he'd be worrying about what to wear to a fortieth birthday party in a honky-tonk bar? With a snap of his fingers, he remembered that he had a clean, light blue striped polo in his duffel bag. "There's my answer," he mumbled, and popped open his trunk. A minute later, he tugged his T-shirt over his head and located the polo. It was a little bit wrinkled, but he shook it out and was about to pull it on when he heard the soft, husky voice of Jessica Robinson close by.

"Let's just walk, Madison. It's such a lovely night."

"I agree," Madison answered, and then said, "Look, there's Ty McKenna. Let's go say hello."

When Ty didn't hear Jessica respond, he knew she was going to try to scoot across the street without speaking to him, so he turned around and waved. "Hey there, ladies." He felt a bit silly standing with his shirt dangling from his fingertips, but when Jessica's eyes widened a fraction, he tightened his ab muscles. He exercised nearly every day, but eating Jessica's food made it harder to keep his weight down, so he had been working out more intensely in the weight room and had bulked up with more muscle than he normally had. "Where y'all heading to?" he asked innocently, and glanced in question at Jessica.

"Y'all?" Jessica gave him a cool arch of one eyebrow. "Really?"

"Mom!" Madison said, and shot her mother a frown. "Sorry. She's hormonal," Madison added in a stage whisper.

"Madison!" Jessica sputtered, and pressed her lips together. "I simply didn't like him poking fun at the Southern way of speaking here."

"I wouldn't do that," Ty quietly assured her, and meant

it. He wondered why she had such a burr up her butt where he was concerned, and right then and there, he made a pact with himself to steal a hot kiss from the cool-as-a-cucumber birthday girl. He vowed that he'd have her melting faster than the candles on her cake. Then he took his sweet time tugging the shirt over his head, giving her an extended view of his bare chest.

"Nice abs," Jessica surprised him by saying. But before he could decide whether or not to thank her or if she was poking fun at his attempt to show off, she turned on her heel. "Come on, Madison. That martini is calling my name."

"*Y'all* going to Sully's?" Ty called after them.

"Yes," Madison answered when her mother kept on walking. "It's her—," she began but was given a shot to the ribs in warning.

"First martini is on me," Ty shouted.

"Okay, but you might want to turn your shirt around first," Jessica tossed over her shoulder without breaking stride.

Ty looked down and grinned. Damned if it wasn't on backward. So much for being a stud muffin. More like a dork muffin with sprinkles on top. "I just wanted to see if you were paying attention," he called after them, and when Jessica's shoulders shook up and down, he smiled. Laughter . . . It was a start. "Guess you were!" he added, and then shook his head while he turned his shirt around. He wished he were sitting in Sully's, waiting for her to be surprised, but then frowned. He just bet that Jessica wanted no part of this birthday-bash business, and was hit with an unexpected longing to be at her side, holding her hand so he could give her a reassuring squeeze. Jessica Robinson put on a tough-girl act, but there was a vulnerable quality in her expressive amber eyes that brought out a protective side Ty didn't even know he had. He might go to Wine and Diner several times a week to sample the amazing menu, but, to be honest, there was much more to it than that. Jessica was an intelligent, vibrant woman, and lately their conversations had broadened from talking about food and baseball to a variety of other subjects. He often stayed long after his meal was over and could usually entice her to join him for coffee. On top of that, he found her sexy as hell. All he needed to do was get her to let her guard down.

"Damn . . ." Ty shut the trunk of his car and then leaned against the back fender. He crossed his arms over his chest and tried to make some sense of the situation as he watched mother and daughter walk away. He could see Madison's hands waving while she talked, and wished he knew what she was saying to her mother. Jessica's head shook, making her sleek ponytail swing back and forth, and Ty suddenly wondered what her deep golden blond hair would look like loose and falling in soft waves past her shoulders. He imagined the silky texture brushing against his bare skin, and groaned.

Ty was no stranger to lust and knew his way around a woman's body, but usually as soon as he felt any warm and fuzzy feelings, he'd run like the hounds of hell were after him. Ty inhaled a deep breath and stared down at his Nikes. It wasn't that he was a womanizing jerk, like Jessica surely thought, but he ran because of baseball. His pro-baseball father had repeatedly cheated on his mother throughout his major-league career, turning her into a sad little shell of a woman until she finally wised up and left his sorry ass, taking half of everything, including his sizable MLB retirement. And while there were some really good guys in baseball, Ty had seen so many cheat while on the road, somehow thinking it was their right or was even expected of them as a professional ballplayer. Ty ground his teeth together just thinking about it. Like it came with the territory and was somehow part of the contract.

After blowing out a sigh, Ty kicked a rock across the

parking lot. His mother might have finally escaped, but all the money in the world couldn't make up for years of misery, and he had made a personal vow never to do that to a woman . . . and the simplest way was to never get attached or fall in love.

Of course, Ty realized that the women who threw themselves at pro athletes were to blame as well, and he had no problem with a hit-it-and-quit-it mentality with chicks who were in it for the thrill and nothing more. That being said, Ty had chosen his bed partners carefully, and more often than not, the eye candy on his arm never landed between his sheets.

Ty drew in another breath of spring-scented air and shoved his hands in his pockets. He hadn't really cared much about his player reputation until he saw the wary mistrust in the amber eyes of Jessica Robinson. He was drawn to the woman in ways he couldn't even explain, and his casual questions about her to Noah had gotten at least a few answers. She had come to her aunt Myra's diner sixteen and pregnant, and had raised young Madison in Cricket Creek before going off to culinary school and settling down in Chicago. Noah had said that Jessica had never been married and was dedicated to her daughter and her career, but apparently was back here to take over the diner. Ty understood and respected all of that, but she was a beautiful, vibrant, talented woman and deserved so much more.

Ty scuffed his shoe against the concrete and then watched the sky turn orange and purple over the Ohio River. He had sunk some serious money into the baseball complex, but instead of feeling anxious about the investment, he felt good. This was a solid little town with good-hearted people. The kids trying out for the Cougars had been overlooked or let go from minor-league teams and were getting a second chance to fulfill their dreams. For the first time in a long while, Ty felt a sense of purpose, and he smiled.

Life was good. . . . Now all he needed to make his night complete was a long, hot kiss from the birthday girl. With that in mind, he slipped behind the wheel of his car and headed over to Sully's Tavern.

# 3

## *Surprise!*

"*M*OM, MAY I GIVE YOU SOME ADVICE?" MADISON ASKED while they waited at the curb for the light to turn green.

"Do I have a choice?"

Madison grinned. "No."

Jessica angled her head at her daughter and wished she already had that martini in her hand. "Shoot."

"Have some fun with Ty McKenna."

"What?" Jessica hoped she wasn't blushing.

"Mom, the man is hotter than a firecracker. Funny. Sexy as sin, and, *hello*? He's totally into you. Have some fun. Flirt." Madison leaned closer and whispered, "Kiss him. . . ."

"Ma-di-son!"

"What?" Madison raised her palms skyward. "He's single; you're single. He's interested. What's holding you back?"

"I told you, he is a notorious player."

"So was Noah Falcon, and he and Olivia are happy as clams," Madison insisted.

"I never did understand that saying. Why are clams considered to be happy?"

"The saying came from John G. Saxe in his 'Sonnet to a

Clam.' The full phrase is 'happy as a clam in high water,' since it can't be found by predators then. Mom, why are you shaking your head?"

"First, because someone wrote a sonnet to a clam. And second, because you knew the answer."

Madison shrugged. "I am full of useless knowledge, unless, of course, I'm ever on *Cash Cab*."

"Maybe someday you will be."

"Yeah, but with my luck, I'll be with Aunt Myra. She'll answer before I get the chance to open my mouth and get the answers all wrong, but then argue with Ben Bailey and get us kicked out before we even reach our destination. Hey, did anybody ever tell you that you are queen of changing the subject?"

"Yeah, you."

"It's true. Mom, listen. Ty McKenna's glory days are over. And, like Olivia, you are a woman of substance. Maybe you're just what Ty McKenna needs. Did you ever think of that?"

"I don't think of Tyler McKenna at *all*," she insisted, and added a prim little sniff. *Liar, liar, pants on fire.*

"No, your pants are not on fire."

"It's really creepy when you read my mind," Jessica said with a slight grin. They started walking across the street. "Okay, I'll admit that the man is . . . sexy." What she wouldn't admit was that it had been so long since she had even had a date that Jessica was simply scared. Her teen pregnancy had taken her out of the dating pool early on. Culinary school and then long days at Chicago Blue Bistro had left her little time for a social life, so she had never really mastered the art of flirting. She was so confident in other areas of her life, but not when it came to men. And sex? Dear God, it had been *years*. Ty McKenna was used to beautiful, chic women who knew their way around a bedroom. Jessica shook her head. She would be laughable.

"Come on, stop shaking your head. You need to go for it. You're not getting any younger."

"Gee, thanks." She shook her head. "I can't believe we're having this conversation."

Madison stopped and pulled her to the side just before they arrived at Sully's. "We're not your typical mother and daughter. We're like the Gilmore Girls."

Jessica had to chuckle. "Yeah, but you're more like crazy Lorelai, and I'm sensible Rory."

"Mmmm, true. But there was that season when Rory cut loose. Maybe this should be your season to do that."

"Madison, I have Wine and Diner to run."

"Yeah, but it doesn't have to consume your life. You deserve more," Madison replied. "Plus, my matchmaker radar says you two would make a great couple." She crooked her index fingers at the top of her head like antennae. "I've seen the way you look at him when he walks into the diner. You love it when he comes in to eat. Admit it."

"Oh, you and Olivia with your matchmaking schemes!" she scoffed, admitting nothing.

"Hey, she hooked up Jason and me, and I got Olivia and Noah together. And just look at Aunt Myra and Olivia's father, Owen. No one could have seen that coming, but quiet Owen is the perfect man for our crazy aunt. Mom, it is your turn!"

"Oh, Madison, you tried last summer when Ty came into town and we chaperoned the Cricket Creek prom. Remember? It was . . . awkward," she said, even though it wasn't really true. The night had been fun. And that kiss . . .

"You kept needling him!"

Jessica rolled her eyes. "He totally deserved it. The man is so full of himself."

"Well, maybe you're just the chickie to take him down a notch. Ever think of that? Huh?"

Jessica groaned, but a tiny voice in the back of her mind

wondered if there was something to what Madison was saying.

"I just want to see you happy."

Jessica put her hands on her daughter's shoulders. "Sweetie, I am happy." Wasn't she? Of course she was! *Okay, maybe. Well, sort of . . .*

"Oh, Mom." Madison paused and put her palm over her mouth, sniffed, and then said, "You've worked so hard and given up so much for me. . . ."

Jessica's eyes filled with hot moisture. "Madison, I love you more than anything in this world. I wouldn't change a thing." She squeezed her daughter's arms and looked her in the eye. "Not *one* thing," she repeated firmly. "You got that?"

"Got it." Madison nodded hard, and then they hugged.

"Now let's go get that drink," Jessica said gruffly. She stepped back and linked her arm through Madison's.

"Let's do it!"

A moment later, Jessica pushed open the big wooden door to Sully's. It was dark. Weird . . . She was met with a still silence for a second, followed by the lights turning on and a huge "Surprise!"

"Ohmigod!" Jessica put her hands on her cheeks while her heart pounded like a jackhammer. The tavern was packed. Colorful balloons bobbed in the breeze of the paddle fans, and streamers twisted across the ceiling. A big HAPPY BIRTHDAY banner was strung from one end of the bar to the other. Everyone clapped, whistled, and cheered like crazy. When Madison pulled her in for a huge hug, Jessica said, "I'm so gonna get you for this." Then she added, "It's a good thing I love you so much."

"It was out of my hands, Mom. The entire town was in on the plans. I'm not the only one who loves and appreciates you."

"Stop or I'm gonna cry!" Jessica pleaded in her ear.

"You're allowed to cry," Madison said with her usual uncanny insight.

"I know!" she answered in a shaky voice. But she rarely did. Crying meant giving power to the people she had trusted the most and who had cut her to the core. Crying meant giving in to weakness when you had to be strong. When the pregnancy test had come back positive, she had curled into a tight ball of sorrow on the cold, hard tile of her bathroom floor and had cried until tears would no longer fall. But when her parents had failed to come to her side, she wiped her eyes. And since that day, she almost never gave in to tears. She would not cry!

Okay, maybe she would.

Jessica pulled away and almost had her emotions under control when she spotted Aunt Myra and Owen sitting on tall stools up at the bar. Her beloved aunt had her arm linked through Owen's and was swiping at her eyes with the back of her other hand. Jessica gave them a trembling smile and a wave, and when Owen leaned in and placed a tender kiss on Aunt Myra's forehead, Jessica had to forcibly swallow hot tears gathering in her throat. Soft-spoken Owen and her outspoken aunt made an unlikely pair, but were so in love that it made Jessica's heart swell with pure joy.

"Love can find you at any age," her aunt had recently said to Jessica, and had given her a meaningful look that she knew was meant to give her hope, but had only made her sad. As a child, Jessica had loved fairy tales and happy endings . . . but she had given up on finding her own Prince Charming a long time ago.

"Aunt Myra has been planning this for weeks," Madison whispered in her ear.

Jessica narrowed her eyes. "So that's what you two have been whispering about! I thought she had been telling you more of her dirty jokes! I'll have to get her back good too," Jessica added, and then shook her head accusingly at her aunt, who raised her palms upward innocently, causing the crowd to laugh. The three of them had tackled life together, Aunt Myra with her hardworking ethics and bawdy humor, Madison with the innocence of a child but old-soul insight. They were a team, and although Jessica was so thrilled that her aunt and daughter had found love, she was feeling somewhat lost without them, and no amount of work seemed to ease her loneliness.

But even though she was trembling with nerves and emotion, seeing the room filled with smiling faces on her behalf touched Jessica's heart. Now, more than ever, she was glad she had made the decision to return to Cricket Creek.

Bar owner Pete Sully, who could be a stand-in for Charlie Daniels, came lumbering forward and thrust an ice-cold longneck into Jessica's hand before giving one to Madison. "Happy birthday," he said gruffly, and then turned and raised his own brown bottle in the air. "A holler and a swaller for our birthday girl, Jessica Robinson!"

Beer bottles shot upward, followed by a loud, "Yee-haw!" and then a collective tilt up to the lips. Jessica joined in and took a long pull from her cold beer. It felt so good to toss back her head and laugh, and when she turned to Madison and tapped her bottle against her daughter's, there was happiness shining in the depths of Madison's blue eyes. While her life hadn't been easy, Jessica had been truthful when she told Madison that she wouldn't change a thing. But that didn't ease the hurt of her parents disowning her and ignoring the existence of their only granddaughter. Jessica smiled to the crowd and wished she had parents sitting there beaming back at her, but her father had been an angry, judgmental man who had been forced to marry the waitress he had gotten pregnant. He had broken her mother's gentle spirit, and Jessica despised him for it. When William Robinson had found out that Jessica was pregnant, he had darkly announced that the apple didn't fall far from the tree and that his daughter was no better than white trash. Jessica had always found his uppity outlook on life odd, since he had come from poverty and had built his fortune from the ground up.

And so Jessica had packed her bags and left, never to return to the big, pillared house on the hill that was so full of beautiful furniture and ugly memories, and she hadn't spoken to them since. Once in a while, Jessica would catch a whiff of Chanel No. 5 and she would look up, hoping her mother had finally come to see her and Madison. After a while she had given up hope, but to this day, the aching hurt remained.

"I want to propose a toast!" Madison announced over the noise of the crowd, and then waited for silence. She swallowed, glanced at Jessica, and said, "Actually, two toasts . . . so y'all stay with me on this, even if I start to choke up. Okay, first I want to salute my mother, who is the most amazing woman on the planet. She is selfless, hard-working, talented, and beautiful from the inside out." Madison blinked rapidly and continued. "I am good with words, but I could never, *ever* find the ones to express how proud of you I am. Happy birthday, Mom. I love you."

Madison turned and hugged Jessica while cheers and whistles thundered in the background. After taking a swig of her beer, Madison held up her hand. "My second toast is to Cricket Creek, Kentucky. Times might still be tough, but we decided to thumb our noses at the economy and build a baseball stadium instead! Thank you, Noah Falcon, for coming home and making it happen. I already have season tickets! And, Jason, I promise to learn the right time to shout, 'Good eye!'" After the laughter died down, Madison said, "Noah, stand up and take a bow. Olivia Lawson, you too. We all know the real reason Noah built the stadium was to impress you. Right, Noah?"

Jessica laughed when Noah stood up and put his arm around Olivia Lawson, the sweet drama teacher whom he had starred with in Madison's play last summer. When Noah tilted his handsome head sideways and nodded his agreement, the crowd burst into laughter, followed by applause. Noah tipped his Cougars baseball cap and then said, "There's a box of hats over by the birthday cake. Make sure you get one, and if we run out, I have more in the trunk of my car."

Madison nodded and then held up her hand for silence again. "Okay, one more announcement before the music starts. I said no presents, because I knew Mom would get ticked if y'all wasted money on droopy-boob gag gifts, but you can make a donation to the Beautification of Cricket Creek fund instead. The money will go toward flowers and seasonal decorations on Main Street and in the city park. And speaking of cake—the lovely confection was baked and donated by Mabel Grammar from her amazing bakery, the other reason that Noah Falcon stayed in Cricket Creek," she added with a wink. "And she will be making my wedding cake, unless Jason rethinks his decision to marry me."

"Never, baby!" Jason shouted, and the crowd roared their approval.

"Okay, I really will shut up now," Madison promised. "Oh, one more thing . . ." She paused and then shouted, "Just dance!" She pointed to the DJ, and the Lady Gaga song of the same name started thumping through the speakers. Madison grabbed Jessica's hand and tugged her onto the dance floor. Jessica laughed as she tried to keep up with Madison's robotlike dance moves.

Jessica crooked her finger for Aunt Myra and Owen to join them. Owen shyly shook his head, but her aunt sashayed up to the dance floor, grabbing Olivia along the way. The four of them danced in a circle, bumping hips and laughing like crazy. Jessica observed that Olivia, Madison, and Aunt Myra seemed to glow with happiness, and she wondered what it felt like to be so in love that it showed physically.

At the end of "Just Dance," they left the dance floor and picked up their longnecks for a much-needed swig. But when "It's Raining Men" started playing, Aunt Myra laughed. "We have to dance to this! Come on, girls!" she shouted over the music.

"You're right, Aunt Myra!" Madison clinked her bottle to her aunt's. "Let's go!"

After another swig, they thumped their bottles down in agreement before dancing and singing their way back onto the dance floor.

"It's raining men!" Jessica did a little spin while raising her hands in the air, and shouted, "Hallelujah," at the exact moment when Ty McKenna walked through the front door not more than fifteen feet away.

"I had hoped for that very reaction from you," he quipped with a grin, and although Jessica pretended to get all huffy, her aunt Myra had the nerve to laugh. "I guess my prayers were answered," he said as he took long strides toward her. "Or maybe yours were," he added when he was closer to her ear.

"You need to get over yourself," Jessica retorted, but as always, a little thrill shot down her spine at the mere sight of him. His warm breath tickled her skin, and her wildly beating heart had little to do with the dancing.

"It's you I can't get over," he said so that only she could hear. Jessica opened her mouth to give him a sassy comeback, but the smile on his face seemed sincere, and her sharp words died in her throat. She sternly reminded herself that he was a flirting machine, but the flutter in her stomach refused to go away. "Ladies, may I steal the birthday girl for a few minutes? Seems to me that I owe her a martini."

Ty gave them a dimpled grin that no woman could refuse, causing them to nod mutely, except for Aunt Myra, who said, "Whatcha owe her is a long, hot kiss."

"Aunt Myra!" Jessica sputtered.

"I'm just sayin'." Aunt Myra flipped her long braid over her shoulder, causing the multiple bracelets on her wrists to jingle. In her midfifties, she remained a free-spirited hippie with a sweet Southern flair, but was always outspoken and truly loved to raise eyebrows. Down-to-earth Owen was in for quite an adventure, but he appeared to be loving every minute of it.

Ty winked at Aunt Myra. "I was thinking the same thing."

Jessica glanced at him to see if he was serious or being flippant, and for the life of her, she couldn't decide, so she looked to Olivia and Madison for help. Olivia mouthed *Go!* and widened her eyes in an are-you-crazy way that almost made Jessica laugh. Madison, like her aunt, was much less subtle, and made visible shooing motions with her hands. "I—I should mingle," Jessica protested, but in truth she was not a good mingling person. But then again, she was clueless at flirting. *Damn!*

Ty crooked his arm in invitation. "I like to mingle. Let's get that martini and mingle together. What do you say?"

"I seem to remember that you can work a room," she replied darkly, and reminded herself that he was a womanizer and she shouldn't fall for his abundant charms. She was thinking of how to politely back away when he reached out and tucked her arm through his. The warmth of his smooth skin made her fingers tingle, and the steely, hard bulge of his biceps made her want to squeeze the muscle and sigh with feminine appreciation. He smelled divine too . . . clean with a hint of something expensive and masculine.

"Relax, Jessica," Ty said in that low and soothing voice that made her want to lean against him and purr. But instead she held on with a light touch and tried to appear cool, calm, and collected, even though she was none of those things.

Friends smiled, waved, and gave her high fives as she headed to the bar. She wouldn't lie. It felt great to be on the arm of a sexy, handsome man. *Not too shabby for a fortieth birthday,* she thought and told herself to relax like Ty had suggested and simply have a good time. *Really, what harm is there in that?*

When Pete Sully spotted her, he slapped his dish towel over his thick shoulder and hurried over to her side of the bar as fast as a guy his size could manage. "What can I get for you, sugar?"

"I'll have a Kentucky Bourbon Barrel Ale," Ty answered with a grin.

"You ain't anywhere near sweet enough to be called sugar, Mr. Triple Threat," Pete said in his sandpaper-rough voice, but then reached over and shook Ty's hand. "I was talkin' to the beautiful birthday girl. Sugar, another beer or anything you want is on the house."

"Thank you, Pete," Jessica replied, and then looked at Ty with surprise. "You know about Bourbon Barrel Ale? It's a favorite of Kentuckians, but only well-known throughout the Commonwealth. Kentucky Ale, Kentucky Light, and Bourbon Barrel are considered the triple crown of beer around these parts. I'm going to serve it on tap at Wine and Diner. Pete, instead of a martini, I'll have the same."

Pete nodded. "Excellent choice, if I must say so myself. Kentucky Ale just took the silver medal in the World Cup of beers, I'll have you know."

"It sure deserves it," Jessica agreed.

Pete gave her a wink. "Beautiful and knows her bourbon and her beer." He gave Ty a look that said he'd better be a gentleman, before turning to fill their order.

Ty arched a dark eyebrow. "Apparently, Pete thinks he's your bodyguard."

Jessica shrugged one shoulder. "It can get a bit rowdy around here on any given night. But he looks out for Madison and me."

"Good for him."

"Not that I can't take care of myself," she felt the need

to add, along with a lift of her chin that she hoped conveyed that she did not need a man for protection or anything else, for that matter. So what if he smelled divine and she really wanted to touch the golden skin exposed by the three open buttons of his shirt? The image of him bare-chested slid into her brain, and she physically shook her head, making her ponytail flip back and forth. It landed playfully over her shoulder, and she hoped it was a flirty move. She reached up and touched the whippy ends, adding to the flirt factor, but then felt silly and folded her hands on the edge of the bar. "So, you like the Kentucky Ale, huh?" *So much for flirting . . .*

Ty nodded, and she envied how at ease he seemed. Did the man ever get intimidated by anything? "Noah turned me onto it a few weeks ago when we were debating what beers to have on tap at the stadium. I understand it's a microbrewery out of Lexington, but is really becoming popular."

"You're right," Jessica said. "It's being marketed in some grocery and liquor stores and is popular at festivals and events. Many high-end restaurants now carry it on tap. It's my plan to use as many Kentucky products and recipes as possible and showcase them on my menu."

"Sounds like a great idea." He nodded, but Jessica wondered if he was merely being polite. "Both tourists and locals should get a kick out of that."

"I'll include the history," she added, and then trailed off, thinking she was going to put him to sleep any minute now. Thank goodness their drinks arrived so she could quit babbling on and on! And yet when Pete placed the snifters in front of them, she thanked him, turned to Ty, and said, "Snifters are the only real way to serve Kentucky Bourbon Barrel. The narrow opening concentrates the aromas and the seductive nose of a smooth, aged bourbon. The glass also adds to the elegance, reminding you that this is a sipping beer much higher in alcohol content. I bought several dozen for the diner." *Babble,* Jessica thought with an inward groan, and then glanced away while she took a sip. She searched her brain for something else to talk about other than something Wine and Diner–related and came up empty. In a bit of a panic, she looked around for Madison and Olivia, but they were back on the dance floor, dancing to "I Will Survive." Aunt Myra was in the middle of the circle, shaking it like a saltshaker and singing every single word at the top of her lungs. Noah, Owen, and Jason were at a nearby table, probably chatting about baseball, and were too engrossed in the conversation to allow her to catch their eyes.

"You can taste the subtle flavor of vanilla and oak from aging in the charred barrels," Ty surprised her by commenting. "This could actually pass for an after-dinner drink," he added with an appreciative nod

"I've thought the same thing."

"Why are you looking at me with such wide eyes?" he asked with a tilt of his head. "You should know by now that I appreciate excellent food and drink." When he lifted his snifter to his lips, Jessica marveled at his long, masculine fingers cradling the delicate glass, and for some reason found it incredibly sexy. She had the sudden urge to slide her hand up the corded muscle of his forearm to the biceps that strained against the short sleeve of his shirt, but then frowned, thinking that the ale must be going straight to her head.

"I suppose that's why you eat at Wine and Diner several times a week," she commented with a slight smile.

"Not the only reason," he answered slowly, making her heart beat faster.

"You are one smooth operator," she teased with Bourbon Barrel boldness, and would have put her hand on his arm, but his smile faltered and he glanced away.

"You think so, huh?"

"I know so. I've seen you in action."

Jessica expected a comeback, but after a moment of silence, he took a sip of his drink and then said, "Hey, I think I'll head over and talk some baseball with Noah. I shouldn't keep you from your guests anyway." He pushed away from the bar.

"Okay," she said, and then swallowed another sip of her drink, thinking she truly sucked at the whole flirting thing. Had she offended him? "I should mingle," she said with a nod that was more enthusiastic than she felt, and glanced down at her snifter.

"Save a dance for me later?" he asked.

Jessica looked up in confusion, but nodded and forced a smile. "I'm certain that Madison has a full playlist of dance music." She lifted her snifter. "After I finish this, I'm sure I'll be busting a move. Just don't let me break-dance. Please?"

"I promise," he said, and Jessica held her breath when he seemed about to say something else. But he picked up his drink and turned away.

Jessica wanted to grab his arm and demand to know what she'd said that bothered him, but maybe he had simply lost interest in her ramblings about beer and wanted to talk baseball instead. She sighed, thinking that she was pretty damned dull at the ripe old age of forty. Maybe she deserved some droopy-boob gifts and reading glasses, after all. She looked over at the dance floor, considering joining Madison and company, but just when she took a step away from the bar, a low, masculine voice stopped her in her tracks.

"Please don't tell me you're leaving."

Jessica turned around and looked into amazing sky-blue eyes and one eyebrow raised in question. He tilted a beer bottle up to a full, sexy mouth made for sin and then gave Jessica a slow grin that made her swallow hard. With shaggy, blond, streaky hair and a tan you wanted to touch, Mr. Blue Eyes looked like he should have just walked off a California beach with a surfboard tucked beneath his arm. She was about to answer him when she realized he couldn't have been more than in his midtwenties if he was a day, and therefore had not been talking to *her*. She looked over her shoulder and expected to find some sweet young thing standing behind her, and was grateful not to have made a fool out of herself yet again.

"Will you stay if I get you another one of those?" He nodded his shaggy head at her snifter and looked at her in question. So he was talking to her!

Either the low lighting made her appear younger or Surfer Dude already had his beer goggles on. Or maybe he was a stripper hired by Aunt Myra to add to the birthday photo album? Dear God, Jessica hoped not. If so, she was going to need another snifter of Bourbon Barrel Ale and then some. "Sure," she finally answered, and handed him her nearly empty glass. "It's my party, so I have to stay." She tapped her finger toward her chest so there would be no mistake that she was the over-the-hill birthday girl. If he *wasn't* a stripper, she wanted him to know that she was the geezer that lordy, lordy, had just turned freaking forty. That should chase him away quicker than she bored Ty McKenna.

"Ahhh, you must be Jessica," he said, and pointed to the table holding the huge cake that said her name in script. "Saw it when I came in, but I'm not above crashing a party." He extended his hand. "I'm Logan Lannigan. I'm here to play with . . . the cougars."

"Really? What position do you play?"

He leaned in close and said in her ear, "Any one you want. Because you are one sexy cougar."

Jessica opened her mouth, but nothing came out. So he wasn't a stripper—thank you, God—and he knew she was the birthday girl.

Well . . . should she be offended that he thought of her as a cougar, or flattered? Did he deserve a slap or a hug?

"Not that I would have ever guessed that you were anywhere close to forty," he commented, as if reading her mind.

"Thank you." *Okay,* Jessica decided, *he deserves the hug.* Could everyone read her doggone mind? Was she that transparent? But anyway, it was a good response, so he got instant brownie points for that. Still, she shouldn't be flirting with someone as young as him. Should she?

*God, no! Step away from the Bourbon Barrel Ale. . . .*

She was about to send cutie-pie Logan on his way, but out of the corner of her eye, she saw Mr. Triple Threat watching with apparent interest. *Hmm, no longer bored,* she thought to herself, and tried to muster up a flirty smile. Surely she could pull off a smile, couldn't she?

"Come on, Jessica," Logan pleaded in her ear. "What do you say?"

Jessica was going to give his chest a shove, regardless of who was watching, when John Fogerty's voice came over the speakers singing, "Put me in, Coach. I'm ready to play . . . today."

"You ready to play, sweet, sexy cougar?"

Jessica laughed and suddenly felt carefree again. "Sure!" she answered, and let him lead her onto the dance floor. What could a little dancing hurt anyway?

Madison squealed with delight when Jessica wiggled her way onto the dance floor. Her daughter's eyes widened when she saw Logan, Aunt Myra gave her a high five, and Olivia shook her head but laughed. Jessica blushed, but decided to just have some fun.

"This is Logan Lannigan. He plays with—I mean *for* the Cougars." *Dear God . . .*

Logan gave her a wink but then nodded. "Pitcher," he announced.

"Welcome to Cricket Creek," they all shouted over the music, and then started singing along to the John Fogarty baseball classic. "Look at me! I can be . . . *center field!*"

A couple of other young guys whom Jessica didn't recognize joined them, and she surmised they must also be potential players when they pointed at their chests while singing along. Jessica knew that this week was going to bring decisions for the final roster, and she would hate to be in their cleats. This league was meant to give them another shot, and if they didn't make the team here, their futures in this profession would most likely come to an end. And so she put her arms around them and started singing along to the timeless song of the boys of summer.

When the song ended, Madison leaned over and said, "Mom, don't go too far away. I have a really fun surprise for you."

"I hope it's a stripper!" Aunt Myra announced.

"Aunt Myra!" Jessica chided, but her aunt just shrugged.

"What? I want a stripper for my sixtieth birthday. Y'all can make a note of it." She pointed at Logan. "And I want it to look like him."

"Myra!" Olivia shook her head. "What would my father think?"

"*Pfft*. Your daddy already knows I'm plumb crazy," she answered with a wave of her hand. "Part of my charm, don't ya think?"

"I sure think so," Logan chimed in, and got a nod from Aunt Myra.

"Well, now, aren't you as cute as Christmas. I like you."

Jessica rolled her eyes and turned to Madison. "So, just what is this surprise you're talking about?"

"*Duh*. I'm not going to tell you. Just don't venture too far away."

"Am I going to like this surprise of yours?"

"I guarantee it."

Jessica didn't point out to Madison that her guarantees weren't always money, but the light shining in her daughter's eyes told Jessica that this was going to be something good. At least she hoped so.

"Can I refresh your drink?" Logan asked, and nodded toward the bar.

"No, thanks," Jessica replied with a smile. "I'm going to go over to the buffet table. I need some food." When she started to walk that way, she fully expected the young hottie to head on to younger pastures, but he fell in step beside her.

"Mind if I join you?"

She kind of did mind, but going to the buffet table required passing by Ty McKenna, and so she shook her head. "Of course not." She went as far as to link her arm through his and then felt sort of silly, but the deed was done so she had to, as Madison would say, just roll with it.

While dipping a carrot stick in ranch dressing, she wondered what the big surprise was going to be and glanced in Madison's direction. She was chatting on the phone, nodding and smiling, giving Jessica hope that something exciting was about to happen. She tried to sneak a peek at Ty, but as luck would have it, he looked in her direction at the same moment. He arched one eyebrow and gave her a smoldering look that made her heart pound, but Jessica lifted her chin a notch and then turned her attention back to Logan. Although she nodded and responded to the young ballplayer's flirty questions, all she could think about was Ty McKenna seated behind her. She tried to keep her focus on Logan, but she kept wondering if Ty was still looking her way. And it took everything in her power not to turn around and find out.

# 4

## Risky Business

"Ouch!" Ty grumbled when Noah kicked his shin beneath the table. "What the hell was that for?"

"You gonna let Logan Lannigan put the moves on Jessica? You know that boy is after one thing." Noah took a long pull from his beer and thumped the bottle down onto the round table.

Ty shrugged. "Not my business." He tilted his own beer up to his lips and took a casual, I-don't-care swig, when in truth he was both pissed and worried, and then even more pissed that he was worried.

"Ty, Jessica is no match for his slick moves. And she's been drinking. Something I know she doesn't do much. You need to keep an eye on her, bro. Kick Lannigan's hotshot ass, if need be. Well, at least pose that threat."

Ty tilted his head to the side and was glad that Owen and Jason had gone over to get some cake. "Why, again, is this my problem?"

"It's obvious that you're into Jessica. Come on, you haven't been able to take your eyes off her, so why are you sittin' over here while she's over there? What gives?"

"She pissed me off," he admitted, even though *hurt my*

*feelings* was probably closer to the truth. But he wanted to keep his man card intact.

"How? I know she puts on a tough-cookie act, but in reality Jessica is a sweetheart."

"Except when it comes to me." Ty stared at the label on his beer bottle and then leaned closer, so that no one but Noah could hear. "Noah, when I put it out there that I can't get her out of my mind, she basically blew me off by responding that I was a smooth operator. That she's seen me in action."

"Has she?"

"Well, yeah. Back in Chicago. So what? Those days are done. I know I had a big rep, but most of it was blown up and the rest of it wasn't even true." Ty inhaled a deep breath. "Look, I wanted to play baseball and not have any baggage ruin my career, and I sure as hell wasn't going to screw over some trusting woman the way my jackass father did to my mom. I saw way too much of that crap. So I played around and never got serious. Nobody got hurt." He shrugged and picked up his beer. "It was better that way. End of story."

"I hear ya. I pretty much had the same reaction from Olivia. She thought I wasn't anything more than beefcake and baseball."

"So what did you do to convince her that you're for real?"

"Starred in a play with her." Noah grinned. "Built the stadium and saved the town she loves from going under."

"Great." Ty scrubbed a hand down his face. "Just what am I supposed to do?"

Noah lifted his shoulders. "You're the manager. Bring some excitement to Cricket Creek by giving us a championship season. That will impress Jessica for sure."

"No pressure there," Ty answered with a long sigh. "You know this is all your damned fault. Bringing me here to this cute-ass little town. Being so gag-me happy with Olivia. I'm starting to want the very things I avoided all my life. Thanks, Noah. Thanks a whole hell of a lot."

"You're welcome," Noah replied, but instead of grinning, he seemed serious. "Now go keep that young shit from pawing all over your girl."

"She's not my girl. It's not my business," Ty stated flatly, but his heart was thumping double time.

"Then change that fact and make it your business."

When Ty looked over and saw Logan pop a strawberry into Jessica's mouth, he muttered a low expletive.

"She's no match for him," Noah warned.

"Really?" Ty drained his beer. "She had no problem shutting my sorry ass down."

"Ty, she didn't shut you down. She stated a fact."

"It wasn't a fact. It was a perception."

"Yeah, one that you admit you created. Can you blame her?"

Ty lifted one shoulder and then took a silent swallow of his beer. "Why the hell am I going after a woman who has made it clear that she wants no part of me?"

"For exactly that reason. Ty, you were used to women throwing themselves at you. It comes with being a celebrity. Jessica isn't like that and you know it. She doesn't have an agenda. Olivia was the same way, and it's one of the reasons I love her so much. But you're dead wrong about her not wanting any part of you."

"You think so?" he asked, and then shook his head. "God, I sound like such a girl."

"Then man up." Noah leaned forward on his elbows and sighed.

Ty shook his head firmly. "I'm staying out of it."

"Are you seriously going to let your pride get in the way of doing the right thing?" He angled his head toward the buffet table. "Look. He's all over her."

"She can take care of herself."

"Ty, she's out of her element."

Ty reluctantly glanced in Jessica's direction and then gritted his teeth when Lannigan suggestively slid his hand up Jessica's arm. "You're right. This is bullshit."

"It's about damned time," Noah agreed with a firm nod.

"I hope I don't regret this," he muttered, but he scooted his chair back and made a beeline for the buffet before he knew exactly what he was going to do once he got there. A big dose of jealousy swirled around with his need to protect Jessica, and for the first time in a long while, Ty felt unsure of how to handle himself.

When Jessica looked up at him, he pretended to be interested in the food and reached for a plate. "Excuse me," Ty said, making Lannigan have to step away from the table so that he could stand closer to Jessica. "I'd like to have some of the, uh, spinach dip." *Damn.* He didn't like spinach dip. . . .

"Sure, Mr. McKenna," Lannigan said, making Ty feel like an old geezer. When a slow song came on, Lannigan turned to Jessica. "You wanna dance, birthday babe?"

The seductive Sinatra ballad had Ty gritting his teeth again. "Actually, Jessica, I need to talk to you."

"May I ask about what?" Jessica looked at him with a slight frown.

*Think fast.* "Um, it's a business situation."

"Does it have to be now?" Her eyebrows shot up.

"It's a pretty pressing matter. Lannigan, do you mind?" Ty asked, but gave him a level look that suggested he had better not mind.

"No, sure, Mr. McKenna," Logan replied. But then he leaned in close to Jessica's ear and continued loud enough for Ty to hear, "Save the next slow one for me. Okay, baby?"

"No problem," Jessica replied, but her smile faded when she turned to Ty. "So what's this urgent business matter you need to speak with me about?"

Ty cupped his hand over her elbow. "Let's get some fresh air and I'll explain."

Jessica hesitated, but then nodded. "All right."

"Thanks. I won't keep you long." Ty put his hand on the small of her back and led her outside to the patio overlooking a bend in the river visible through the budding trees. Pete had yet to set the tables up for his summer beer garden, so they were the only two out there. "Too cold?" he asked.

"I'm fine," she assured him, but then leaned her hip against the railing and looked at him expectantly. She appeared so lovely in the light of the moon that he wanted to gather her into his arms and kiss her. "So, what's up?"

"I was rescuing you," he said, deciding to go for the direct approach.

"Rescuing me?" She tilted her head, making her ponytail slip over her shoulder. Ty wanted to reach out and touch it. "From what?"

Although Ty got the distinct impression this wasn't going to go well, he was invested and continued. "From Logan Lannigan."

"So . . ." She raised her eyebrows and put her hands on her hips. Not a good sign. "You thought I needed to be rescued from Logan?"

"I thought you might have been tired of him pawing all over you. Come on, Jessica. He was after one thing and it wasn't birthday cake."

"Really?" She tilted her head farther. "And what might that be?"

"Every young dude's dream. To score with a beautiful, mature woman."

"Mature?" She drew out the word.

*Oh, boy . . .* "You know, that whole cougar thing." His smile felt more like a wince. "Hey, I did say *beautiful.*"

"For a woman my age."

"I didn't say that."

Jessica sucked in her bottom lip as if in thought, and Ty braced himself for the missile she was sure to fire. "So, it's perfectly acceptable for *you* to have a sweet young thing on *your* arm, but the reverse isn't okay for me?"

Oh, this was going to hell in a handbasket at warp speed. He was going to kick Noah's ass all the way into next week for talking him into this big mess. "Look, I didn't want him to take advantage of you."

"I am forty years old. *Mature.* I am beyond being taken advantage of."

Ty cleared his throat. "Granted, but it must be flattering and—" He stopped at her quick intake of breath.

"Flattering?" Her usual sultry tone became higher pitched. "You have a lot of nerve," she ground out, and turned on her heel. But he stopped her with a gentle grip around her arm.

"Wait, you're taking this all wrong. I was simply looking out for your best interest."

"Really? You weren't paying much attention to me until Logan showed up. I guess it's all about the chase, huh? Once a player, always a player, and I'm the only game in this town."

"Fine. Think whatever you want of me. I don't care," he lied. "But, Jessica, he's doing his damnedest to try to get you into bed," he stated bluntly.

"So?" Jessica recklessly tossed back. "Again, what concern is that of yours?"

*I care about you.*

He wanted to say it, but he had spent so many years avoiding such sentiments that the words died on his lips. As his heart pounded and he felt both anger and confusion, it hit him that this damned drama was another reason he avoided relationships at all costs. "You're right," he said tightly. "It's not my concern."

"Exactly." Her chin came up, but those amber eyes got to him. He felt unwanted emotion stab at his gut, and he longed to pull her into his arms and hold her tightly. "In fact, I owe him a dance."

"Fine," Ty responded curtly. He dropped his hand and stepped back, but when she turned to go once more, his heart overruled his brain and his arm shot out. He pulled her closer.

"What do you think you're doing?" she demanded hotly, but the slight quaver in her voice gave her away. He gazed at that perfect mouth that had been driving him crazy for weeks. She wore barely there nude gloss that made her lips appear moist and kissable.

"Do you have your phone on you?"

She swallowed and nodded.

"Give it to me."

"Why?" After stepping back, she reached in her pocket and handed it to him. "Do you need to make a call?"

"No, I'm punching my number in for you," he replied, and after doing so, he gave it back to her. "If Lannigan gets out of line, just give me a call and I'll kick his ass." He cupped her cheek in his hand. "Or anybody else's, for that matter," he added gruffly.

"It's not your business or your concern. Remember?" There went her chin again, but her voice had turned soft, yielding.

"I'm making it my concern." He rubbed the pad of his thumb over her full bottom lip. "Call me if you need me. Okay?" He wanted to kiss her so badly that he ached with need, but when she finally nodded, he dropped his hand.

"Evidently, Madison has another surprise up her sleeve. I should get back in there." A heartbeat of silence went by while neither of them moved.

*Kiss her!* He inched closer and her eyes widened a fraction, and he stopped just short of drawing her into his arms. "Okay, but remember what I said," he reminded, surprised when she nodded instead of giving a short retort back.

"I will," she replied softly. And when she turned away, Ty felt such a sense of loss that he almost reached for her again. He shoved his hands in his pockets instead. He watched her walk away, but she paused at the door, and when she looked over her shoulder, his damned heart lurched in his chest. "Oh, and, Ty?"

"Yeah?"

"That whole caveman thing about kicking somebody's ass on my behalf?"

"Yeah?" he asked again, but with uncertainty. She was going to slam him for sure. He swallowed and braced himself.

"It was hot."

Ty's jaw dropped, and he watched her open the door with a quick *whoosh*. "Well, damn," he murmured, and then stood there blinking like an idiot. "That was unexpected." After a moment, he leaned against the railing and then smiled while shaking his head slowly. Jessica Robinson had him so tied in knots that he didn't know what the hell to think.

Ty stood there and let the cool breeze clear his head. He couldn't believe he had the nerve to stick his nose in and say the things he had just said to Jessica. Where she was concerned, his good sense took a flying leap out the window. But the thought of a young hotshot like Logan Lannigan taking advantage of her set his teeth on edge. Baseball and babes were all players Logan's age thought about. He should know; he had seen enough of it.

But her comments hit home. He must have really looked like a jackass to her, coming into Chicago Blue with a different woman on his arm each time, most of them several years younger than he. His past was over, but would Jessica ever believe it?

Hearing the music thumping through the windows reminded him that Jessica had been going inside to dance with Lannigan, and Ty didn't know how he would handle seeing her swaying in the young man's arms. This jealousy thing was new territory for him, and it got his blood pumping. Should he beat Lannigan to the punch and ask Jessica to dance first? Cut in? Ask someone else in an effort to make her jealous? Would she even get jealous? He shook his head, unable to decide, and then chuckled softly. "Wow. Noah was right. I've got it bad for her." Instead of the usual urge to retreat, Ty wanted to get closer, and not just physically. He really enjoyed talking to her about food when he ate at Wine and Diner. He loved the passion in her voice, because he understood. Baseball was like that for him—it was his world. But for the first time, he longed for something more in his life than just baseball.

With that in mind, he decided to go for it and snag Jessica for a dance before Lannigan got the chance. But just when he headed across the deck, he heard a car door slam, followed by a hot curse from a cool female voice. "Gravel parking lot? Are you kidding me?" she grumbled, and then leaned over and shook a rock from her shoe.

Ty halted in his tracks. *Wait. Don't I know that voice?* He walked over and looked around the corner of the building into the parking lot and nodded. "Arabella Diamante . . . ," he murmured when he spotted the young hostess from Chicago Blue Bistro. The little spitfire kept first and second seating running with smooth efficiency—no easy task in the popular, posh restaurant. Lucky for him, Bella loved baseball and always hooked him up with a good table. Ty grinned, remembering that Bella could be hell on wheels and didn't take any guff from anyone, no matter who. Giving her attitude was sure to get you a seat next to the kitchen. He heard her curse again and chuckled. "Oh, boy. I do believe the extra surprise has arrived."

# 5

## Stayin' Alive

*B*ELLA BENT OVER AND GROANED WHEN ANOTHER PESKY pebble slipped inside her peekaboo, studded sling-back sandal. When she shook the pebble out, her hair fell across her face. "Whoa!" She managed to lose her balance, landing her bare foot on a sharp rock. "Ouch! Damn!" She dropped the decorative pink bag holding Jessica's birthday gift and glared down at the gray gravel as if it were to blame for all of the problems leading up to this very moment in her twenty-five years of life.

"Stupid rocks!" She blinked back hot tears and then tried to get her sorry-ass self under control. "Okay. *O-kay*. Just chill!" She swallowed hard. After all, the first twenty-four years were pretty darned good. It was only the past few months that had sucked, especially this past week.

Bella slipped her sandal back on, picked up her present once more, and flipped her hair over her shoulder. But instead of walking over to the front door, she stood there and contemplated getting into her Lexus and leaving. She glanced left and right without moving her head, not wanting anyone who might happen to be watching to think she was passing judgment, but come on. . . . Except for a sleek silver Audi, a white van with GRAMMAR'S BAKERY painted on the side, and a shiny red corvette, the rest of the parking lot was pretty much filled with pickup trucks and motorcycles. Not exactly her kind of place.

Bella looked down at her now-dusty sandals and sighed.

When Madison had said *casual attire*, Bella had chosen the plain black sheath and added a deep red shrug for a pop of color. The studded sling-backs added a bit of a funky flair and height to her mere five-foot-three-inch stature. By looking at the neon Budweiser beer sign, Bella guessed that she was way over-the-top for Sully's Tavern, but she was already late, so digging through her suitcase for jeans wasn't an option.

"Damn," she grumbled, and swallowed hard. She was clearly overdressed and out of her element. It wasn't that she was intimidated or scared. Bella was pretty much fearless when it came to handling herself, and even when she was afraid, she could put on a pretty good show of pretending otherwise. But she was tired from the five-hour drive from Chicago that had turned into more than six, due to getting lost twice, even with the GPS her mother had forced her to use. Ironically, it was her mother's fault for calling her every single hour to ask how she was doing, causing her to miss a turn twice, causing the snooty, know-it-all GPS voice to implore, "If possible, make a legal U-turn."

Oh, and how was she doing?

Well, she was doing crappy!

Discovering her sous-chef boyfriend was cheating right under her nose with a waitress at Chicago Blue had resulted in a dessert-tray food fight that had gotten Bella fired. Not that she cared. A cherry tart smashed in the face of her cheating ex held a certain amount of satisfying irony. Plus, the nut-job head chef who replaced Jessica Robinson had turned the menu into an overpriced, pretentious hot mess that created a very real hell's kitchen. They could have seriously been a reality show. Oh, and since she lived with Dastardly Ex-boyfriend David, she was now officially jobless and homeless. Wasn't that just peachy?

"Fun times," Bella muttered under her breath while staring at the front door of Sully's Tavern. Her mother, who'd never liked David anyway, said this was the perfect opportunity for Bella to use her marketing degree to help her mother take her online jewelry business, Designs by Diamante, to the next level and open a real brick-and-mortar store, but Bella was afraid that in this tough economy, the timing might be off.

"Well, hell." She had thought of nothing other than her troubles for the past six hours, but she inhaled a deep breath and squared her shoulders. Lively dance music spilled out into the parking lot, and the neon Budweiser sign seemed to be winking at her in silent invitation. Plus, she dearly wanted to see Madison and meet this Jason Craig cowboy, or whatever he was, that she was engaged to. And, oh, how she missed strong and steady Jessica, who was like a mom and friend rolled into one sweet package. While Bella loved her mother, Nicolina Diamante tended to get emotional when Bella needed someone to just simply understand. Jessica Robinson was an amazingly levelheaded listener.

Although they hadn't talked much in the past few months, Facebook had allowed Bella to keep in touch with Madison, and she had followed the progress of Wine and Diner and the construction of the baseball complex. In truth, she would never in a million years have thought her friends would have ended up back in this small town to stay, but she had learned a hard lesson lately that life could take some unexpected twists and turns. She sighed again and stiffened her spine. Yes, she was going to have to buck up and head on into the party. And Madison had mentioned that the owner made a kick-ass martini, something she could really use right about now. But when she looked up at the rustic exterior, she had some serious doubts, and glanced longingly back at her car.

"Arabella Diamante? Are you coming in or not?" inquired a deep voice that Bella thought she recognized.

*Wait! Ty McKenna?* She watched the tall figure come from the shadows of the building and walk toward her, and had to smile. Sure enough . . .

"Well, hello, Mr. Triple Threat. I thought that was you." Even in her heels, she had to tilt her head back to gaze up at him. "Madison told me that you're the new manager of the Cricket Creek Cowboys."

"Cougars."

"Right, Cougars. How's life in a small town been treating you?" She gave her hair a flip and tried to muster up some sass.

He shrugged those spectacular shoulders of his. "Not too shabby."

"So are you here for Jessica's party?"

"I crashed it."

"Wait." Bella raised her palms in the air. "You weren't on the A-list? Here?" She sliced one hand through the air. "What's up with that?"

Ty leaned back against a fat tree trunk and crossed his arms over his chest. "The birthday girl isn't exactly fond of me."

"What? Everybody likes you. Um, especially women." It was true. Ty McKenna had an easygoing, fun-loving personality. Like most pro ballplayers, he had a bit of an ego, but never seemed to take himself too seriously. And although Bella had seen him in Chicago Blue with lots of different arm candy, she had always thought he was selling himself short with shallow women instead of someone worthy of his time. Someone like Jessica Robinson . . . And then it hit her. "Ohmigod, you're into Jess!"

"Guilty," he admitted with a scowl.

*"Hmmm."* Bella gave him a slow smile. "Jess always did get a little flustered when she knew you were eating at Chicago Blue."

Ty snorted. "I think you're mistaking flustered for pissed," he commented, but seemed to be a little pleased at the notion.

Bella tapped her index finger against her cheek. "Maybe it's kismet that you both ended up here."

"Right. So, then, why is she in there dancing with a young-as-shit ballplayer? He's been panting after her all night."

"So what are you doing about the situation?" Bella tilted her head sideways and looked at him in challenge.

"Look, I already tried talking some sense into her, and she got pissed." He glanced toward the tavern and sighed.

"Wait." Bella frowned, and then her eyes widened. "You did *what*?"

"Let her know that the cocky kid was trying to score with an older, beautiful woman."

"Older?" Bella added a wince to her frown. "No, you did not."

"'Fraid so." He sighed and then raked his fingers through his hair. "Hey, but I did call her beautiful. That should count for something. And I was genuinely concerned for her welfare."

"You were jealous."

"That too," he admitted with a certain sense of wonder in his voice.

"Oh, wait. There's more, isn't there?"

Ty raked his hand down his face and then winced. "I kinda said that I would kick Lannigan's ass if he got out of line."

"What are you—twelve?"

"Hey, she said my badass attitude was hot," he announced with some swagger.

"And you thought she was serious?"

"Oh . . . well, yeah. I mean, I guess," he said with more than a little confusion. Had she been poking fun? "Hell, I don't know."

"Ah, a first for the mighty Ty McKenna. Well, stop your girly pouting."

"I'm not pouting. I don't pout."

Bella rolled her eyes. "Okay. Glowering? Call it what you want, but I have some good news for you."

"Really?" He appeared so hopeful that Bella knew he really was interested in Jessica.

"Yep. There's more than one way to skin a cat."

"What are you getting at?"

"Come on, Triple Threat." Bella crooked her French-tipped fingernail at him. "Let's make Jessica jealous."

Ty pushed away from the tree trunk. "Do you think it will work?"

"There's only one way to find out." She hefted her Coach purse over her shoulder and then slipped her arm through his.

"So, are you just here for the party?" Ty asked as they headed for the front door.

Her smile faded. "Why do you ask?" Had everyone heard about her now-notorious food fight?

"Well, Jessica is looking for an experienced hostess at Wine and Diner. I thought she might be trying to snag you away from Chicago Blue."

Oh, thank God he didn't know she had been fired during a fury of flying desserts. "Come on, Ty." Bella looked up at him and shook her head. "Do you seriously think I could survive in this small town? I'd go stir-crazy. I honestly don't know how you're doing it."

Ty shrugged. "It's growing on me. Life does move at a slower pace here, but I've found that's not such a bad thing."

"Really?" Bella looped Jessica's decorative gift bag over her wrist and pointed to the front door. "This little honky-tonk is your night life?"

"Hey, at one time, Cricket Creek was actually a pretty lively tourist town, with thriving shops and bed-and-breakfasts. I'm told that the marina was always packed with boaters. The community theater is top-notch too, but in this sluggish economy, everything has suffered."

"And you hope the baseball complex will bring the town

back to life? Isn't that taking a pretty big chance, all things considered?"

He gave her a crooked grin, and Bella wondered how Jessica could resist his charm. "Isn't that what life is all about? Taking chances?"

"No!" Bella pulled up short at the front door. "I told you I'm all about sure things, and I'm not at all sure about going in this bar. Ty, would you look at me? I'm way overdressed. I'm going to stick out like a sore thumb."

"Oh, you're going to stick out, but not like a sore thumb. You're as pretty as ever, and those young ballplayers are going to be falling all over themselves to get a glance."

His statement made her throat constrict. *Apparently, not pretty enough.* She swallowed hard and remained silent.

"Bella, look. You'll make an entrance."

"That's my mother's gig, not mine."

Ty laughed. "Speaking of, how is Nicolina? I used to love it when she would hang out at the bar at Chicago Blue. She's quite a character."

"Driving me crazy, as usual."

"Okay, enough stalling. Let's go on in there. It will be fun. Trust me."

Bella arched a carefully plucked eyebrow at him. "Oh, like you haven't promised that before." When he laughed again, Bella's spirits lifted a little. It would be good to see her old friends and forget her woes for a while. "Let's do this."

"Don't forget, we're making Jessica jealous," he reminded her, but then tilted his head in question. "Hey, wait. Don't you have a boyfriend? A chef or something? Jessica would never buy into you cheating."

Bella snorted.

"Oh . . ." He gave her a look of sympathy.

"Don't even ask."

"Take the hostess job at Wine and Diner. You know that Jessica would be thrilled to have you."

"Ty, I can't live here."

"At least give it some thought. The change of atmosphere might do you some good, and you can always move back."

"I'll think about it." Her heart thudded. Maybe he was right. A change might do her a world of good. "I'll go over there tomorrow and check it out."

"Fair enough. Right now you need to come on in here with me, grab a drink, and kick up those ridiculous heels of yours," he said, but when he put his hand on the door, she held back.

"Wait. Jessica is my friend, and it's her party. I don't want her to get pissed at me for fawning all over you." She shook her head. "Maybe making her jealous wasn't such a good plan after all. It seems I'm the queen of bad plans. Do yourself a favor and don't listen to any more of my rotten ideas."

Ty chuckled. "I thought you were all about sure things."

"Yeah, but not sure-to-go-wrong things."

"Well, at least look at me adoringly with those big brown eyes of yours, okay?"

"Oh, all right," she relented with a slight nod. "No harm in that, I suppose."

"Are you finally ready to go in there?"

Bella squared her shoulders. For some strange reason, she had a gut feeling that going through that door was somehow going to alter the course of her life. Crazy, she knew, and it was probably only due to her emotional state of mind, yet she couldn't shake the feeling.

"Bella?" Ty raised his eyebrows.

"I'm ready. Let's do this," she finally answered.

He gave her a reassuring smile. "Here we go."

When Ty pushed the door open, Bella braced herself for the stench of stale beer and cigarettes, but she was surprised by a pleasant, smoke-free atmosphere that smelled like fried food, bourbon, and beer and actually made her hungry. Although the interior was rustic, with wide-plank hardwood floors and sturdy-looking oak tables and chairs, the red-checkered tablecloths added a splash of color and the retro beer signs blinked with fun charm. Sully's had an if-walls-could-talk kind of feeling and Bella felt a little of the nervous flutter in her stomach subside. Balloons and streamers created a festive, welcoming air.

Ty leaned over and said, "Not exactly Chicago Blue, is it?"

"Nope." Bella shook her head. "But it is kind of cool." Instead of the delicate sound of clinking glasses, the soft tinkle of a baby-grand piano, and muted conversation, Sully's rocked with solid thumps, rowdy music, and lively laughter. A moment later, Bella spotted Madison on the crowded dance floor in a circle of women doing John Travolta moves to the Bee Gees' disco classic "Stayin' Alive." Then she saw Jessica dancing with a gorgeous, tanned-and-toned guy who looked like he just stepped off a California beach. Bella felt an unexpected strong pull of attraction before she remembered that she hated men forever and always, and looked away. She felt Ty's biceps tense beneath her hold, and glanced up at him. A muscle jumped in his stubble-covered jaw, and she had to chuckle.

"What's so damned funny?"

"Seeing the mighty Ty McKenna fall so hard."

He shifted his gaze from Jessica. "Noah wished that same damned karma on me. Don't you know that mean people suck?"

"Yeah, they do," she said, and felt her smile melt into a frown.

"Oh, damn it, Bella. I'm sorry. I'm so wrapped up in myself that I forgot that you're going through some shit."

She gave him a slight grin. "That's okay. Focusing on your shit is distracting me from my sorry-ass, so-called life."

"You're welcome."

Bella laughed and if felt good. "But seriously, I think it's great that you're into Jessica. She's an amazing woman," Bella added, and nodded toward the dance floor.

"A lot of good it's doing me." He shrugged. "If that's what she wants, let her have it," he growled as Surfer Baseball Boy twirled Jessica around and then dipped her.

"Really?" Bella gave Ty a jab to the ribs and nodded at his hand. "So, tell me how you got that World Series ring with that kind of defeatist attitude. I still have plenty of hero worship for you. Don't let me down."

"Then look at me with that hero worship and make her perky little ass jealous. And speaking of ass, if Lannigan puts his hands on Jessica's booty, there will be hell to pay."

"Oh, a bar fight. That would impress Jess."

Ty inhaled a deep breath. "Do me a favor and keep me under control, okay?"

"I'll try," Bella said, and then squeezed his biceps. "Oh, come on. Enough of the wallflower nonsense. Time for my big entrance," she announced with more moxie than she truly felt. Funny how getting dumped messed with a girl's confidence.

"You got it," Ty answered, and they walked farther into the room.

A moment later, Madison spotted Bella. She let out a squeal before grabbing her mother's hand and hurrying over. Bella breathed a sigh of relief when Hannigan . . . Lannigan, or whatever his name was, headed to the bar instead of coming with Jessica. She couldn't help but notice that he had a very cute butt.

"Look who I found wandering around in the parking lot," Ty announced with a grin.

"You made it!" Madison gushed, and gave her a huge hug. "I am so glad you came!"

"Me too!" Jessica said, and made it a group hug. "Madison said she had another surprise for me. Sweetie, it's so good to see you!"

"Hey, what about me?" Ty complained from outside the hug fest.

Bella pulled back and then laughed. "Well, get on over here," she said, and made room so that Ty was on Jessica's side of the group hug.

"I thought you'd never ask," Ty said, and then put his arm around Jessica and squeezed.

"*We* didn't," Jessica said, but Bella noticed color in her cheeks that didn't match her grumble. She gave Ty's chest a shove and then stepped away. "Bella, it's so great to see your lovely face! I'm so thrilled that you made the trip."

"I wouldn't have missed it for the world." Just seeing these two lifted her spirits. "I got lost a few times, or I would have been here sooner. I have a GPS, but Mom kept calling me and I made a wrong turn or two. I swear the chick in that little box actually got pissed at me. She kept saying 'recalculating' in a snippy tone."

"Well, I'm glad you arrived safely," Jessica commented as they all took a step back. She shook her head when Bella handed her the pink bag. "Oh, thank you, but you shouldn't have."

"Bella, I said no gifts," Madison added with a shake of her head. "Um, and casual attire."

Bella gave her a deadpan look.

"Okay. I guess that slinky dress is casual attire for you."

"I'm still a clotheshorse. This is tame for me." She rolled her eyes and turned her attention to Jessica. "Mom and I wanted you to have this gift, even though I'm still mad at you both for moving."

Jessica accepted the gift but said, "Let's go out on the back deck, where it's not so noisy. I want to hear all about the crazy chef at Chicago Blue."

"Okay." Bella exchanged a look with Ty that didn't go unnoticed by Jessica. *Ah . . . a spark of jealousy.* She suppressed a smile and put her hand on Ty's forearm. "Come on out with us. You'll want to hear the dirt I'm going to dish," she said, even though he already knew her sad tale.

"Do you mind, Jessica?" Ty asked. "I'd like to hear all about it."

For a moment, Bella thought Jessica was going to protest, but she shrugged her slim shoulders. "I guess not. After all, you were a fixture there."

Ty grinned. "Ah, so you did notice me."

"You made sure that everyone noticed you," Jessica shot back. "I'm surprised that there's anything to gossip about now that you're gone."

"I sure missed you, Mr. Triple Threat," Bella said, and looked at him with adoring eyes. "Who wouldn't?" she cooed, and got a questioning look from Madison.

"How's David?" Madison asked in a tone that told Bella she had better let her know what she was trying to accomplish.

"We broke up," Bella replied glumly. "I'm feeling pretty low and could use a shoulder to cry on." She thought about batting her eyes, but didn't think she could pull it off without laughing. "A big, strong shoulder."

Jessica's eyes widened a fraction. "Um, Madison, why don't you take Bella to meet Jason and then come out onto the back deck in a few minutes? I'll wait to open your gift. Ty, would you mind coming with me?"

"Sure," Ty answered.

"Great," Jessica replied sweetly, but her smile was tight.

As soon as they walked away, Madison grabbed Bella's arm and all but dragged her into the ladies' room. She leaned her hip against the sink and folded her arms across her chest. "Girl, are you going to tell me what *that* was all about?"

"You promise not to tell?" Bella asked.

"No!"

"You have to promise, Madison!"

"Oh . . . okay. Geez, do I have to pinky swear?" Madison rolled her eyes and sighed.

"Excellent idea," Bella said, and thrust her pinky finger at Madison.

Madison hooked her finger and tugged. "I swear. Spill!"

"I was coming to Ty's aid and making your mother jealous."

"Oh . . ." Madison gave the word about ten syllables, and then smiled.

Bella nodded. "Yeah, but I love Jess, so I didn't want to get her mad at me, so in a flash of inspiration I decided to play all sad and vulnerable. And Jess can't really call Ty out on it, since she's got her own little cougar thing going on with Hannigan."

"Lannigan." Madison leaned back and gave her legs a little kick. "Brilliant! You did a bang-up job."

"Not really," Bella admitted.

Madison raised her shoulders and palms upward. "What are you talking about? Mom bought it hook, line, and sinker. And those two have been tiptoeing around their attraction since last summer, when Ty came into town. My matchmaking radar has been on full alert."

Bella grinned. "Since when do you have matchmaking radar?"

"I don't know. Guess it's always been there. It seems it's a Southern thing that bubbled to the surface with a little help from my friend Olivia. She and Noah Falcon starred in my play last summer. I knew they were meant for each other way before they ever did. Boy, oh, boy, did they fight it!"

Bella nodded. "You do really know how to read people. I guess that's why you're such a great writer. I hated to miss your play, but I couldn't get away from work."

"Well, I'm glad that you were able to get off work for the party."

"Um, yeah . . . about that . . ."

Madison's eyes widened. "Oh, my God. Did you quit?"

She scrunched up her nose. "Mmmm, more like fired."

"Fired?" Madison squeaked.

"Yep, shit-canned."

Madison leaned forward. "No way."

"Yes, way." Bella pressed her lips together and nodded grimly.

"Wait. So was the sad-and-vulnerable thing really an act?"

"Not so much."

"Oh, Bella."

"David cheated."

Madison sucked in a breath. "That scum-sucking, low-life rat bastard!"

Bella swallowed hard and fanned her suddenly hot face. "Yep, I'm jobless and homeless. Dateless. Clueless."

"Hey," Madison said firmly, "this isn't the feisty Arabella Diamante that I know and love talking. Add *fearless* to that list!"

Bella dug deep for a smile, but it wobbled at the corners. "I'm trying, but the truly scary part is that I never saw it coming. Am I that stupid? Really?"

"No!" Madison shook her head. "You're that loving and trusting and would never suspect something that would never occur to you to do. Don't you dare beat yourself up over his fucking bad behavior," Madison said fiercely.

"God, I've missed you and Jess."

Madison gave her a hug and then placed her hands on Bella's shoulders. "Mom needs a hostess at Wine and Diner. You should take it."

Bella swiped at the corner of her eyes and nodded. "That's what Ty said." She inhaled a deep breath. "Madison, no offense, but I don't think I could live in a small town. I just wouldn't fit in."

"That's what I thought too. But I was wrong."

"Right . . . you fell in love. Speaking of, when do I get to meet this hometown hottie?" She cleared her throat and forced another smile.

"Hey, are you okay?"

"No." She inhaled another deep breath, and once again squared her shoulders. "But I'm gonna be, or my mother will drive me bonkers until I am."

Madison laughed. "I just adore your mom."

"And I adore yours."

Madison raised her hands upward. "Hey, move her here too!" she joked, but then her eyes widened. "Ohmigod, there are some amazing boutiques on the riverfront that Jason is finishing. One of those would be perfect for a jewelry store!"

Bella's heart beat faster at the notion, and she once again got a tingling feeling that tonight was somehow going to be life altering. But she arched one eyebrow at Madison. "Nicolina Diamante in Cricket Creek, Kentucky? This town would never be the same."

"Hey, we're doing our best to shake things up around here. Bring it on!" Madison gave Bella's shoulders one last squeeze. "Listen, I'll show you around tomorrow and you can give it some thought. But right now, let's go find Jason. I'm dying to introduce you."

# 6
## *It's My Party . . .*

JESSICA PASTED A SMILE ON HER FACE AS SHE MADE HER way through the crowd toward the back door, but she was trying to keep her simmering anger from going to a full boil. Confrontations brought back the horrific memory of the day she gave the news to her shocked parents that their sixteen-year-old daughter was not only pregnant, but also carrying the child of Clayton Massey, the classic boy from the wrong side of the tracks whom she had been forbidden to see. Young, forbidden love had been a heady escape from the cold environment of her parents' strained marriage, but she hadn't been prepared for her father's rage, her mother's desertion, or Clayton's disappearance. She could have tried harder to find him or asked for child support, but if he cared so little for her welfare, then she had opted to simply forget that he existed. Of course, it was possible that her father either scared him or paid him off, or both.

But she hadn't cried . . . Well, at least not in front of them, and she would certainly stand her ground with Ty McKenna now. That didn't mean it was going to be easy, but she had learned a long time ago to hold her own, and she was going to let Ty McKenna have it! If she hadn't stood up to the wrath of her father that fateful day, she would have crumpled like a rag doll, and so she had developed a spine made of steel. To Jessica, bending meant breaking, and so she never waffled, and she wasn't about to now. After walking out of ear- and eye shot, she whipped around to face him.

"Let me make myself perfectly clear. Arabella Diamante is like a daughter to me. Stay the hell away from her." Jessica tried not to flinch when Ty's eyes widened at her harsh words, but in her experience, getting to the point instead of beating around the bush was the way to get an important message across.

"Bella has been my friend for a long time," he answered quietly. "I wouldn't do anything to hurt her."

"Really?" Jessica inhaled a deep breath of the crisp night air to clear the alcohol and anger from her brain. "Taking advantage of her infatuation would hurt her."

"Jessica, listen. About that . . ." Ty reached an imploring hand in her direction, but she pushed it away.

"No, *you* listen." She took a step closer and tapped his chest, wishing she were taller so she could look at him eye to eye. "Don't use your superstar-bullshit charm on her. It's the last thing she needs right now."

Ty flinched at her direct hit, but after a heartbeat of silence said, "Look, I understand your concern. But this isn't what it seems."

"Ha. How many times have you used that one?" She flipped her ponytail and waited. The fact that he was being so calm for some reason only fueled her anger, and so she tapped his chest again. "Too many to count?" His chest felt rock hard and warm, and despite her anger, she felt a pull of attraction. She swallowed and would have snatched her hand away, but he caught her fist and trapped it against his shirt. She could feel the rapid beat of his heart, and something flashed in his eyes that made her wonder if she was dead wrong. Dear God . . . what was she doing? She opened her mouth and thought perhaps she should apologize or at the very least hear him out, but the look in his eyes shifted, making her take a step backward.

Oh, boy. He was pissed.

Jessica came up against the wall and shivered when the cool cement seeped through her thin blouse. Ty inched closer, crowding her space, and she wanted to tell him to back off . . . except despite his anger, she really didn't want him to. He placed his palms on either side of her head in a masculine show of power that both infuriated and excited her at the same time.

"Let *me* make *myself* perfectly clear. Both Bella and her mother are my friends. I would kick anybody's ever-loving ass who even *tried* to hurt either one of them. No matter what low opinion you've formed of me, I promise you that Bella could come to me stark naked, and I wouldn't touch her."

Jessica swallowed hard but didn't know how to respond, so she remained silent. She wanted to believe him, to trust him, but it made her feel as if she were on a cliff ready to jump into deep water. She looked into his unwavering gaze and knew she would be safe, and yet couldn't take the plunge. Some of what she was thinking must have shown in her expression, because, although anger still flashed in his eyes, he gently trailed his fingertip down her cheek.

"Funny thing is that Bella was trying to make you jealous on my behalf," he said softly.

Jessica's heart took a nosedive in her chest. "Oh . . ."

"Yeah, but you've got your sights set on Lannigan, the very reason for Bella's little misguided charade," he added just as softly, but with a sad edge.

Jessica wanted to open her mouth to protest, but as Ty continued to run a gentle fingertip down her cheek, words failed her.

"But while you're kissing the *kid*, let me give you a little something to remember," he said gruffly, and before Jessica could protest, he lowered his head and captured her mouth with his.

At the mere touch of his lips, a heady jolt of desire coursed through her veins like warm, thick honey. Jessica put her hands on his chest to push him away, but she melted into the kiss and instead fisted her hands in his shirt, pulling him even closer. When their tongues tangled, Jessica's heart thudded. She slanted her mouth, giving more, taking more. . . .

Needing more.

With a soft moan in the back of her throat, she let go of his shirt and threaded her fingers through his thick hair, sinking deeper and deeper into the hot, demanding kiss.

When he finally pulled back, she felt light-headed and breathless, yet wanted an instant replay. But when she reached for him, he pushed away from the wall with one swift move.

"Happy birthday, Jessica," he said gruffly, and then turned away. But instead of going inside, he headed for the steps. Jessica tried to get her scrambled emotions under control, but by the time she found her voice, he was already gone.

With a sigh, she leaned against the wall and closed her eyes, reliving the kiss. God, it had been forever since she had kissed like that, and it left her shaken and yet longing for more. She touched her fingertips to lips that still tingled and inhaled a trembling breath of night air. She shivered, wishing he were still there, keeping her warm with another amazing, bone-melting kiss.

But he was gone, leaving her with an immediate sense of loss.

"Damn," she whispered, when unwanted emotion suddenly bubbled up in her throat. Ty McKenna was handsome, smart, and sexy as hell, and made no bones about the fact that he wanted her. "What in the world am I doing?" There were women who would kill to be in her shoes, and she had just pushed him away! Oh, she used the excuse that he was a not-to-be-trusted player, but in truth she believed that just like with Noah, those days were over. For almost a year he had been coming into Wine and Diner, exhausted from his daily work helping to design the stadium, and now with team tryouts. During that time, she hadn't seen him with a woman, and her heart always kicked into high gear the moment she spotted him in the restaurant.

Jessica sighed and swiped at a stupid tear that leaked out of the corner of her eye. She was falling hard for Ty, and it made her shake in her boots. While leaning her head against the rough wall, she fisted her hands and wanted to scream in frustration. She was so damned afraid to open up her heart! The rejection by her very own parents and the disappearance of Clayton had left scars so deep that she didn't think she could ever heal.

Jessica heard footsteps and opened her eyes, hoping that Ty was indeed returning, but it was Madison and Bella heading her way.

"There you are!" Madison said with a shake of her head. "Mom, why are you over here in the corner?" She and Bella hurried closer. "Ohmigosh, Mom, have you been crying?"

"No!"

Madison exchanged a glance with Bella and then peered at her mother closely. "You have so."

Jessica's chuckle sounded more like a gurgle. "It's my party, and I'll cry if I want to."

"Mom! Did Ty say something to upset you?"

"No . . . Yes . . ." She bit her bottom lip and glanced away.

Bella stepped forward. "Oh, Jess, this is totally my fault! I came up with the stupid plan to make you jealous, so I gushed all over him. I am such a doucher!"

Jessica chuckled in spite of her misery, making Bella give Madison a worried glance.

"No, Mom hasn't gone off her rocker." Madison shook her head, making her curls bounce. "She laughs every time I say *doucher* too. She won't say it, but Aunt Myra does, and she laughs even harder."

"Oh," Bella said, and then turned to Jessica. "Well, then, what's wrong? Come on and tell us!" She raised her eyebrows and jammed her thumb over her shoulder. "Or do you want me to leave?"

"Of course not," Jessica answered. "Bella, you're like a daughter to me."

"Then explain," Bella urged. "What did Ty do?"

Jessica inhaled a deep breath and then blurted out, "He kissed me!"

Madison raised her eyebrows. "And?"

"I liked it!" she admitted, and felt color rise in her cheeks.

"A kiss from Ty McKenna!" Madison slapped her leg. "Now, there's a birthday present!" She laughed, but then sobered. "Hey, wait. Then why were you crying?"

"And where did he go?" Bella wanted to know. "You want me to hunt him down?"

Jessica closed her eyes and swallowed. "I chased him away."

"Why?" Madison asked gently.

Jessica looked at her daughter and felt like even more of a dumb-ass. She hesitated and then revealed the one thing she had always hidden from Madison. "I am so afraid," she slowly admitted.

"Oh, Mom, I was too," Madison said softly, and put her hands on Jessica's shoulders.

"Yes, and that was my doing!" she said hotly. "I raised you to be so strong and so damned independent and not to rely on anyone but yourself." She shook her head. "I was wrong to make you think it was a sign of weakness to ever need anyone in your life. I am so sorry."

"Mom," Madison said firmly, "I think I turned out pretty good. Don't you?"

"Yes."

"Well, then, quit beating yourself up. You might be forty years old, but you've still got living and learning left to do."

"What should I do?"

"Chase after him," Bella chimed in.

Jessica widened her eyes. "I can't do that!"

Madison crossed her arms over her chest. "Mom, weren't you the one who told me not to have *can't* in my vocabulary?" She pointed to Jessica's thighs. "You have two legs. Use them."

"No! I will not chase after him!"

Madison sighed. "You won't be chasing him. You'll be . . . tracking him down. Take him a piece of cake or something."

"No!"

"Then you're not getting your birthday gift," Bella said stubbornly, and scooped up the pink bag.

Jessica chuckled and reached for the bag, but Bella held it out of reach. "You can't be serious."

Bella angled her head. "Not usually, but this time I am. No chase—I mean, tracking down—then no gift." She waggled her eyebrows. "And it is lovely. Mom created it especially for you."

"You're not playing fair," Jessica protested, and looked to Madison for support.

Madison pressed her lips together and then said, "Mom, don't be a douche *nozzle!*"

"You two are impossible!" Jessica felt her lips twitch and she laughed. "So if I chase—I mean, track down—Ty, I get my gift?"

"Win-win," Bella answered. "So . . ."

"Give me the present," she answered, but Bella hesitated.

"She never goes back on her word," Madison assured Bella, who then handed over the bag.

"Happy birthday!" Bella folded her hands together in anticipation while Jessica opened it up.

"Oh, it is exquisite!" Jessica breathed softly as she lifted the delicate coral-and-turquoise bracelet from the box. "It matches my necklace! Bella, Nicolina is truly gifted," she said, and hooked the bracelet onto her wrist. "I wish she could have come with you."

"Me too," Bella admitted. "She was simply up to her eyeballs in orders. Mom does a lot of jewelry for weddings, and this is the season. But now off with you!"

"Go, Mom!" Madison made shooing motions with her hands.

"I can't leave my own party."

"It's winding down anyway, except for the die-hard partiers. I'm going to run in there and get you some cake, and then you're going to march right over to Ty's condo. Okay?"

"Do I have to?" Jessica groaned, and put her hand to her stomach. "Really? Come on, girls. It's my birthday. Give me a break."

Madison sighed. "Bella, you hold her here while I get the cake. Don't let her out of your sight."

"Gotcha." Bella turned to Jessica. "Okay, girlfriend. You're not going anywhere on my watch," she promised, but then softened. "Seriously, Jess, you can do this. Ty McKenna is just a dude."

"Right." Jessica nodded and then tried for a smile when Madison appeared with a plate full of cake and a shot glass. "What is that?" she pointed to the drink.

Madison raised the glass. "Some good ole Kentucky bourbon in the form of Woodford Reserve. Small-batch, premium bourbon made in the heart of Kentucky. Pete said only top shelf for you." She held up the cake. "Liquid courage and a peace offering. And I brought your purse, so you're good to go."

Jessica eyed the amber liquid. "I can't do a *shot*!"

Madison rolled her eyes. "There you go with that whole *can't* thing." She thrust the bourbon at Jessica. "Just do it."

Jessica looked imploringly at Bella, but she nodded at the shot glass. "Go for it, Jess."

Jessica took the shot glass and blinked at it. Finally, she sniffed the contents. "Wow!" The sweet, smoky aroma sliced through her brain like smelling salts clearing her head. "I can't do this. . . ."

"Mom!"

"Oh . . . okay!" She tossed the bourbon back in one big swallow, thinking it wasn't so bad, just burned a little, but she actually liked the smooth oak-barrel flavor . . . and then it splashed into her stomach and spread through her system like warm fingers reaching all the way to her toes. She suddenly felt mellow, relaxed, and ready to face Tyler McKenna.

# 7

## *The Icing on the Cake*

TY TUGGED ON A PAIR OF BLACK SWEATPANTS THAT READ
COUGARS down one leg. The merchandise for the gift
shop had been rolling in, adding to the general excitement
that in a little more than a month, the first season for the
Cricket Creek Cougars would begin. Of course, Bella had
been right. This venture was a risk, but he didn't care. He'd
rather invest in something worthwhile and lose his ass than
squander his money on meaningless bullshit.

While Ty and Noah worked hands-on with the team and
staff, silent partner Mitch Monroe took care of the money
end of the project. Young but hardworking Jason Craig
kept the nearly complete construction running smoothly,
and local landscaper Owen Lawson was doing a bang-up
job with getting thick grass to grow on the field. Season-
ticket sales had been going strong, and corporate sponsors
were showing interest. All in all, everything was coming together, putting Ty in the best frame of mind he had been in
for a long time.

Until tonight.

Right this minute, he was frustrated as hell. His little
prove-it-to-you kiss had backfired big-time. Just thinking
about locking lips with Jessica got him going all over again.

Ty raked a hand down his face and groaned. "Damn." His attraction to her went beyond physical. He admired her culinary talents and work ethic. Ty grinned. And when she let her guard down, she entertained him with her sharp sense of humor. But his grin faded when he thought that at this very moment, she was probably dancing with hotshot Lannigan. He suddenly regretted his decision to leave the party, but his emotions had gotten the best of him.

With a sigh, Ty padded on bare feet into the kitchen. The smooth, cold tile sent a slight chill up his spine, but he didn't mind. After spending years in hot leather cleats, Ty loved the freedom of bare feet. He opened the refrigerator door and peered at the meager assortment of food: olives, spicy mustard, hot sauce, pickles, one lonely apple taken from a basket of fruit sent to the stadium, bottled water, and expired milk. The rest of the shelves were laden with beer. *But not just ordinary beer,* he thought in his own defense. Ty was a big fan of microbreweries and placed a high value on flavor, complexity, and quality. He picked up a bottle of Moose Drool from Big Sky Brewing and grinned. Noah thought he was a beer snob, but in reality, Ty appreciated the handcrafted passion that went into brewing the best beer possible. Ty fully understood dedication and the need for success, but what he was just beginning to get was that there was so much more to life, namely sharing it with someone you love.

"Wow," he said with a sad sigh, and then put the bottle back onto the shelf. Other than the spinach dip, he hadn't eaten, and his stomach growled in angry protest. He stood there scratching his chest and was contemplating opening the jar of olives when his doorbell rang. Ty frowned and shut the refrigerator door. If it was a pizza-delivery dude at the wrong door, he might just have to claim the order.

He took long strides across the living room in case the delivery dude figured out his mistake, and tugged the door open. He was so dumbfounded to see Jessica standing there that he stared at her in silent confusion instead of inviting her in. Finally, she thrust a plate at him.

"I brought you . . . uh . . ." She looked down at the plate as if she had forgotten what was on it and then added, "Cake."

"Thank you," he finally managed, and took the plate from him.

Jessica hefted her purse higher on her shoulder and said, "Well, enjoy. Good night." It wasn't until she pivoted on her heel so fast that her ponytail whipped across his chest that Ty located his lost senses.

"Can't you come in for a while?"

She halted her quick head-down exit and turned around slowly to face him. "I—I should go. You—you look ready for bed," she added, and then her cheeks turned a cute shade of pink. "Please don't touch that line," she pleaded with a slight grin. "Wow, I suck at flirting."

"Is that what you're doing?"

"Apparently not."

Ty grinned back. There it was again, that unexpected splash of humor. "On the contrary."

"Really?" She appeared so pleased that Ty chuckled.

"Have you had any cake yet?"

"No. But I did have a shot of bourbon." She raised one finger in the air, and he realized she was tipsy. *Oh, that explains a lot.*

"That'll put hair on your chest," he teased, but at his comment, her gaze dropped to his bare chest, and she visibly swallowed.

"I guess you've been drinking bourbon too."

Ty chuckled.

"I'm glad you're not into that whole shaving-your-chest trend."

"Good to know."

She closed her eyes briefly. "I don't know why I felt the need to share that with you. I should go," she added in a voice barely above a whisper.

"Why, Jessica?" he asked, and when she raised her gaze to meet his, he witnessed a flash of fear that made him want to gather her in his arms and hold her until it melted away.

"Because . . ." she began, but then seemed to be at a loss for a valid reason. "It's late," she finally answered. "I have to—" she continued, but Ty reached out and grabbed her hand. Her eyes widened when he tugged her inside the condo, and she stumbled forward and bumped against him, nearly knocking the cake out of his hands. "What do you think you're doing?" she sputtered, and Ty had to hide his smile. *Yes!* He wanted spunk, anger, passion, humor—anything but fear.

Oh, and Ty understood. He had steered clear of serious relationships for fear of hurting someone the way his father had crushed his mother. Jessica had been hurt. It was high time that they both put those fears to rest and took a chance. He closed the door with his foot and tugged her toward the kitchen.

"Hey!" she continued to protest, and pulled on his hand. "Let me go!"

"You have to eat cake on your birthday!" he said, and then placed the plate on the table. As soon as he released her hand, she fisted it on her hip and gave him a good glare.

"I don't appreciate being manhandled."

Ty raised his palms in the air. "Fine. I'll keep my hands to myself."

"And you need to put a shirt on."

"Why?" He reached down and swiped his fingertip through the icing and then slowly licked it off. She watched as if fascinated. "It's my place and there's no rule that you have to wear a shirt, but if it's bothering you or something, I'll go and put one on."

She raised her chin a notch. "No, never mind. The sight of your bare chest isn't really bothering me."

Ty took a step closer, and to her credit, she stood her ground. "I think it is. I think you're getting *hot* and bothered."

"You are so very, very, absolutely, totally wrong."

"I think you protest way too much. That could only mean one thing."

"What?"

"That I'm right."

She snorted. "Yeah, right." She frowned. "Wait. I mean, wrong."

"Then touch me," he challenged, and took another step closer.

"No! Give me a fork. I want my cake."

"Chicken?"

"No, I want cake."

"Are you afraid to touch me, Jessica?" He decided to go ahead and challenge her fear head-on.

"Oh . . ." She tilted her head and gazed up at him, and he waited, fully expecting a sharp protest. "Yes," she answered so softly that at first he thought he hadn't heard her correctly. "Ty, it's been so long that I wouldn't even know where to begin."

God . . . his heart ached with her honest admission. He knew it was the alcohol that allowed her to speak so freely, and for that reason he should back off. "Jessica, I'm sorry. I'm being an ass." He started to turn away and get the fork that she had requested, but she reached up and placed one cool hand on his warm skin.

"No. I mean, *yeah*, you are but . . . oh . . ."

Ty looked down.

It was just a hand. On his chest. No, it was *her* hand.

And her small act of courage reached in and grabbed his heart much like the exhilaration of making an impossible diving catch and coming up with the ball.

He looked down into those whiskey-colored eyes and he was lost—no, make that captivated. God, she was such a beauty with those full lips, high cheekbones, and perfect nose. And she was talented, smart . . . funny. She should ooze confidence. Own it. But her lips trembled and she swallowed hard. Ty thought she was going to pull away, and he wanted to trap her hand against his body, but he refrained. This was up to her. He wouldn't force it.

Her shoulders rose and fell with each breath she took, but instead of removing her hand, she placed both palms against his skin. She smoothed her hands over his pecs in a slow, outward sweep and then back in. When her fingernails grazed his nipples, his muscles contracted involuntary, making his abdomen a hard ridge that seemed to fascinate her. She sucked in a breath when she came to the waistband of his sweats. The bulge of his erection was all too visible and left no doubt that he was going commando. He wanted her to touch him there, stroke him, and when she didn't, a low groan escaped him.

"Jessica . . ." He tilted her head up to look at him. Her cheeks were pink, and she licked her lips. "Touch me."

"I can't," she said in a breathless voice, and then grinned slightly.

"What?" he asked gruffly.

"Madison reminded me earlier that I always told her that *can't* wasn't a part of her vocabulary. She called me out on it."

"Smart girl," he joked, but his voice sounded strained.

"Yeah." She tilted her head, making her golden ponytail slide over her shoulder. She smoothed her hands upward and then back down, coming even closer to his rock-hard penis, almost as if daring herself.

"God!" Ty sucked in a sharp breath. He knew she wasn't being a tease on purpose, but still. . . . "You're driving me nuts."

She looked up, startled, and pulled her hand back. "Oh! I'm sorry. I should really go!"

"Would you stop saying that? Jessica, I've been drawn to you since last summer when we went to that prom for Olivia and Noah." He shook his head. "No, even before that. I caught glimpses of you at Chicago Blue. And yes, I love your amazing food, but I eat at Wine and Diner almost every night to see you. Surely you must *get* that."

"I—"

"Don't say it. There is no reason you should go unless you really want to." He looked into her eyes. "Do you?"

She searched his face and then glanced away. "Oh, Ty, I'm way out of my league here. Do I have to spell it out for you?"

He raked his fingers through his hair. "Yeah, you do."

"I have devoted myself to Madison. To my career." She lifted one shoulder. "Sure, I dated here and there, but . . ." She closed her eyes and swallowed. "It's been years since I've been with a man." She put a hand to her mouth. "My God, I can't believe I'm telling you this. Damn that shot of bourbon!"

Ty cupped her cheeks with his hands. "You're not telling me anything I haven't already guessed."

"Oh, great . . ." She laughed without much humor. "I feel like the forty-year-old virgin. I mean, okay, I *know* the mechanics, but I would be a bumbling, fumbling fool."

"You've got to be kidding me."

"No, really, it has been *years*."

Ty laughed shortly. "That's not what I meant." He took her hand and gently placed it against the hard ridge of his erection. "That's what you do to me. Jessica, you've got nothing to worry about."

Even more color rose in her cheeks. "Yes, that might be what I do to you. But what would I do *with* you?"

Ty gave her a slow grin. "As they say here in Cricket Creek, anything your li'l ole heart desires. Do as little or as much as you wish. Happy birthday. I'm all yours," he offered in a teasing tone to keep the mood light, but in reality he meant what he said and he didn't mean just for tonight. He just wouldn't let her know it yet.

Her chest rose and fell, but she remained silent.

"Hey, I'll be your guinea pig. To get you back in the game." *As long as you only play with me,* he thought.

"Ah . . . taking one for the team?"

Ty laughed, but when her smile trembled, he sobered. "I want you to know you are a beautiful, desirable, sensual woman. I don't care how long it's been. You are capable of bringing a man to his knees."

Frowning slightly, she shook her head and looked away.

Ty gently cupped her chin and tilted her face back in his direction. "Let's start with a simple kiss. If you want to stop there, I won't push. Deal?"

# 8

## *Sealed with a Kiss*

AS SOON AS JESSICA NODDED, TY DIPPED HIS HEAD AND sealed the deal with a kiss. But there was nothing simple about his lush, moist mouth locking with hers. Oh no, the man kissed in layers: sweet and tender at first, then coaxing, playfully teasing with a lick across her bottom lip, a gentle nip before sliding into an erotic tangle of tongues.

Jessica found herself pushed back against the kitchen wall, kissing Ty like she had been pouring rain all this time instead of having years of drought. When she wrapped her arms around his neck, he slid his hands beneath her butt and lifted her up. With a groan, she hooked her legs around his waist, shamelessly clinging to him like kudzu on a tall oak. He kissed her deeply, endlessly, and held her up as if she were weightless. With a soft moan, she threaded her fingers through his hair, pressing her soft breasts into his hard chest. He smelled amazing, and she simply couldn't get enough.

Jessica suddenly felt as if she were floating, and realized he was carrying her through his condo. Thank God for small favors, because she most likely would have had difficulty walking. Guessing his destination, she knew she should protest at least a little, but Jessica couldn't bring herself to pull her mouth from his.

When he halted and finally ended the knock-you-naked kiss, Jessica raised her heavy eyelids and peered over his shoulder. Light spilled out from a half-open door to the bathroom, casting a soft glow in the spacious, nicely appointed room. A paddle fan suspended from a vaulted ceiling swung in lazy circles above a massive bed. *Gulp.*

*Oh, boy.*

His heated gaze met hers in silent question.

*"Um . . ."* Jessica's heart pounded, and uncertainty reared its ugly head.

"No pressure. We'll take this only as far as you want to. Okay?" His voice was a low, sexy rumble.

"Yes." Oh, she knew how far she wanted to take this, all right. She wanted to jump the man's bones! Jessica swallowed, nodded as she tried to control her breathing. Asking for a paper bag to control hyperventilating might spoil the mood . . .

He set her gently on her feet but kept his arms around her. "Hey, let me ease some tension," he coaxed while rubbing her shoulders with long, strong fingers. His mouth found the tender, sensitive spot just beneath her earlobe and he showered her with warm, soft kisses, sending a hot tingle down her spine. Her head tilted sideways, feeling too heavy for her neck, giving him better access to wherever he wanted to kiss. He unbuttoned a few buttons and eased her blouse over one shoulder and then continued his sensual trail of kisses on her bare skin. "Just relax."

"Easy for you to say, Mr. Stud Muffin."

He chuckled, but then tilted her head to look at her with serious eyes. "Most of that was hype, Jessica. You and I are on a totally different level that doesn't even begin to compare. I'm not taking this lightly."

"I believe you," she replied, and then, making her decision, she reached back and tugged the band from her ponytail.

"Oh . . . wow." He threaded his fingers through her hair. "It feels even better than I imagined."

"You think about me?"

"All the time." He looked up at the ceiling and then back down. "Noah gets ticked off at me when I drift off into Jessica-land. I let him believe I'm thinking about the team roster." He tucked a lock of hair behind her ear and gazed at her thoughtfully. "But it's always about you." He rubbed the pad of his thumb over her bottom lip. "And I love hanging out at the diner. I feel as if I've gotten to know you over the past year. Coming to see you is the highlight of my day."

"Really?"

"Absolutely. And I hope you feel the same way."

Jessica recognized truth in the depths of his brown eyes and was so moved by his admission that words once again failed her. The fact that she was always on Ty's mind sent a thrill coursing through her body. Could this really be happening to her? Love? Her heart pounded, but then an unexpected, sharp stab of fear sliced through her joy. *Love equals pain. Run like the wind.*

"I'm sorry." After a quick intake of breath, Ty dropped his hand. "I'm pushing, telling you too much, going too damned fast. What the hell am I thinking? Assuring you I'm not a player, and then I carry you into my bedroom. No wonder you're looking at me like you want an escape hatch. Wow, talk about sucking . . ." he said, but when he started to turn away, Jessica gave him a swift shove, knocking him onto the bed. He fell so hard that he bounced. "Hey, I said I was sorry," he protested, but when he made a move to get up, Jessica shook her head, giving him pause. "I guess I deserved that."

"Yes, I'm pissed at you. And!" She tapped her chest so hard that there would surely be bruises. "At my chickenshit self!" She closed her eyes and blew out an exasperated breath. "Oh, boy."

"Talk to me, Jessica."

She opened her eyes and looked at him for a thoughtful moment. "My parents disowned me when I was a scared, lost teenager. My boyfriend deserted me in my time of need. From that point on, I vowed never to need anyone. Ever. So I devoted myself to raising my daughter. Furthering my career. End of story."

"You deserve so much more than that."

"Really?" She inhaled a deep breath. "I was doing just fine! And then you had to come along and make me feel . . . Want. God, *need* things that I thought were long buried."

"Interesting choice of words."

She looked down at him accusingly. She wanted to smack him. Kiss him. And then smack him again. "Wait. What?" She angled her head in question.

"Buried?" He came up to his elbows. "Yeah, feelings that were buried alive and wanting to get out. You can be pissed at me all you damned well please, but you know what? I take it back. I'm not sorry. You needed to be pushed. Prodded. And as for going too fast? Damn, I let *you* push me away for nearly a year. Screw that noise. I've waited long enough."

"Really, now?" she sputtered, not even knowing what she meant. She glared at him, wanting to run, but felt as if her feet had developed roots. *Wow, he has a great chest,* she thought in spite of her anger. *Wide shoulders . . .* "Oh, stop!" she muttered out loud.

"No!" He pushed up to a sitting position, making muscles ripple and bulge. "And you don't own fear, Jessica."

She looked at him expectantly. He appeared so big and strong and sure of himself. This was a man who played baseball in front of sold-out stadiums. "What are you afraid of, Ty?" she asked softly.

"Hurting someone." His gaze flicked away. "You want to know why you never saw me with the same woman twice?" He didn't wait for her to answer. He ran impatient fingers through his hair and said, "Because I didn't want to crush a woman the way my cheating-ass father did to my loving, loyal mother. Yeah, he was a major-league baseball player, but also a major-league asshat. All my friends treated him like a damned hero and thought I was the luckiest kid alive to have a superstar baseball player for a father." He snorted. "I was afraid I had those same genes and would follow in his footsteps."

"Oh, Ty."

"I used to hear her cry at night, Jessica." He closed his eyes as if trying to erase the memory, and then sighed. "Look, there are some really great guys in baseball, but I also saw a lot of ballplayers cheat on their wives. I didn't want to be one of them. So I never stayed with a woman long enough to let her care about me. That's my fear."

She swallowed hard.

"So when does it end, Jessica? Isn't it about time to quit letting the mistakes of others rule our own lives? Damn, I look at Olivia and Noah, see their happiness, and I want that. Don't you?"

She thought of the *Modern Bride* magazine and felt emotion well up in her throat, but refused to answer.

"At least give yourself the chance. Give *me* the chance. That's all I'm asking."

Jessica gazed down at the gorgeous man looking imploringly up at her. "I must be crazy."

"To give me a shot?"

"No." She took a quick step closer to the bed. "Not to."

It seemed to take a moment for her answer to sink in, and when it did, he smiled slowly. "Now you're talking." He arched one eyebrow. "After all, you're not getting any younger."

"Gee, thanks." Jessica gave his shoulders another quick shove, sending him tumbling backward, but when he made a move to get up, she pointed a finger at him. "Don't move a muscle."

"Why? Just what are you planning on doing?" he asked with a hint of suggestion.

"I . . ."

*You can do this.*

"I'm waiting." He looked at her with challenge in his eyes.

"Well, for starters"—Jessica put her hands on her hips and raised her chin a notch—"I plan on taking you up on your generous offer to let me have my way with you."

"It was rather gracious of me, wasn't it?" His mouth twitched as if suppressing a smile. "I am such a nice guy. I'll keep my hands to myself and let you explore to your heart's content. I'm all yours. Have at it." He leaned back on his elbows in silent invitation.

"Okay," Jessica said in the same matter-of-fact tone, but then stood rooted to the spot. She caught her bottom lip between her teeth and wondered just where to begin. *What have I just gotten myself into?*

"Come here," he urged softly, and patted the bed.

"What am I doing? This is crazy."

"I know." He grinned. "But fun."

"Fun?" She murmured the word with a sense of wonder.

"Yeah . . . *fun*. Not work. Not worry. Just plain, good, old-fashioned fun. Are you up for it?"

"Apparently you are," she quipped with a grin of her own.

Ty glanced down and then cocked one eyebrow. "I won't even try to deny it."

Jessica tossed her head back and laughed. *Really* laughed with sheer joy, and, God, it felt good. *This is fun,* she thought, and just then something shifted inside her. A weight that she didn't even know she had been carrying suddenly lifted, leaving her feeling light and free to simply enjoy the amazing, handsome man just waiting for her touch.

*Happy birthday to me. . . .*

Jessica shook her head, thinking that life could be really crazy at times. Who would have ever thought that she would be climbing into bed with Tyler McKenna?

"Please don't tell me you're having second thoughts. Damn, Jessica, you're hurting my ego."

"Good! Your inflated ego needs to be popped!"

"Get over here. Or I might just have to break my own rule and grab you."

"Really, now? Well, maybe I'll just have to tie you to the bedpost." As soon as she said it, she clamped a hand to her forehead and her eyes widened. "Sorry—must still be the bourbon talking."

Ty shrugged. "Do it if you want to. I don't mind being at your mercy."

"Really?" Her heart thudded at the erotic image that skittered through her brain. *Oh. Dear. God.*

"Sure." He angled his head toward a walk-in closet. "You can look around in there. Use a necktie or something?"

"Okay." With an eager smile, she turned on her heel. She couldn't really wrap her brain around the fact that she was going to tie him to the bedpost, but doing something so out of character, so daring, gave her such a heady sense of exhilarated freedom that she decided to just do it.

Lordy, lordy . . . she'd gone crazy at forty!

Jessica put a hand to her mouth as she looked around the neat and tidy closet and found the tie rack. With shaking fingers she picked up an orange one (did he really wear that?) and a blue one, swallowed hard, and then hurried back into the bedroom before the bourbon buzz faded and her good sense returned.

# 9
## All Tied Up

*WAIT . . . WHAT?* TY WATCHED JESSICA WALK TOWARD HIM with a tie dangling from each hand. Ty thought she had been teasing, and he had simply played along.

"Scoot up to the pillows," she said with the air of one used to giving orders. Wait . . . she wasn't *really* going to tie him up, was she? "Good. Now put your hands against the headboard."

Ty inhaled a deep breath. Apparently, she was.

Jessica kicked off her shoes and then scrambled onto the bed and knelt next to him. "Okay, now put your hands against the posts," she requested in the same tone, but he noticed that her fingers were trembling. And yet she managed a quick, impressive slipknot that he couldn't get out of, thereby truly putting him at her mercy. *Oh, boy.*

"Okay," he agreed, but was hit with a sudden bout of uncertainty. Ty was used to being on top, in control and in charge. Instead, he had to trust her, and that was something that didn't come easy to him. Too many people had used him, betraying his trust. As a professional athlete, Ty was used to being treated like a commodity, a franchise rather than a flesh-and-blood human being with feelings and emotions, who bled red just like everybody else. And while he was eternally grateful for his success, he wanted to shed the Mr. Triple Threat persona and simply be Tyler McKenna.

Allowing Jessica to bind him to the bed gave him an oddly vulnerable feeling, something foreign to his nature, and yet sent an exciting blast of anticipation humming through his veins.

*This is nuts.*

*What is she going to do?*

About a dozen suggestions popped into Ty's brain, but this was her gig and so he remained silent. She nibbled on the inside of her bottom lip, making him want to know what was going through her mind. After a contemplative moment, she leaned forward. The billowy tunic gaped, showing him a hint of cream-colored lace and a mouthwatering view of her cleavage. He dearly longed to bury his face there, but the ties restrained him from getting close enough. *Damn.* Not being able to touch her made his desire to do so even more intense.

He studied her while she contemplated her sweet torture. She really didn't look her age and he couldn't blame Lannigan for hitting on her. At that thought, he ground his teeth together. Unlike hotshot Logan Lannigan, youth had passed him by. Ty had strands of silver in his hair, crow's feet from squinting into the sun, and a three-inch scar on his chin from a collision at home plate. He did his best to keep in shape, but he had a bum knee that gave him fits, and a shoulder that ached when it rained. The Toby Keith song "As Good as I Once Was" popped into his brain, and yet Jessica gazed down at him as if drinking in the sight and liking what she saw.

"Touch me," he finally said in a gruff, needy voice.

"Oh, but where?" She arched one eyebrow and pressed her lips together.

"I have a particular suggestion, but at this point anywhere will do," he replied in a strained voice. Her eyes widened a fraction, and Ty knew that she suddenly realized the feminine power she had over him. She could tease him into a damned frenzy, and the slow smile she gave him told him that she knew it.

Oh, damn, he was in trouble now. . . .

She scooted closer, tossed a pillow out of her way with a determined flick of her wrist that almost made Ty laugh. Oh, but then she leaned in mere inches from his chest. He could feel the warmth of her body, smell her light floral scent. He clenched his jaw, and his muscles tensed when she lifted her hand, bringing the anticipation of her touch to a fever pitch. But then she hesitated. "You're loving this, aren't you?" he ground out.

Her gaze locked with his. "Yes," she admitted softly.

Finally, she ran one fingertip down the center of his chest to the top of his sweatpants. The featherlight touch caused a hot shiver down his spine, tightened his nipples, and sent even more blood rushing south. She continued using just one fingertip, swirling as if painting his bare skin. Her touch tickled, teased, and made him hungry for so much more.

She added the rest of her fingertips, raking lightly with her nails until he arched his back from the sheer sensual pleasure. She paused, traced his collarbone, and then moved up his neck, over the rough stubble on his cheek. She frowned when she traced the scar on his chin, but then moved to his bottom lip, sliding her finger slowly back and forth. When his mouth parted, she just barely touched his tongue, but it sent an intense, hot thrill straight to his groin.

"Oh, my . . ." Without warning she dipped her head, and he braced himself for a hot kiss. But instead she lightly licked the stubble on his chin, making him long for more, and lowered her head and swirled the very tip of her tongue over his left nipple. Her golden blond hair trailed over his sensitive skin, and when her hand brushed against his rock-hard erection, he sucked in a breath. She tugged his waistband downward but only an inch or two, making him want to yank his pants off and offer his package to play with . . . but he was helplessly tied to the damned bedpost!

"Whose idea was this?" he grumbled, drawing a low chuckle from her. He watched the top of her golden head and longed to thread his fingers through her hair. He was frustrated . . . but so incredibly turned on, and when she placed butterfly kisses down his abdomen, it was almost his undoing.

"Jessica . . ." He tugged at the ties and arched his back. "Enough!"

"Really? I was just getting started." Jessica looked up and met his heated, desperate gaze, knowing exactly what he meant but showing no mercy. She placed her hands on his chest and then slid her palms up across his shoulders, over his extended arms, and then back to his biceps. His heart pounded when she slowly leaned forward, and, God, *finally* pressed her mouth to his, soft and sweet at first and then with a hunger that matched his own. He needed to, had to touch her!

"Untie me."

She shook her head. "No."

"Jessi—" he began, but his voice stopped working when she slowly started unbuttoning the rest of her blouse. He swallowed and watched, mesmerized as she unbuckled her belt and tossed it to the floor. It landed with a soft *plop* next to her shoes. With a breathy sigh, she let her sleeves slide off her shoulders, revealing a sexy push-up bra edged with lace. Her lovely Nicolina Diamante necklace enhanced her beauty—delicate, original, and yet natural—and matched Jessica's personality.

"Holy shit . . ." Ty whispered when she came up to her knees and unzipped her jeans, exposing matching panties.

And then she stopped.

"Oh no, you don't. Keep going."

Color deepened in her cheeks and she caught her bottom lip between her teeth.

"Please."

Her chest rose and fell and she closed her eyes as if gathering her courage. Ty wanted to urge her on, but he remained silent, giving her the time she needed. It had obviously been a long time since she had exposed herself both physically and emotionally, and he wasn't about to force the issue. And yet this was sweet torture . . .

Finally she reached behind her back and unhooked her bra, letting her breasts tumble free.

When he sucked in an audible breath, she opened her eyes. "I'm not very . . . big."

"Ah, pure perfection, if you ask me. Bring those here," he pleaded. "I need to taste them."

Her eyes widened slightly at his request, and she made his thudding heart pound even harder when she straddled his legs, bringing her breasts up to mouth level. She placed cool hands on his shoulders and braced herself. He could feel her slight tremble and knew this was taking some major-league courage on her part. Ty wanted to purge the fear from her system and replace it with mindless need. With that goal in mind, he leaned forward and captured one dusky nipple with his mouth.

"Oh!" she said in a sexy tone even lower than her normal throaty voice. Her skin felt like cool velvet against his warm tongue. He licked the pebbled sweetness, and when he sucked, she inhaled sharply and gripped his shoulders tighter. She pressed closer, offering more, and he took her deeper into his mouth, laving, sucking, and nibbling until she tilted her head to the side and sighed.

The need to have his arms wrapped around her intensified, and he tugged his wrists until the bedpost groaned in protest. He pulled back and looked at her with pleading eyes, but she shook her head.

"Not . . . *yet*."

"You're killing me." He looked at her rosy, wet nipple and groaned. "Seriously killing me."

"I know." And to torture him even more, she scooted away and got up from the bed.

"Where are you . . ." he began, and then swallowed hard. "Oh, my God," he breathed when she shimmied out of her jeans and stood there in nothing but that mere wisp of cream-colored lace panties. She was toned from kitchen work, but with delicious curves instead of the wafer-thin look that women starved for and he had never found appealing. He'd take soft curves over sharp angles any day of the week. When she looked at him shyly, as if wondering about her sex appeal, he shook his head. "Wow. Forty and fabulous."

She blushed at his compliment. "Really?"

"Absolutely. Now bring that luscious body back here, and untie me while you're at it."

She scooted back onto the bed but made no move to untie him. Instead, she straddled his legs, leaned in, and pressed her soft, moist lips to his. Her bare breasts against his chest had him moaning against her mouth. She threaded her fingers through his hair and kissed him hotly, deeply, and when she rocked her lace-covered mound against his raging erection, he arched his hips, wishing he could reach down and touch her moist heat. When she pulled back, he thought she was finally going to untie him, but instead she shimmied out of her panties and tossed them to the floor. *Oh, God.* Then she leaned down and tugged his sweatpants over his hips and down his legs in one swift, efficient move that had him grinning.

The breeze from the paddle fan felt cool against his warm body. His dick stood at full attention, as if begging for her hand, her mouth . . . her sweet body. "Touch me."

She placed her palm on his chest, and Ty was about to protest, but she slowly slid her hand downward, and his voice was nowhere to be found. All he could make was useless groaning noises. She continued her sensual assault, caressing him everywhere except where he wanted it most.

He could have pounded nails with his dick and was wondering how to politely tell her so when she suddenly curved her delicate hand firmly around his shaft.

*Mother of God, have mercy on my soul. . . .*

Ty sucked in a sharp breath, drawing her attention.

Her eyes widened. "Am I hurting you?"

He thought she was teasing until he saw real concern in her eyes, reminding him that she was unpracticed and unsure. "Yeah, it hurts so good," he said with a strained chuckle. When she moved her hand up and back down, Ty was afraid he was going to embarrass himself and lose it. When a pearl of moisture popped out on the head of his dick, she swirled it around with her thumb. This simple movement was so sinfully sexy that he watched with fascination. "Please. I have to touch you. Feel your skin."

"Okay," she said, wringing a sigh of relieved joy from him. But she took her sweet time hovering mere inches from his body and yet not touching him. When her breasts grazed his chest, he had to grit his teeth.

And then he was free.

For a second he was stunned like a bird realizing the door to the cage was open, but then lowered his arms and wrapped them around her. With a sigh of pure pleasure, he rubbed his hands up her back, loving the exquisite sensation of her soft, smooth skin, and she seemed to melt into his embrace. "Jessica . . ." He threaded his fingers though her hair and kissed her like he could never get enough. After being denied, it felt so wonderful to have his hands on her body.

With his lips still locked with hers, he rolled her to her back, and needing a little payback, he threaded his fingers through hers and pinned her hands to the bed. For a moment he hovered above her, taking in the beauty of her flushed face. Her hair fanned out onto the navy blue pillows, and she met his gaze with shy determination. She was a study in contradictions . . . confident yet unsure, strong but vulnerable. After months of trying to get her to open up to him, it was rather surreal to have her naked in his bed. He moved his mouth to her neck and nuzzled her there before taking the soft shell of her ear into his mouth. She moaned, squirmed beneath him, and tugged at his hands, but he chuckled. "Payback," he told her, and then took a rosy nipple into his mouth. When she gasped, Ty released his grip, and she immediately shoved her hands into his hair. She arched her back, offering her body to him, and he gladly accepted.

In all of her forty years of living, Jessica had never felt this kind of passion. When his teeth nipped and tugged, hot desire chased the last shreds of her inhibitions. She arched her back shamelessly and parted her thighs, giving him access to where she burned for his touch. When his long fingers found her slick heat, a hot shot of shockingly intense pleasure had her clinging to his shoulders and longing for sweet, blessed release. He sucked harder on her nipple, seeming to draw pleasure from within. His finger dipped into her body, and with a throaty cry, she arched up against his hand. He pumped gently and then withdrew, and began small circles that drove her crazy.

"Ty . . ." she pleaded, needing, wanting. Him. That thought drove her over the edge, and she climaxed with deep, aching shudders. He let her ride it out and then kissed her sweetly, tenderly, lovingly. He turned away while she was still reeling with pulsating aftershocks, but by the time she found her voice to call him back, he returned sheathed in a condom. The fact that she hadn't considered protection gave her pause, but when his mouth met hers, her fear melted and passion took over.

His kiss was a hot tangle of tongues, bringing her sated body back to full-blown arousal in no time flat. He caressed her sensitive breasts, sending a shock right though her, and her thighs parted in silent invitation for him to make love to her.

He entered her in one sure stroke, and she loved the feeling of him buried deep. He moved slowly at first, and she could tell he was holding back. She smiled, knowing he was trying to please her over his own needs. Her heart thudded, pulse pounded, and she matched his sweet, slow seduction with some heat of her own. He kissed her, stroked her, until she was mindless with need. With a cry, she wrapped her legs around his waist and urged him to go faster, deeper. She clung to him, and when he thrust deep and shuddered, he took her right with him.

He chuckled weakly and pressed his forehead to hers. "Dear God . . ." She noticed that he trembled slightly and was moved by the fact that he was just as blown away as she was.

Jessica put her palms to his cheeks and kissed him softly. "I know it sounds trite, but that was amazing. I don't know how else to put it."

He smiled and nodded. "I agree," he said gruffly, and then rolled to the side, bringing her with him. She snuggled into the crook of his shoulder with her head on his chest. "Will you stay with me tonight?"

Jessica nodded and then sighed. This wasn't just birthday sex. She wanted him. Needed him. And if she wanted to be honest, she had been falling for him for months now. *Tonight is just the icing on the cake*, she thought with a little contented smile. *Birthday humor. Gotta love it.*

But then a cold shot of fear clawed at her heart. As if reading her mind, Ty kissed the top of her head and hugged her closer. Jessica hoped she could learn to trust enough to allow herself to live, to laugh . . . damn, to have fun! And above all else . . .

To finally let her guard down and to love without holding back.

# 10

## *The Hangover*

$\mathcal{B}$ELLA INHALED A DEEP BREATH AND SNUGGLED CLOSER TO the warm body next to her. "Mmm, David," she purred, thinking it felt so nice to be in his arms. Maybe that whole jobless, homeless, getting-cheated-on thing was just a nightmare. She'd wake up to everything being normal. With that in mind, she placed a possessive hand on David's chest and rubbed leisurely back and forth. Wait . . . she stopped caressing when she encountered smooth skin instead of crisp hair. Bella refused to open her eyes, hoping that David had finally shaved his chest. *Interesting*, she thought, and then trailed her fingers over his warm skin, but instead of a wiry, lanky build, Bella's fingers found sculpted muscle.

*Oh, boy . . .*

She opened her eyes a mere slit and witnessed a strong jaw covered in golden stubble rather than black.

Bella winced. *Oh, please . . . don't tell me.* Swallowing hard, she raised her gaze to shaggy blond hair. Yep, Logan Lannigan. She swallowed again and tried to recall the events from Jessica's birthday party, but it was fuzzy. Had she really gotten that hammered? She didn't feel all that hungover. *Think!* Okay, she remembered dancing. Laughter. Jell-O shots! Wait, did she sing karaoke to the Dixie

Chicks' "Goodbye Earl" with Madison and Aunt Myra? *Um . . . yes.* She remembered walking from Sully's back to Madison's condo—no, wait. She rode piggyback with her legs wrapped around Logan, after she had complained that her high heels hurt her feet! It was like a blurry movie running through her head, but the one burning question remained: Did she have sex with the man lying next to her? She had no blurry memory of *that*.

Sunlight sliced through a gap in the drapes, and she dearly longed to raise her head and get her bearings, but she didn't want to wake Logan. His chest rose and fell beneath her palm. *Good. He is sound asleep.* Maybe she could slip silently from the bed and sneak out of . . . good God, where exactly was she? Holding her breath, she oh so slowly started to slide her hand away from his warm skin, but just when she smelled success, he reached up and trapped her hand against his chest.

"Mornin', sunshine." He opened his sky-blue eyes and gave her a crooked grin. "Just where are you sneakin' off to?"

"I . . . uh."

He reached over to a bottle of water on the nightstand and came up to one elbow to take a swig before offering it to her. "Thirsty?"

"Yes, thanks," Bella replied uncertainly. She rose and took a grateful swig and then handed it back to him. He guzzled the rest, and when he twisted and leaned to put the bottle back on the nightstand, the sheet slipped below his waist. She swallowed and tried to sneak a peek to see if he was naked, and caught a glimpse of a very nice ass. Apparently, he was sleeping in the buff. Not good news for her no-sex theory.

Bella looked down and realized she was in his Cougars shirt. *Oh . . . snap.* "Um, I have a tiny question." She pressed her lips together and held her finger and thumb an inch apart.

"Okay." Logan came up to his elbows with a delicious

show of rippled muscle. Surely she would remember having sex with that gorgeous body. "Shoot."

*Did we sleep together?* The question remained on the tip of her tongue. "Where, um, are we?"

He arched a tawny eyebrow. "Your condo."

"M-my condo?"

"Well, *our* condo."

Her heart pounded like a jackhammer. Was Cricket Creek one of those little towns where you could get married in a tacky little chapel with a blinking neon heart? "Oh, right," she said, trying to play it cool even though a bead of sweat rolled between her shoulder blades. She licked her lips and then said casually, "Nice that it's furnished, huh?"

"I know, and with high-end stuff. I'm used to GW."

"GW?"

"Goodwill. But, damn, there's even a flat-screen TV in the joint." He nodded his shaggy head happily and had the nerve to look sexy as hell, all sleep rumpled and . . . naked. "Yeah, all we have to do is keep it tidy so Madison can show it."

His little nugget of information triggered a memory, and she all but snapped her fingers. "Oh, it's nice that Madison snagged the job showing the model unit, since she doesn't start teaching until the fall semester." She smiled, so proud of her sudden recollection. "And we ate birthday cake back at her condo!" She blurted this random memory without sliding it into the topic of conversation. "With Madison and Jason." If she could remember that tiny detail, surely she would remember getting married. And having sex. She looked at his golden, tanned chest. Especially the sex.

He grinned and then casually scratched his chest. "Just how much of last night do you remember, Bella?"

"Everything," she scoffed. "I don't even feel that hung-over."

"You bitched and moaned, but I insisted that you hydrate. Luckily, our fridge was stocked with bottled water. Hydration is the key to not feeling like shit the next day."

*Our fridge* sent a little slice of uh-oh through her brain. "Sounds like you've been there before."

"Yep, a time or two." He grinned. "You can thank me now or you can thank me later." He arched an annoyingly knowing eyebrow. "So, you remember everything, huh?"

"Absolutely." The memory had to be there somewhere. She just had to get her brain to function, and she was sure last night would all come flooding back . . . unless her brain was taking pity and shoving some shocking event from her mind. Like getting married, for example.

"Really?" He leaned in and ran a fingertip over her bottom lip. She tried not to be affected by his touch, but a shiver of awareness ran down her spine. "Everything?" He drew out the word suggestively.

"Okay, *some* things." He was really starting to annoy her. "Maybe *other* things weren't so memorable."

"Is that right?" He looked at her mouth for a long, hot moment.

"Oh yeah." She nodded slowly. "I don't care how many Jell-O shots I sucked from those little plastic cups. If we had"—she almost said *made love*, but stopped herself—"done the deed last night?"

"Yeah?"

"I would have remembered."

His lopsided grin turned into a full-blown smile that flashed straight white teeth against his golden tan. "Bella Diamante, I do believe I am going to thoroughly enjoy living with you."

"Um." Her eyes widened. "About that. We're not"—she stopped and pressed her lips together. *Married* just would not come out of her mouth—"uh, *hitched*, are we?"

"Hitched? You mean, like, married?"

She gave him a jerky nod and looked up at him wide-eyed.

*     *     *

"Baby, there isn't enough alcohol in the universe that would get me to tie the knot." The image of his mother and father screaming at each other filtered into his brain and he had to suppress a shudder. "The only diamond I'll ever care about is on the baseball field," he added.

"Thank God." She breathed a sigh of obvious relief and allowed tense shoulders to slump against the feather pillows.

"Hey, I'm not such a bad catch!" he protested.

She gave him a deadpan stare. "I'm talking off the field."

"Okay, I am," he admitted with a chuckle. "How in the world could we have gotten married last night anyway? Don't you need a license and blood tests and stuff?"

"Hey, maybe I'm not thinking quite so clearly this morning." She blushed and then lifted one shoulder. "But I had a friend who went to Gatlinburg, Tennessee, for a weekend and came back to Chicago on Monday very much married." She raised her left hand and pointed to her ring finger. "And it happens in Vegas all the time," she said defensively. "I was just covering all the bases."

"Ah, baseball analogies. Maybe you are my soul mate," he joked, but something sad in her eyes hit him hard in the gut, and he wished he had kept his damned mouth shut.

"Soul mate?" she muttered darkly. "*Pfft*. Like there is such a thing. I am so done with dudes," she ground out, but the anger in her voice failed to match the haunting hurt in her warm brown eyes. "I mean no offense, but who needs them?"

"Well, I could think of one particular need," he said, drawing a deeper blush from her.

She wrinkled her nose. "There are battery-operated devices for that."

He ran a gentle finger down her chin. Damn, she was smokin' hot with bed-tousled, chestnut brown hair tumbling over her shoulders. Just a tiny little thing like Eva

Longoria, but sexy and sultry and sporting a don't-mess-with-me attitude that Logan thought was a major turn-on. "Oh, but a poor substitute for the real thing. Luckily, you now have a live-in boy toy."

Her brown eyes widened. "Wait, Logan. So that part is true?"

He was momentarily distracted by hearing his name on her lips. He had never been too fond of Logan, thinking it sounded too frat boy–ish for a ballplayer, but hearing her sultry voice utter his name made him long to hear her say it again . . . but with passion. *Wait . . . what?* He gave himself a mental shake. What the hell was he thinking? Baseball was his one and only passion. Okay, so Bella had gotten to him last night with her tearful tale about Dastardly David, as she called him, who had dicked her over. And, yeah, he'd like to beat the guy to a pulp just for shits and giggles. But that was as far as this was going to go. This uncharacteristic softness he felt toward Bella Diamante would soon pass. And if their situation was going to work, he needed to keep his hands and other body parts away from her body parts.

"Logan?" she persisted, looking a bit lost and vulnerable, swallowed up by his too-big shirt. And, well, sexy. "Just what have I gotten my sorry self into this time?"

Logan scooted over and leaned against the pillows next to her. "Well, for starters, you accepted the job as hostess at Wine and Diner."

"Oh . . ." She frowned, but didn't seem too terribly upset by the prospect. "I kinda remember that."

"Your friend Madison is pretty darned persistent."

Bella nodded. "Yeah, we were tight back in Chicago. I've missed her and Jess. So . . . what is the rest of the story?"

He sliced his palm through the air. "Madison offered you this furnished condo as long as we show it as the model."

"We?" Bella angled her head at him and toyed with the edge of the sheet. "How did this become *we*?"

"Simple economics," Logan answered with a slow shrug. "The rent here is discounted for baseball players, but still a hefty twelve hundred bones a month. So we decided to become roomies."

Bella put the heel of her hand to her forehead. "Wow. Note to self: Do not drink on an empty stomach."

"I warned you about the Jell-O shots you and Madison were slurping. They were strong. But you said, 'There's always room for Jell-O,' and then you and Madison laughed like crazy. Your favorite flavor was purple."

Bella groaned. "Oh, would you please stop!"

"It's all good, Bella. You were funny."

"Yeah, but now I've moved in with a complete stranger!"

"It was Madison who suggested it." Logan reached over and moved her hand. "Listen, it won't be so bad. I really am pretty tidy, and I promise to leave the toilet seat down." Her wrist felt so tiny in his big hand, and an unexpected pull of something he couldn't quite name washed over him. He felt possessive . . . protective, and he barely knew the girl. Weird . . . and yet he couldn't shake it.

"Yeah, but . . ." She closed her eyes and swallowed hard. "We can't do *this*." She opened her eyes and swung her hand in an arc across the bed.

"Okay . . ." He pulled a face. "Don't worry. There's another bedroom. And, hey, you made it quite clear last night that you think men are dogs. And then Madison got mad because she likes dogs, so you amended it to 'Men are all cockroaches.'"

"Hey, if the shoe fits. Or in your case, the cleats."

"There you go, going all baseball on me again. Damn, girl."

Bella grinned in spite of this insane situation. "I'm a huge Cubs fan and I love Wrigley Field."

"You're killing me, but quite frankly, I don't need the distraction of a chick." He inhaled deeply. "Baseball means more to me than anything, Bella. This team is my chance to make it back to the minor leagues." He flexed his left arm forward and showed her a four-inch scar on the inside of his elbow. I had Tommy John surgery last year. Should have bounced back, but my dumb ass started throwing sooner than I should have and fucked it all up."

"Why did the trainers let you come back too soon?"

He shoved his fingers through his hair. "I lied about the pain. But I had been playing with pain for so long that it was normal for me. This is the kind of injury that comes from overuse. It even happens to kids in Little League. They call it Little League elbow." He shook his head. "Comes from wanting to win over concern for the kid."

She put a hand on his forearm and gave him a look of compassion. "I'm guessing this happened to you?" she asked softly.

"Yeah, my old man was a wannabe. Lived vicariously through me. Up and moved us to Texas so I could play ball year-round. Called me a pussy when I said my arm hurt too much to pitch."

Bella gasped. "That son of a bitch!" she cried harshly, but her touch on his arm remained light and soothing. She was a passionate little force to be reckoned with, and Dastardly David was a complete ass clown to let her get away.

"Yeah, well, reinjuring my arm led to a bad attitude that was rotten enough to begin with, and I was released from my contract."

"I'm sorry. That had to suck."

"You have no idea." He rubbed the sudden tension in his neck. His bad attitude hid a hell of a lot of disappointment and fear.

"Turn around."

"What?"

"Scoot around and put your back to me," she insisted.

"You're a bossy little thing," he grumbled, but did as she requested. A moment later, she was up on her knees, massaging his neck. "Ah, damn, that feels amazing. Seriously," he said as her magic fingers melted the tension away from his entire body. "Where did you learn to do this?"

"My mother would bend over a table for hours, making jewelry, and the muscles in her neck would tense up. I've been massaging her neck for years. I hated to see her in pain."

"Mmm, well, you know what you're doing." He meant for his statement to come out matter-of-fact, but her touch coupled with compassion made his voice gruff. He was used to being told to suck up the pain, rather than a tender and caring touch. And, God, it felt good.

"Better?"

"If I say yes, are you going to stop?"

Her low chuckle slid over his skin like a warm caress. "No," she said as she rubbed the pads of her thumbs in circles. "Not until I feel the knots in your neck subside."

"Listen, I'll do dishes if you do this. Deal?"

"Add take out garbage."

"Deal." He reached over his shoulder and shook her hand.

"So, have you already been added to the roster?"

"Not officially, but I know I will be. I've been through this enough times to know." He sighed. "I'll be honest—I hate playing for a team that isn't even minor-league level, but Noah Falcon is amazing and he can teach me a lot about pitching. So I'm going to have to work hard and then get the hell out of here as soon as I can."

She leaned over his shoulder. "Well, I don't think you endeared yourself to Ty McKenna. He's really into Jessica, Logan. And, hey, look. Jess is my friend too. She works her tail off, and hasn't had it easy. If you screw things up for her, I'll kick your sweet ass all the way into next week."

"Oh, so you acknowledge that my ass is sweet. Very nice."

She rolled her eyes and then gave his back a shove. "Whatever. But that brings me to the next stipulation. We need to keep our hands to ourselves. Except for this, no more . . . um, *touching*," she said, and then plopped back down onto the bed.

"Look." Logan swiveled around to face her. "You've sworn off men, and I'm going to be married to baseball. You'll be working a lot, and I'll be on the road for lots of games. We'll be like ships passing in the night," he said with a reassuring smile. "No big deal."

She rubbed her lips together. "Good. Glad we're on the same page. We'll just have to roll with it." She stuck her hand in his direction. "Let's shake on it."

Logan looked at her delicate hand once more. She had a cool, funky ring that must have been designed by her mother. Last night Madison had been hell-bent on getting Bella's mother to move here and open a jewelry store. "I'd rather seal the deal with a kiss."

"Logan! That would be defeating the purpose." She tilted her head and gave him a deadpan look, and edged her hand closer just as he leaned forward. Her fingers brushed against his chest, sending a jolt of awareness straight to his groin. When her eyes widened slightly and she pulled her hand back quickly, he wondered if she felt it too.

Logan was floored by his reaction. Women had always just been a form of entertainment to him. He wasn't a total ass about it, but he took what was offered. But watching his parents fight had left a bitter taste in his mouth where relationships were concerned, and he vowed never to let someone have that kind of hold over him. And yet he thought he could get used to sharing breakfast with Bella Diamante. Or even better . . . a bed. Having her delectable body off-limits wasn't going to be easy. But he grasped her hand in good faith. "Deal?"

"Deal." For such a delicate hand, she shook his with some strength. But her sudden frown bothered him.

"Hey, I fully admit that I can be an ass. But you can take

me at my word." He raised both palms in the air and wiggled his fingers. "I'll keep these to myself. Of course, if you feel the need to touch me, go right ahead."

"Well, then?"

"Yeah?" Logan looked at her expectantly, and for a moment he thought she was going to back out.

She inhaled deeply, outlining her breasts against the cotton shirt. *My shirt* . . . Damn, but that was sexy. Logan did his best not to notice, but he had to discreetly tug a pillow over the sudden tent in the sheet.

"I don't know why, but I believe you." She rolled her eyes. "Not that I'm a very good judge of character," she added in a lower tone. She remained silent for a moment and then shook her head. "Wow."

"What, Bella?"

"I was just wondering how I'm going to break my living arrangements to my mother."

"Just tell her it's a business arrangement," he suggested.

"You don't know my mother."

He looked at her and grinned. "I can only imagine. What about your dad?"

A shadow crossed over her lovely features. "He ran off when I was just a kid. I barely remember him."

"Dumb-ass," Logan muttered. There is was again. Concern for her. But oddly enough, it felt good to care about someone. He told himself that it was just a reaction to being in bed with a gorgeous woman who had a vulnerable set to her full mouth, and dark eyes that a man could lose himself in.

"Yeah," Bella said with a slight lift of one shoulder. "My mom deserved better. She drives me nuts, but she is a talented, beautiful woman."

"Apple doesn't fall far from the tree."

Bella looked at him in surprise, and he really wanted to kick Dastardly David's ass for taking away her confidence. He was surprised at himself, though, because he never said sappy things like that. But at her shy smile, Logan knew why: It was because it wasn't a sappy come-on. He meant it.

Well, damn. He had better watch it. She had already been hurt, and he sure as hell didn't want to be on her list of cockroaches. "Hey, listen. Are you hungry?"

"Starving."

"Let's go round up some greasy, bad-for-us hangover food. What do ya say?"

"I say that sounds like a plan." Her sad face suddenly brightened.

"What?"

"I'm no longer homeless and jobless! Wow, and I actually have a plan." She tipped her head. "Granted, it's a crazy plan and my mother will throw a fit, but it's a plan nonetheless. I think this might just work for us, Logan."

"Ya gotta like it when a plan comes together," he said, and wanted to kiss her, but then sternly reminded himself of the no-touching rule. But then she did something that blew him away.

She smiled.

Not just a regular curve of the lips, but a megawatt, Julia Roberts smile that lit up the room. It was the kind of smile that could make a man do just about anything to see again and again.

Of course, he wasn't that sappy kind of dude.

*A smile,* he thought with an internal roll of his eyes. *Holy crap. What the hell is happening to me?*

Her smile faltered and she put a hand on his arm. "Hey, are you okay? I mean, if you're having second thoughts, I totally understand." She looked at him with warm, honest eyes and it hit him hard. She was a good-hearted chick. He simply had to keep his wits about him and his hands to himself. He would be her friend—like a big brother—and look out for her well-being. Keep her away from ass clowns like him.

"Yeah, I'm fine. Just starving. Low blood sugar, I guess.

Let's go over to Wine and Diner and get some grub and get your car over here."

"Okay," she answered with another smile and a squeeze of his arm. "I need me some chocolate-chip pancakes!"

Logan smiled back but winced inwardly. *Big brother, my sweet ass.*

# 11

## The Name of the Game

TY TURNED HIS SWIVEL CHAIR AWAY FROM HIS DESK AND gazed out the picture window overlooking the Ohio River. He and Noah had spent the day hammering out the final roster, and now he had the crappy job of cutting the hopefuls, but also the fun of welcoming the chosen ones to the team. He still had misgivings about Logan Lannigan, but the kid had too much talent not to give him a chance. But Ty was going to lay the law down to the hotshot pitcher and nip any bad behavior in the bud.

Ty rehearsed his speech in his head one more time and then spun his leather chair away from the view and back to his desk. Finally, he picked up the phone and told his secretary to send Lannigan into the office. Ty wasn't surprised at the bored expression on Lannigan's face, but what the kid couldn't hide was the wary hint of uncertainty in the depths of his eyes.

"Have a seat," Ty crisply ordered, and pointed to the chair directly in front of his desk.

"Thanks," Lannigan said, and folded his tall frame into the leather chair. He casually draped his arms over his thighs, but there was a tension around his mouth that betrayed his nonchalant stance. The kid was nervous. *Well,*

*good. He damned well should be.* First the shithead had hit
on Jessica, and Ty had learned just a little while ago that not
only had he spent the night with Bella, but they were also
moving in together. What the hell was Bella thinking? Not
that it was really his business exactly, and while he couldn't
come right out and forbid the arrangement—or whatever
the hell it was—he could get his point across in a read-
between-the-lines kind of way, if he could keep from
punching the smirk off the kid's face.

"Congratulations, Lannigan. You made the team," Ty
announced in a tone that was flatter than he intended. But
when the kid raised one eyebrow slightly, he wanted to
jump across the desk and throttle him.

"Thanks," Lannigan replied in a not-quite-bored tone,
but without the excitement of the other players. It pissed Ty
off. The only saving grace was the almost-undetectable ease
of his rigid shoulders that once again negated his badass
attitude. This was his second chance, and the kid damned
well knew it.

Ty pressed his fingertips together in a steeple and gave
Lannigan a level stare. "Look, I am well aware that you
think that playing in this league is beneath you."

"Why would you say that?"

"It's written all over your face." Ty flattened his hands
on the desk and leaned forward. "But let me explain something to you. A lot is riding on the success of this team."

"I get it."

"Do you? Noah and I have invested our time and a
helluva lot of money, but more important, this entire town
is counting on it. Do you understand?"

"Yes," Logan replied quietly, but a muscle jumped in his
jaw.

"You're not the only player looking for either a first or a
second chance at the big show. Most won't get it. You probably will. But if you bring this team down with an attitude,
I'll kick your ass off the field so fast you'll get whiplash."

Okay, that last bit wasn't part of the speech, but the kid's insolence was getting under Ty's skin.

"I get it," he said just as quietly, and his chest rose and fell beneath his T-shirt.

Ty leaned back in his chair. "And while your personal life is none of my business, I expect you to conduct yourself in a professional manner. This is a small town with small-town values. I want my players to be an example to the community and be athletes that kids can look up to and emulate."

"Uh, most of your *community* was at a local bar last night, getting hammered."

"It was a party, Lannigan," he defended through gritted teeth.

Logan arched an eyebrow. "I'm just sayin'."

Ty wanted to reach over and rip that damned eyebrow off his face and toss it out the window. Except for one thing: Ty had been a late bloomer and was littler than most of his high school teammates. He had always had a bit of a chip on his shoulder and felt the need to prove himself with a cocky attitude much like Lannigan's.

"Are we finished?" Logan asked, and put his hands on the armrests, as if eager to get the hell out of the office.

Ty wanted to mention Bella, but it really wasn't his place, so he sighed and then nodded. "Yes," he replied, and stood up and extended his hand. "Welcome to the Cricket Creek Cougars."

Lannigan took his hand and shook with a firm grip. "Thanks. I appreciate the offer. No matter what you think of me, I can promise that I will work my ass off."

"Good. You damned well better," Ty answered, but was pleased with the kid's declaration. "I'll be honest. We need you, Lannigan. But we will get your arm back in shape and you won't pitch before we think you're ready. I won't win at the expense of your health. I want to see you make it back to the minors too." Ty meant it. It was what he and Noah wanted to see happen as often as possible.

"Thanks," Logan said, and something shifted in his eyes. The wariness, the hostility, vanished, making Ty wonder how many coaches or even if his parents had pushed this talented kid too much, too far, and if when he finally had his big shot, his overused arm gave out. And to add insult to injury, he was brought back too soon. "I appreciate that."

"You bet." Ty released his hand and watched the kid walk across the office, but when he put his hand on the doorknob, Lannigan paused and turned around.

"Sorry about hitting on your girl."

Ty shrugged. "I probably would have done the same thing at your age."

"She's hot."

Ty angled his head.

"Guess I should have kept that to myself."

"Just keep your hands to yourself, Lannigan."

At his comment, a look Ty couldn't quite read crossed Lannigan's face, and he said, "Hey, about Bella. Look, I know she's your friend, and for the record, we're just roommates."

"Didn't you just meet last night? How does that happen?"

Lannigan tilted his head and ran a hand down his face. "Jell-O shots. It seemed like a good idea to us both last night. Madison pushed for it. Anyway, it's purely a business arrangement. Not that I had to tell ya, but I wanted to put your mind at ease, because I can tell that you really care about her."

"She acts like one tough cookie, but she's going through some shit right now. Don't take advantage."

"I won't. As a matter of fact, I'll take it one step further. I'll kick any dude's ass who tries to mess with her," he added hotly.

Ty had to press his lips together to keep from grinning. The kid was reminding him more and more of himself . . . and Lannigan already cared about Bella. "Hey, I understand where you're coming from." Ty walked over and clamped a hand on Lannigan's shoulder. "I've known Bella for a few years. I was a regular at Chicago Blue, where she was the hostess. It's nice to know someone is looking out for her."

"I hear a *but* in there somewhere."

"But good luck." Ty couldn't hold back a grin this time. "Because Bella's a handful."

Lannigan gave him a lopsided grin back. "I already have that figured out, but thanks for the heads-up, Coach."

Ty sat down and then swiveled around to the window view, and exhaled a sigh of relief. He felt much better about that whole exchange and smiled. Logan Lannigan wasn't quite as cocky as he pretended to be, and Ty could relate. The kid was good, but had worked hard, and it was some scary shit watching a dream of a lifetime slip through your fingertips. And while Ty had been telling him the truth—that he wouldn't sacrifice the health of any of his players for a victory—the fact remained that a winning season was important. But he welcomed the pressure and the challenge. It was the name of the game.

Ty inhaled the smell of fresh paint and new carpet while watching a barge heading slowly down the river. The sinking sun glinted off the water, and he felt a sense of peace wash over him just watching the lazy progress. But at the same time, he felt a sweet surge of anticipation. Opening day was just weeks away!

When Ty's stomach rumbled he was reminded that he had skipped lunch. But then he felt another rush of anticipation that had nothing to do with baseball. It was time for a little dinner at Wine and Diner. With that thought, a vision of Jessica popped into his mind, and he slowly shook his head. He never imagined that a woman could have a hold on him the way that she did . . . and it felt amazing. Ty leaned back and chuckled. "Damn . . ." He had been teasing Noah about being whipped, but now he totally understood.

Although Ty had carefully distanced himself from serious relationships, he had always wondered what it would feel like to be in love, but the intensity of the emotion blew him away. He would do anything for Jessica. But he also knew that he needed to take things slow or he might scare her away. Little by little, inch by inch, he was going to remove that fear lingering in the depths of her eyes. He wanted Jessica to look at him the way Olivia looked at Noah. It would take some time, but he was a patient man when it came to getting what he wanted. And he wanted a relationship with Jessica Robinson more than anything. That thought startled him at first, but he smiled. "So this is love," he whispered. "Well, damn."

When his stomach rumbled again in protest, Ty pushed up to his feet and rubbed his midsection. "Meat loaf and mashed potatoes, here I come."

Since he had been cooped up in his office all day, Ty decided to walk to Wine and Diner. He had to smile at how many people honked and waved or stopped him to chat about how pumped they were that opening day was fast approaching. He loved seeing hope and excitement on the faces of the townsfolk, and he was going to work his everloving tail off to make the team a success.

When Ty entered Wine and Diner, he was pleased to see a line waiting to be seated. "Well, hey there, Bella." When she looked up from the hostess podium, Ty greeted her with a grin. "Kinda like old times."

"Well, hello again, Ty McKenna. Welcome to Wine and Diner!" Bella tucked her pen behind her ear, and Ty was glad to see her smile. "Just you tonight?"

"Yep, okay, maybe it's not like old times."

Bella laughed. "Not even close," she commented in a low tone.

"You doing any better today?"

Her smile faltered a bit. "Heading in that general direction, I hope."

"That's good to hear," Ty said, and took the menu she handed him, even though he knew it by heart.

"There's a twenty-minute wait unless you want to sit at the bar."

"You know I have no problem bellying up to the bar."

Bella laughed. "Well, at least *some* things never change. Not that there's anything wrong with that," she added with a wink.

"Lead the way." Ty of course knew where the bar was, but allowed Bella to do her job and followed her through the main dining area. He got waves and nods from now-familiar faces, and although he wasn't a hometown boy like Noah, he liked the fact that he was being treated more like a resident than a celebrity. Fewer people were calling him Triple Threat, and referred to him as Coach instead. Cricket Creek was beginning to feel like home, and after the transient lifestyle of a pro baseball player, the thought of putting down roots was appealing.

Although everything had been updated, Jessica had kept the essence of the original diner intact. Square Formica tables swirled with shades of smoky gray filled the booths lining the walls of the room. The chairs and benches gleamed with deep red leather upholstery, and the hardwood floor had been refinished and restored. A long counter with swivel stools formed an *L* shape directly in front of the bustling kitchen. Round trays of food were constantly being shoved up for the servers, who bantered back and forth with the cooks in diner lingo that entertained the customers. Ty knew that Jessica urged them to create a fun, energetic atmosphere that brought people back time and time again, and it was working. Jessica was smart and savvy. *And sexy,* his brain added, making him smile.

"Wow, that's temptation under glass," Ty commented to Bella when they passed a glass case displaying mouthwatering desserts that could be bought by the slice or by the entire pie or cake, some of which were made at Grammar's Bakery across the street.

"Oh, I know!" Bella said over her shoulder. "That Mile-High Coconut Cream Pie has been calling my name. It's a good thing the condo complex has a workout center. I'm going to need it!"

"Tell me about it," Ty agreed, and patted his stomach.

Country and bluegrass music filtered through speakers, while lively conversation hummed throughout the room. Silverware tinkled, glasses clinked, and a sprinkling of laughter gave the restaurant the modern-meets-throwback feel that Jessica was going for. He smiled, remembering the many conversations about the new menu and decor they had had over the past few weeks. Jessica pored over every detail, but wasn't opposed to listening to his suggestions. Having been valued only for his athletic ability over the years, her heeding his advice was a good feeling. Adding Bella to her crew was going to keep the bigger crowds under control.

Ty eyed plates with big, juicy burgers and hand-cut French fries, double-deckers, and open-faced roast beef. But Jessica had also added some modern flair to old favorites and included some bistro-style entrées that she had perfected at Chicago Blue. Tonight's special was Jessica's amazing meat loaf, green beans, and mashed potatoes, the kind with the skin still on, and his stomach rumbled just thinking about it.

"Smells great in here," Ty commented.

"I know." Bella nodded and gave her long, dark hair a flip over her shoulder. "I plan on trying everything on the menu. Jessica was working on some summertime fare this afternoon. Corn-and-bean salsa. Oh, baby, it was spicy hot, but so good."

Ty followed Bella into the new addition at the rear of the building. Although there was still a retro look, the tables were covered in white linen and rolled napkins. Fat candles flickered in muted lighting, and the music was soft rock instead of the bluegrass in the main dining room. A gorgeous bar built by Jason ran the length of the room, and mirrored lighted shelves displayed top-shelf liquor, with the emphasis on Kentucky bourbon. A wine rack butted up to an exposed brick wall, and a stone fireplace was the focal point in a lounge area at the rear of the room. French doors led to a patio that was a work in progress that Jessica wanted to have ready for an opening-day outdoor party.

"Do you still want to sit up at the bar?" Bella asked. "The couple at the end has a table that's ready."

"Yeah, that works," Ty answered. No need to take up a table when he planned on staying until Jessica was finished for the night. Just the thought of seeing her made him grin.

"Do you want me to find her?" Bella asked with a knowing arch of an eyebrow.

"Who?"

"Right," she said with a tilt of her head. "I'll let Jessica know you're here."

"Am I that transparent?"

"Yes, and I think it's so cute," she said, and wrinkled up her nose. "I always hoped you'd end up with somebody with some substance instead of those airheads you used to hang out with."

"I haven't ended up with Jessica. I still have my work cut out for me."

Bella lifted her chin and tapped him on the chest. "Somehow I think you're up for the challenge."

"I am," Ty answered, and gave Sam, the bartender, a nod when he held up a Kentucky Ale.

"Good, because Jess is worth it," Bella said with the conviction of someone who cared. She really was a sweetheart, and he had a hard time wrapping his brain around anyone treating her poorly.

"I agree," Ty answered, and then sat down on the vacant leather-backed stool.

"How are ya doin' tonight, Coach?" Sam asked as he popped the top off the beer and handed Ty the cold bottle.

"I'm doin' great, Sam," Ty answered before taking a long swig of the cold brew. And he realized that it wasn't just one of those automatic replies when in reality you're doing crappy. He truly meant it. The roster was filled with some solid talent, and opening day was just around the corner. Season-ticket sales were going strong, and local merchants were already feeling a positive impact.

"Glad to hear it," Sam replied. "This whole town is lookin' forward to opening day."

"Me too." Ty took another drink from the bottle and looked around. This was a typical Tuesday night, and yet Wine and Diner was packed with locals who, like Ty, were regulars. But a recent article in *Southern Living* magazine had also been bringing in patrons from miles away. Ty knew that Jessica had been scrambling to keep up and had called in a favor from a staff writer who was a big fan of his—not that he would ever let Jessica know he had a hand in landing the article. He wished there was something he could do to help out. A late-night back rub popped into his brain, almost making him choke on his beer. There had never been a woman who had occupied his thoughts as much as Jessica, and at this point he couldn't imagine his life without her.

"You ready to order?" Sam flicked Ty a glance while making drinks with lightning speed.

"Meat loaf special," Ty answered with a nod, but then sighed, thinking this going-slow thing wasn't going to be easy. Ty was used to going full throttle. It was everything he could do not to head on into the kitchen and drag Jessica into his arms in front of God and everybody. His heart thumped. He was half tempted to do it.

With another sigh, Ty looked up at the flat-screen television and checked out the score of the Cincinnati Reds preseason baseball game, but watched the action without much interest. All he could think about was getting a kiss from Jessica. When his meat loaf arrived, his attention was diverted by the delicious meal and a very nice glass of 2008 Estate Merlot from Elk Creek Winery. Jessica's wine list included several Kentucky wineries, and this one was a favorite of his.

Ty smiled when he spotted Madison heading his way. Jason wasn't with her, since he had been burning the midnight oil on last-minute work over at the stadium. The kid was talented and a hard worker.

"Well, hello there, Ty." Madison greeted him with a bright smile. "Enjoy your dinner?" She glanced down at his nearly clean plate. "Ah, meat loaf and merlot?"

Ty wiped his mouth with his napkin and scooted around to face her. "Well, after all, it is called Wine and Diner."

Madison nodded slowly and raised her palms upward. "My mama is a genius."

"I won't argue that."

"Have you seen her yet tonight?"

Ty toyed with the neck of his beer bottle and tried to appear casual and not like a lovesick puppy. "No . . ."

"Was that a pout?"

"Hold on. I'm a dude. An athlete!" Ty sat up straighter. "I don't pout."

Madison arched one blond brow and gave him a pointed look.

"Okay, yes, that was a pout. But, hey, I know she's busy."

Madison rolled her eyes. "Yes, she *is*, but Mom has very capable people back there, especially at this time of night, when things are starting to wind down. Ty, we close in just a little while. She can leave the doggone kitchen. I told her she needs to get out here and mingle with the customers, and she delegated that job to me." Madison sighed. "I don't mind, but Mom's tired and could use a cold drink. But do you think she would listen? No-oo."

"So she refuses to leave the kitchen?"

"Yes," Madison replied darkly, but then tapped her finger against her cheek. A moment later, her eyes widened. *"Hmm . . ."*

"What?"

She bit her bottom lip and then leaned in closer, away from prying eyes and ears. "I think I might have thought of a plan. Are you game?"

Ty grinned. "What do you think?"

Madison angled her head with her hands on her hips. "I'm thinking yes."

"You'd be right."

"Awesome!" She leaned her forearm on his shoulder and whispered in his ear, "Now, here's what I want you to do. . . ."

# 12

## *The Shape of Things to Come*

JESSICA MOVED HER HEAD FROM SIDE TO SIDE AND THEN rolled her shoulders in an effort to ease the tension. She was elated that Wine and Diner was packed—on a Tuesday night, no less—but waves of exhaustion washed over her. The flattering *Southern Living* article that hit the stands yesterday was such a blessing, but she was running on fumes. She glanced around the kitchen, searching for potential problems, but each station seemed to be running smoothly and they were slowly sliding into cleanup mode. Everyone was weary but remained upbeat, making Jessica smile. This was a good crew.

Jessica felt a little guilty sending Madison out to mingle, but she was bone-tired and her bubbly daughter was so much better in that capacity than she would ever hope to be. And while Jessica was sorry for Bella's recent breakup and the loss of her job at Chicago Blue, having her as hostess, particularly on a night like tonight, was a blessing. Jessica also knew that Bella's mother, Nicolina, would soon blow into Cricket Creek like a hurricane, especially when she learned that her daughter had moved in with a complete stranger! Jessica had been shocked when Madison had given her the news that Bella and Logan were roommates, and none too happy when Madison had also confessed to orchestrating the situation. But Madison had given Jessica the matchmaker look of *I know what I'm doing*, and she knew there was no arguing with Madison's gut feeling.

"Mom!"

Jessica turned at Madison's shout and was brought out of her musings. She mustered a smile and tried not to appear too tired, even though she was, as Aunt Myra would say, plumb tuckered out. Her heart kicked it up a notch when she witnessed the look on Madison's face. "Sweetie, is there something wrong?"

"Well . . ." Madison pressed her lips together and nodded slowly. "We seem to have a disgruntled customer."

"Oh no! Really?"

"Yes." Madison continued to nod.

"Was it the food?" Jessica asked with a frown, and then pulled her daughter out into the hallway, away from the heat and the kitchen clatter. Plus, everyone had worked so hard tonight, she didn't want to bring the crew down.

Madison tucked a blond curl behind her ear. "Actually, it was the service."

"Seriously?" Jessica angled her head in disbelief. She leaned back against the exposed brick wall and sighed. "So what did you do?"

"Offered free dessert."

"Always a pleaser. Good job, Madison," Jessica said, and then pushed away from the wall. "So did it work?"

"Well, I believe so, but he wanted the person in charge to deliver it personally."

"Me?" Jessica splayed a hand on her chest and groaned. "Oh, honey. I'm so tired! Can't Bella do it? She's a charmer when she wants to be."

"He only wanted you. You know, I mean, the owner."

"Where's Aunt Myra?"

"She was helping Bella handle the crowd, but when things slowed down, she was making goo-goo eyes at Owen, who stopped in for dinner. They hightailed it out of here about an hour ago."

"Well, damn!" Jessica felt anger flare up like the flame on a gas stove turned on high. "You know, just once I'd like to drag a disgruntled jackass back here by his ear and shove him into this inferno of a kitchen. I'd like him to see the work and effort that goes into preparing the perfect meal over and over again. Then maybe he'd shut his big mouth! Oh, and the service? Nobody works harder than a good waiter! And our staff is fucking fantastic!"

Madison's eyes widened.

"Sorry about the language," she muttered darkly, but for once she really wasn't. She folded her arms across her chest and narrowed her eyes. "Oh, I would like to take an entire pie out there and shove it in his face! Bet he'd be disgruntled then!"

Madison winced. "Um, maybe you'd better not do that. Really."

"Oh, you know I'm just venting. Okay, my rant is . . . Hey, wait." Jessica looked at Madison closely. "Why do I suddenly smell something fishy?"

Madison raised her shoulders slightly. "Um, maybe it's the halibut? That was excellent, by the way. The sauce—"

"Ma-di-son!"

"What?" Madison lifted her palms upward. "Hey, you'd better sashay out there with that dessert. I believe he requested, um, your Kentucky Nut Pie."

"Let me guess. With extra bourbon-laced whipped cream?" Jessica asked in a knowing tone.

"Maybe . . . Oh, that sounds good. I think I'll go rustle up a slice for Jason. He should be home soon."

"You're meddling again, aren't you?"

"No . . . okay, maybe."

"There is never a *maybe* with you."

"Okay, yes," Madison admitted, and bestowed Jessica with her best don't-be-mad-at-me smile.

Jessica uncrossed her arms and put her fists on her hips. "I don't know whether I should be pissed or relieved."

"I totally vote for relieved."

"Madison, you didn't have to fabricate this. Why didn't you just tell me the truth?"

"Yeah, right! You wouldn't have left the kitchen if I had said that Ty wanted to hang out for a while. Now, would you?"

"No!"

"See!"

"That doesn't make it right!"

Madison put her hands on Jessica's shoulders. "I didn't really make it up," she defended. "Ty McKenna is a customer and he was disgruntled . . . in a manner of speaking."

"You are stretching the truth like a rubber band."

"Who cares?" Madison dropped her hands. "You've been out here with me and the restaurant is running just fine! You work too hard. Take a little time to enjoy the view!"

Jessica snorted.

"Okay, that was reaching. Sounds better when Barbara Walters says it."

"You seriously watch *The View*?"

"Sometimes, until they annoy me by talking over one another." She waved her hand in the air. "That's not the point. You work too much."

"It's the nature of this business. Restaurants have a very high failure rate, Madison."

"Mom . . ."

"And so do relationships," she muttered, and then put a hand over her mouth.

"Too late. You said it out loud. The truth comes out. You're still afraid."

Jessica felt emotion well up in her throat.

"Mom, look. It's okay to be guarded, but not jaded. Believe me, I get it. But it's not okay not to give this a shot. The only failure is in not trying."

"Hey." Jessica gave her a small smile. "When did you become the mother and I become the kid?"

"I'm repeating what you taught me not only through words but through action. Now go take Ty his dessert. He's waiting out on the patio."

"Okay." Jessica rolled her eyes. "Kentucky Nut Pie with extra bourbon whipped cream."

Madison chuckled softly.

"What?"

"Nothing."

Jessica tapped her foot.

"Kentucky Nut Pie was the first dessert that popped into my head. He didn't even ask for it. All he wants is you. But I find it so sweet, if you'll pardon the pun, that you knew his obvious favorite."

"Madison, the man eats here all the time."

"So do a lot of people, and I bet you don't know their favorite desserts. As a matter of fact, you used to only have it here on Derby weekend, but I seem to recall that you suddenly decided to keep it on the menu."

"I have a lot of Kentucky favorites on the menu." She put her index finger to her pinky and started ticking them off. "Kentucky Hot Brown, Kentucky Bourbon Balls, Dead Heat Kentucky Burgoo . . ."

"Yeah, the *new* menu! You kept the Derby Pie for Ty McKenna. Fess up!"

"Okay, busted. So what? He's a loyal customer. Just like you and martini Mondays at Sully's."

"Mom! Stop arguing and get your butt out there, with or without the Derby Pie!"

"I'm a mess!"

"Take your chef's whites off, slap on some lipstick, and get on out there before he dips out. Although I'm sure he knew this was going to take some doing. For pity's sake, you are enough to wear a person out, Mom. I swear!" She made shooing motions with her fingers. "Go! And don't bother with dessert! The man wants some sugar from you!"

"Ma-di-son! You are the only one who would say something like that to your mother."

"You say my name like that a lot, you know. I'm going to call you Jess-i-ca!"

"Okay, I'm going," Jessica promised, but then turned away so that Madison couldn't see the sudden emotion that her innocent comment caused. She hurried across the hallway and into her office, quickly closing the door. She put a hand over her mouth and willed herself not to sob. Jessica had suddenly remembered that her mother would do the same thing and break her name into syllables whenever she would pop off. When her father had been gone on some business trip or whatever, she and her mother would relax and enjoy each other. Back then, Jessica's humor had been much like Madison's whenever her father wasn't around.

She shook her head. The sudden memory of her mother had taken her by surprise. It hurt to this day that her mother had chosen not to be a part of her life.

"Damn it!" Jessica remembered her conversation with Ty and whispered, "I will no longer let the mistakes of others rule my life!" She sniffed, but then stiffened her spine while fumbling with the buttons on her chef's jacket. When she finally got it off, she tossed it aside, tugged off her checkered pants, and quickly located her black leggings and soft pink tunic. It wasn't fancy, but would have to do. After touching up her lipstick, she hurried into the kitchen and slid a slice of pie into a to-go box and added a generous dollop of her famous bourbon-laced whipped cream. After inhaling a deep breath, she headed out the back entrance and around the corner to the patio.

Jessica smiled. She was on a mission, and Mr. Triple Treat wasn't going to know what hit him.

# 13

## *Mission Accomplished!*

*T*Y REACHED INTO HIS JEANS POCKET AND PULLED OUT HIS cell phone for the fifth time. It was pushing ten o'clock. He had been waiting for Jessica for more than twenty minutes. Madison's little scheme hadn't worked.

Jessica wasn't coming.

With a long sigh, he glanced over to where light spilled from the French doors, hoping once again to see Jessica emerge. "Well, damn," he muttered. Despite his disappointment, he had to admire the surroundings. Even in the muted light, Ty could see that Jason had laid a lovely oval, brick-paved patio, and Owen had done a fantastic job with the landscaping. Green ivy spilled over the top of tall terra-cotta planters filled with a plethora of colorful spring flowers. The soothing sound of gurgling water stemmed from a fountain in the far corner of the patio, and strategically placed trees would eventually add shade and privacy to the outdoor space. The bronzed, wrought-iron furniture had a rustic edge, but the mosaic tabletops added a touch of elegance that was a perfect feel for Wine and Diner.

Jessica had told Ty of her future plans for live music and an expanded patio that would include a gazebo for Madison, who wanted an outdoor wedding. With a shake of his head, Ty wondered if Jessica realized how well he had gotten to know her over the past year, despite her attempts to keep him at arm's length. And after making love to her, she meant even more to him. He chuckled softly, but it suddenly scared him that he might never be able to break down her walls and have her come to him without reservation.

And he wanted nothing less.

Ty glanced over at the table where he had lit two candles. The bottle of Elk Creek merlot and two wineglasses appeared as lonely as he felt. "Well . . ." Ty muttered, and then scrubbed a hand down his face. He suddenly felt a bit of a fool, standing out here, hoping Jessica would join him. And he shouldn't have to resort to playing games while trying to get the woman he cared about to spend time with him. He reminded himself that he was supposed to be patient and to take it slow, but all at once he became frustrated and decided that he should simply leave.

And then he saw her.

While she walked slowly toward him, the light of the windows behind her cast a golden glow. The cool evening breeze molded her billowy blouse to her body, making Ty inhale sharply. He knew he was staring, but could not even begin to tear his gaze from her face.

"Good evening, Ty." Her sultry voice was a warm contrast to the cool night and felt like a physical caress. When she was standing directly in front of him, Ty tried to think of something clever to say, but when he caught a whiff of her perfume, words failed him. Instead, a pathetic little moan came out of his mouth and he had to disguise it with a cough. Her eyes widened slightly. "Are you okay?"

"Yeah," he managed to articulate. "Something caught in my throat."

"Oh." There was something different in the way she gazed up at him. He felt confidence oozing from her and an underlying sense of determination, and when Ty searched her amber eyes for that all-too-familiar flash of fear, his heart thudded.

It was gone.

What he did see was a woman who knew what she wanted and was going for it. And it was damned sexy.

"Well, now . . ." Jessica angled her head slightly, allowing her sleek ponytail to slip over her shoulder. Ty dearly wanted to wrap the silky hair around his fist and pull her head back for a long, hot kiss. "I was told I had a disgruntled customer. Might that be you?"

"Yes," he replied in a husky tone filled with the need to kiss her. But he wanted to play this out and hopefully drive her crazy. He gestured toward the table where candles flickered and danced off the delicate wineglasses. "Would you mind sitting down and discussing my grievances over a nice glass of merlot?"

"Not at all," she replied, and sat down on the cushioned love seat. "Oh, and by the way, I brought you dessert as an apology for your . . . dissatisfaction."

Ty sat down next to her and then leaned over to open the small box. "Ah, Derby Pie?"

She nodded

"My favorite." *Did she remember that?*

"Well, actually, it's my version of the original classic served at the Kentucky Derby. I use pecans instead of walnuts."

"I think it's great to give classic recipes your own personal touch. You excel at that, you know."

"I always have to tinker with a recipe. Besides, we couldn't call it Derby Pie on the menu."

"Really?"

"Yes, the original was created by George Kern at the Melrose Inn in Prospect, Kentucky, and the Kern family holds the copyright. There have been several lawsuits over the use of the name Derby Pie through the years, including one against Nestlé when they put a Derby Pie recipe on the back of a bag of chocolate chips."

"You're kidding."

"Not at all. The Kern family is serious about guarding the secret Derby Pie recipe." She leaned in closer. "Only a few of the Kern family know it, and one kitchen cook." She held up her index finger with a grin. "I think it would be the coolest thing to create something so amazing that it was a closely guarded secret and kept in a safe."

"Well, the Derby—I mean the *Kentucky Nut Pie*—that you make is to die for, and I can't imagine one better. It really is my personal favorite."

She gave him a steady look. "I know. I kept it on the menu just for you."

Ty was touched by her admission. She was allowing him to know that she had been taking note over the past months as well and wasn't afraid to put it out there. "Thank you, Jessica," he said, and they both knew he wasn't only referring to the pie. "I'm beginning to really like this habit of you bringing me dessert." He wiggled his eyebrows and then swiped his finger in the whipped cream before sucking the cool sweetness off his finger. "Wow, that is amazingly good. Just the right amount of bourbon," he said, letting her know that her cooking was an art and not hit-or-miss. Nothing at Wine and Diner was simply slapped together, and he admired her dedication and talent.

"I aim to please," she answered in a low, seductive voice that made him feel warm despite the evening breeze. She handed him a fork. "Go ahead. Take a bite. I'll pour the wine. Would you like a glass?"

"Don't mind if I do." Ty tried for a casual tone but failed miserably. And he was grateful for her offer to pour, because when he pushed his fork into the crunchy pecans, he noticed that his hands were trembling slightly. *Wow,* Ty thought to himself. He had played baseball in front of thousands in crushingly stressful situations and his hands had been as steady as a rock. And yet just sitting next to Jessica, with the anticipation of what was to come, had him shaking like a rookie taking his first at bat in the major leagues.

The flaky crust hit his tongue, followed by a blast of rich, dark chocolate. The soft, buttery center of the pie rolled over his tongue and he savored the texture and flavor. He pointed his fork at the pie. "What I like about this pie is that the semisweet chocolate and bite of bourbon keep it from being too cloyingly sweet."

Jessica handed him a glass of wine. "I agree. And I prefer pecans over walnuts, although I might try mixing in both."

Ty gave her a shake of his head. "Don't change a thing. This pie is perfect as it is. And you make a tender, flaky crust. My mom was a good cook, but piecrusts always gave her fits. What's the secret?"

"Keeping everything chilled and not overworking the dough, or the texture will be tough. Precise measurements are so important for a perfect crust. Oh, and add just enough water, or it will get too sticky and not be nearly as flaky. . . ." She trailed off and sucked her bottom lip between her teeth. "Sorry! More than you wanted to know." She leaned back against the cushion and shook her head. "I get carried away talking about food."

"What?" Ty reached over and touched her arm. "First of all, I asked you. And you know me better than that. I could listen to you talk about food all night long. Jessica, to me, eating is one of life's pleasures, and you enhance that experience for me."

"You have a good palate. That's for sure, and . . ." She pressed her lips together.

"Don't"—Ty shook his head and softly pleaded—"hold anything back from me. Jessica, please finish your thought."

"I love that about you . . . your appreciation of fine food and the work that goes into making it that way," she said, but instead of meeting his gaze, she took a sip of her wine and glanced away.

Ty's heart pounded and he wanted to pull her in for a

hug, but he refrained. She was a strong-willed woman and needed to open up on her own terms, and he would let her. So even though he sensed she wanted to say more, instead of prompting her further, Ty decided it was time to kick back and have a good time. "Day-um, this Derby Pie—um, I mean Kentucky Nut Pie—is a party in my mouth."

Jessica giggled, making her appear younger, carefree. "So you're no longer a disgruntled customer?"

"Not anymore."

"Yeah, right." Jessica reached over and pinched off a piece of the piecrust. "I am going to get Madison back when she least expects it," she said before popping the pastry into her mouth.

"Hey, I am a customer and I was disgruntled."

"Sure you were." Jessica scoffed. "About what?"

"Not getting a glimpse of you all night long."

"Oh, come on." She took another sip of her wine and then sighed.

Ty felt his heart plummet and he placed his wineglass and pie on the table. "What will it take?"

"What do you mean?"

"What will it take for you to believe me and not think I'm spitting game at you?"

"I don't think that!"

"What was the sigh for, Jessica?"

She set down her wine and scooted to face him on the love seat. "I came out here to knock your doggone socks off and . . ."

"And what?"

"I don't know how to banter. To flirt!" She raised her palms skyward. "I suck!" she said so forcefully that Ty almost laughed, except that she was serious and it went straight to his heart.

"You've got to be kidding me."

"No, I suck, suck . . . *suck*!"

"That's what I . . . like about you." He almost said *love*.

She dipped her head and gave him a pointed look. "That I suck at flirting?"

"Jessica, I've had a lifetime of bullshit from women. I don't need batting eyes and playful pouts. Games." He sliced his hand like a salute to the forehead. "I've had it up to here with all of that meaningless crap. When I pay you a compliment, I'm not flirting. I damned well mean it. And you don't know how refreshing it is to have real, meaningful conversations with you. No pretense."

She grinned. "No bullshit?"

"Exactly."

"So, I should just get down to brass tacks?"

"Damned straight."

"Thank God for small favors," Jessica said, and before he could voice his total agreement, she closed the gap between them and pulled his head down for a long, hot kiss. Damn, she tasted like wine and woman, and he couldn't get enough. The pie had been a party in his mouth, but this was a full-blown celebration. He had been daydreaming about this all day long, but the reality was so much better. He cradled her head, wishing for her hair to be loose and sliding between his fingers. To hell with playing this out. He wanted her more than enough now, and he wanted her in his bed.

"Jessica, are you finished for the night?"

"Not with you," she said, and kissed his neck. "I'm just beginning."

"Damn, that was straight to the point and smokin' hot. Who needs wimpy-ass flirting?" He chuckled but then inhaled a quick breath when she sucked his earlobe into her warm mouth. When she nibbled, a jolt of pure desire shot all the way to his toes. "How quickly can you meet me back at my condo?"

"World Record time. I'll tell Madison to lock up."

"Good." He let out a long sigh.

"What?"

"The only thing better than you bringing me dessert is you being the dessert."

Jessica tossed her head back and laughed. "Oh, I like the way you think."

"Let's get out of here." He sensed that she was finally letting her guard down and saying what she felt, and he loved it. Her personality was shining through, and she seemed tired but as though she was beginning to finally relax. He planned on giving her a back rub that would turn her into warm putty in his hands. She deserved to be pampered. And then it hit him hard that no one had probably ever done that for her. She was always doing for everyone else. He ground his teeth together when unexpected emotion gripped him, but then he smiled.

Jessica Robinson was about to get swept off her tired feet.

# 14

## This Kiss, This Kiss!

"CHECK IT OUT." BELLA GAVE MADISON AN ELBOW WHEN she spotted Jessica scurrying into her office.

"You girls lock up. Okay?" Jessica requested when she emerged a moment later clutching her purse.

"Sure, Mom," Madison replied, and they watched her rush toward the front door and then pause to catch her breath.

"Oh, Bella, awesome job tonight!" Jessica tossed over her shoulder. "See you both tomorrow! I'm, uh, really tired and—"

"Mom, don't even try."

Jessica flushed a pretty shade of pink and pointed at Madison. "I'm going to get you for this. A disgruntled customer. Right."

"Go on and get out of here," Madison urged with a giggle and shooed her mother out the door.

"Wow," Bella commented with a sense of wonder. "I always kinda thought your mom had a thing for Ty, but he was such a player back in Chicago and she wouldn't give him the time of day. Wouldn't it be cool if they stayed together? You know, became an official couple?"

"They will," Madison responded with a firm nod.

"What makes you so sure?"

"My gut."

"You trust your gut?" Bella snorted. "My gut lies to me all the damned time." She frowned down at her stomach. "Are you serious?"

"Yeah, I am," Madison replied with a tilt of her head. "Bella, your gut doesn't lie. You just don't listen."

*"Pfft."* Bella straightened up a stack of menus. "You really are joking, right?" She remembered that Madison had a wicked sense of humor.

"No, I'm not. You just can't let your heart"—she tapped her chest—"or your brain"—she tapped her temple—"screw it all up."

"That doesn't make any sense," Bella scoffed.

"If you've got a minute, I'll explain," Madison offered, and pointed to the stools at the counter.

"Sure. Every minute I spend here is a minute more I get to put off calling my mother. She's left two messages, but I texted her that I was busy hanging out with you guys and catching up on old times." She wrinkled her nose. "Little white lie. But no— *Hey*, I don't want to keep you from Jason."

"Don't worry. I have to stay here and lock up after the cleanup is done in the kitchen." Madison rolled her eyes. "They would have been done by now if they hadn't been tripping over each other, sneaking peeks at you."

"Shut up. I'm just the new girl in town."

Madison handed her a cold bottle of water and then sat down. "Yeah, the new girl who looks like Eva Longoria."

"Right . . ." Bella shrugged, even though she had gotten that too often to count in Chicago. "She's, like, ten years older than me and Mexican, not Italian."

Madison raised her hands in surrender. "Hey, don't shoot the messenger. I finally had Evan the busboy convinced that you *were* Eva Longoria and were doing that TV show *I Get That a Lot*, where celebrities pretend to be everyday Joes. Told him there were hidden cameras. I had him going."

Bella laughed. "Madison, you're crazy."

"I know. And I get *that* a lot." She shrugged. "I've embraced it."

"Why fight a losing battle?"

"I keep telling my mother that."

Bella laughed at her friend. "Okay, so fill me in on how to go with my gut—a gut that will get bigger if I keep eating here. I had forgotten how amazing your mother's food is, and I love it here even more than at Chicago Blue. The Wine and Diner thing is genius. But anyway, go ahead."

Madison put her hand over Bella's and squeezed. "I hate to bring it up, but tell me how your heart and your head felt about David."

Bella took a swig of her water and swiveled back and forth on the round stool while she pondered the question. "Well, he was a broody, edgy, starving artist, and my heart was all over that." She looked at Madison for feedback.

"And your head?"

"I can't draw more than stick people, and I was fascinated by his talent. My brain was intrigued."

"I hear a *but. . . .*"

Bella played with her bottle for a thoughtful moment. "But David couldn't stay focused and would get angry when I stressed the business side of his career. Look, my mother is a talented artist. She sketches her ideas and then works hard on her jewelry, but she knows she has to put effort into selling her creations. My brain warned me this was a real problem with David. I know now that it's part of being mature. An adult. But my heart chalked it up to David being passionate about his work, and my heart trumped my brain every single damned time."

Madison tapped her midsection. "And your gut?"

Bella gave her a long, level look.

"Be honest."

After inhaling deeply, Bella continued. "My gut never did really trust him."

"And your heart and brain ignored your gut."

"Wow . . . Bingo."

Madison tilted her head, making her riot of curls slide over her shoulder. "So, from now on, trust your gut. It will be right every time."

"I'll try. But the brain and heart are difficult to ignore."

Madison nodded. "Yeah, gut instinct, *intuition* . . . divine intervention? Call it what you want, but it is our most powerful tool as human beings and the one we fight the most."

"Why is that, do you think?"

Madison toyed with the napkin holder. "A lot of reasons. Most of the time a gut feeling has no real tangible basis. It's simply a feeling."

"And we don't trust our feelings?"

"Not when we don't want to," Madison replied slowly. "A gut feeling usually has a warning or foreboding. You didn't want to believe that David was cheating, so you ignored the red flags. The old saying that the woman is always the last to know is bull. Even if you didn't know for sure, you had a strong suspicion that he was capable of this behavior."

"Oh, I was such a dumb-ass," Bella admitted hotly, and felt tears spring into her eyes. "Never again!"

Madison reached over and grabbed Bella's clenched fist resting on the counter. "My mother fell into that trap. Don't you dare let what Dastardly David did to you screw up a chance at the real deal. What he did isn't the next guy's fault."

"Yeah, but—"

"But nothing." Madison gave Bella a steady look and waited.

"Don't ask it." Bella's heart pumped, but Madison shook her head from side to side.

"I have to. So, what does your gut say about Logan?"

"You're the matchmaker with the always-right gut feelings. You're so sure about Ty and your mother. You tell me."

"Oh no, you don't, girlfriend." Madison thumped her water bottle down so hard that water sloshed over the top. "Fess up. What is your gut saying to you?"

"That he's an arrogant hotshot who will have the girls in this town falling all over him. That he's talented, and, with the help of Ty and Noah, will make his way back to the minor leagues, where he belongs. That I had better not fall for him, because he will be leaving soon anyway."

"Bella . . ." Madison tapped her midsection. "That's all *stuff*. What is your gut telling you about him?"

"I hardly know him!"

Madison tapped again.

"I'm gonna grab that finger of yours and break it right off," she threatened, but the hitch in her voice took away the heat. "Besides, I don't believe in love at first sight. That's plain bullshit. Not that I love Logan. We're just living together . . . rooming together, and it was at your—" She stopped and stared. "Insistence," she added softly. "Oh, boy, Madison, don't deny that you have some sort of feeling here."

"Okay, I won't."

Bella did a little head bop. "Not that I believe in your matchmaking mojo. It's just one of those quirky Southern things."

"Okay, I feel ya."

Bella lifted one shoulder ever so slightly. "But just out of curiosity . . . you know, for shits and giggles?" She swallowed and then asked in a tiny voice, "What is your gut feeling about Logan and me?"

"Well . . ." Madison looked at her for a contemplative moment, as if reading her love aura or something. "It doesn't matter what my gut thinks."

"Ma-di-son!"

"Why does everyone say my name like that? Is it on my birth certificate that way?"

"It damned well should be!"

"Well—" Madison began, but they were distracted by the bell jingling over the front door.

"We're closed," Bella called over her shoulder, and was about to apologize when she spotted Logan coming into the diner. He walked toward them with the grace of a superior athlete.

"I know." He shoved long fingers through his shaggy hair, which appeared just-showered damp.

"Oh." Bella tried to appear nonchalant, but a whiff of his spicy aftershave had her pulse racing. It didn't help that his black baseball-cut T-shirt molded to his chest and biceps like second skin. "So, what's up?"

"I noticed that your car was parked over at the condo."

Bella nodded. "I walked to work. It was such a pretty day, and after that stack of chocolate-chip pancakes, I decided I needed the exercise."

Logan shrugged, making muscles do delicious things beneath his shirt. "Yeah, but it's dark now, so I drove over here to pick you up."

"You didn't have to do that," Bella said, and flicked a glance over at Madison to see her reaction. She didn't seem surprised and, in fact, was smiling.

"I know. I just thought the temperature had dropped and . . ." He shrugged again and then shifted his weight, as if suddenly unsure. "But, listen. If I'm interrupting something, I can—"

"I think it was a nice gesture," Madison broke in, and gave Bella a give-the-guy-some-credit look. "And, no. We were just having some girl talk. We're finished here. As a matter of fact, I'm going to head into the kitchen to fix Jason a sandwich before it completely shuts down. It was good seeing you, Logan."

"Same here."

"I'll see you tomorrow, Bella."

Bella gave Madison an I-know-what-you're-doing look, but she gave her an innocent smile back.

"Are you ready?" Logan asked.

"Yes, I just need to grab my purse from behind the hostess stand," she replied, and headed over to retrieve it. She slipped the strap over her shoulder. When she smiled up at him, he seemed to relax. Bella thought it was sweet that he was concerned, but it was his almost-shy uncertainty that got to her the most. Maybe Logan Lannigan wasn't as cocky as he pretended to be.

"I didn't mean to butt into your business," Logan said as he held the door open for her.

"That's my mother's job and she does it well," Bella said with a laugh, but when she passed him, their bodies brushed, and damned if she didn't feel a hot tingle that had her melting like a marshmallow on a s'more.

"Have you talked to your mother yet?" Logan asked as they walked over to his blue Ford Ranger.

"No," Bella answered glumly. "But I'll have to face the music later tonight. She's already called a couple of times."

"You'll feel better after you talk to her."

Bella inhaled a deep breath. "Don't count on it," she said, as he opened the passenger's door for her. "I didn't realize you had a truck."

"Are you surprised?"

"Kinda."

Logan pointed down at his feet.

"Cowboy boots? Really?"

"I'm from Dallas, Bella."

"You don't sound like it. And you look to me like you just stepped off a California beach."

"I have a little Texas twang that comes out now and then. My father transferred there when I was a kid so I could play baseball year-round. Most people living in Dallas are transplants." He smiled. "But I love my boots and my truck."

Bella scooted up into the passenger's seat and watched Logan walk around to the driver's side, while thinking here she was, living with a man whom she knew very little about, and by rights she should feel a measure of concern. But she just couldn't muster much up. Oh, boy, but she knew her mother sure would! If anyone she knew were doing such a foolish thing, she would give them a piece of her mind.

Bella sighed. Apparently, her common sense had taken a holiday, and she should really tell Logan that this living-together arrangement was alcohol induced and should be reconsidered. But when he folded his tall frame into the truck and flashed Bella a smile, her common sense decided to extend its vacation.

"Well, it's official. Ty told me that I made the team."

"Congratulations. Was there ever a doubt?"

"No." Logan put the truck into gear.

"You don't seem too excited."

After steering the truck out onto Main Street, Logan flicked Bella a glance. "Don't get me wrong; I'm grateful for the chance to prove myself, but this isn't where I wanted to be at this stage of the game."

"I understand," Bella said, but felt a sharp stab of disappointment. "You can't wait to head on out of here," she added with more of an edge than intended. It didn't matter what Madison's intuition said. She needed to guard her heart where Logan Lannigan was concerned.

"You sound pissed."

Bella shrugged but remained silent.

"Bella, that's what this team is all about: second chances. Ty and Noah will tell you that."

"I'm sorry, Logan. I'm just in a dark and twisty place right now. Don't mind me."

Logan reached over and covered her hand with his. "I know you're going through some crap."

She nodded and felt her throat constrict. His big hand

felt warm and strong, but she untangled her fingers from his. "Look, it was a nice gesture for you to come pick me up. Really."

"But you don't want me to do it again."

"No, I don't." When they stopped at a red light, Bella turned and gave him a firm, negative shake of her head. "You don't need to be my rebound guy, Logan. And chances are, some smart scout is going to snatch you back up to the minor leagues."

"I have a contract. I have to remain here for the season."

"Regardless, you'll most likely be leaving by the end of the summer. We need to keep our relationship platonic. Picking me up feels . . . too intimate. Like you're my boyfriend, but you're not." She looked at his profile, but he remained silent. "You're feeling me, right?"

Finally, he nodded. "Yeah, I'm feeling ya, Bella. But I promised Ty McKenna that I'd look out for you, and I won't break that promise."

"I don't need anyone looking out for me," she replied hotly. "I might be a little shit, but I can hold my own. We need to live as roommates but stay out of each other's way. Otherwise, this isn't going to work. Okay?"

He was silent for a moment longer, and Bella's stupid heart beat faster. A big part of her wanted him to say that there was no way he could keep his hands off her, and if any other guy even thought of looking at her, he would punch him in the face. *Silly,* she thought with a mental shake of her head. She barely knew Logan, so her attraction to him could only be physical at this point. Madison's whole gut thing was pure bologna.

Logan still didn't answer until he pulled into the parking lot. After killing the engine, he finally turned her way. "Look, I made a promise to myself and to Ty that I'd look out for you like a big brother."

"And I told you I don't need you to do that." *Big brother? Ugh!*

"Maybe, but all the same, I probably won't be able to stop myself. But I'll try."

"Good. We're on the same page," she said, but didn't really mean it. "Okay, let's go on in."

"Wait." Logan reached over and put a hand on her arm. "I have only one request."

"What?" she asked breezily, and tried her damnedest not to be affected by his warm hand on her arm.

Logan cleared his throat and hesitated for a second.

"Logan?"

"Before we start this whole big-brother, platonic thing, I'd like just one kiss."

"What?" Bella asked in a pitch just short of a shout. "Are you kidding me?" she added in a much lower but no less exasperated tone.

He shrugged slightly. "To get it out of my system, so I don't walk around wondering for the rest of my life."

"To get me out of your system?" She angled her head and cocked one eyebrow. "Really . . . and then just dismiss me." She snapped her fingers. "Just like that."

"Okay, maybe that didn't come out just right."

"No, I think it came out just the way you wanted it to." Bella felt anger wash over her. *Men are dogs. . . . Oh yeah, right*—cockroaches. Why did she keep forgetting that?

Logan gave her a sheepish look, as if he knew what she was thinking. "Bella, forget that I asked."

"Oh no, you don't."

"What?"

"Let's get out of the truck so we can do this right."

"No . . . really. I've just been thinking about it and—"

"Well, you won't have to wonder any longer." Bella reached for the door handle and got out of the truck. She put her purse down on the ground and stood there fuming. Well, if Logan Lannigan thought this kiss was going to be a little ole peck, he was so wrong that he'd soon forget he was oh, so wrong. *Get me out of his system? Ha!* Bella was hell-bent on giving him a kiss that would haunt him for a life-time!

"Get on over here, cowboy!"

As soon as he reached her side, Bella fisted her hands in his shirt and yanked him forward. He landed against her with a solid *thump* that knocked her backward against the truck. The door handle bit into her back, but Bella barely felt it.

"Bella, listen!"

"Shut up!" She pulled his head down and pressed her lips to his. Her kiss was born of anger, but what started off hard and punishing quickly melted like butter on a hot griddle. And, God, the man could kiss. His lips were firm but pliant and his mouth was oh, so warm. He tasted slightly of mint, and the spicy scent of his aftershave filled her head. When his tongue tangled with hers, a hot jolt of desire un-coiled in her stomach and spread like wildfire. Bella clung to his shoulders and pressed her body closer. She tilted her head and deepened the kiss, and when she nipped his bottom lip with a love bite, she noted with satisfaction that Logan moaned. Oh, wait. That moan came from her own throat. *Damn . . .*

Bella moved her hands from Logan's shoulders to his chest so that she could give him her planned, quick, dismissive shove and then march away in a huff. But when he threaded his long fingers through her hair, she became lost in the kiss.

Her plan had totally backfired.

But never in a million years would Bella let Logan know it. She finally mustered up the will to end the delicious kiss, but did it by slowly licking her tongue across his bottom lip and then pulling back to look up at him. "So, am I out of your system?" she asked in what was supposed to be a harsh tone but came out soft and husky.

"Not even close," Logan responded, and gently traced his fingertip over her bottom lip.

Bella wanted to suck his finger into her mouth, but she smacked his hand away. "I guess it sucks to be you," Bella said, but it was difficult to be snarky with a hot shiver running down her spine. Hotshot Logan was the kind of guy she should run like hell from, and so she clung to her anger like a lifeline.

"Yeah, it does," Logan admitted with a slight grin, but there was an edge of sadness in his eyes that offset his teasing tone. He opened his mouth as if to say more, but then cleared his throat and remained silent.

Bella was thrown by his reaction, but when she felt herself soften, she sternly reminded herself that he wanted to kiss her and then dismiss her! Purge her from his system or whatever! She swallowed a squeal of pure frustration. When would she ever learn? David could suck her in like Coke through a straw, and she was already repeating the same mistake.

"If it makes you happy, you damned well proved your point."

"Well, sorry about your luck." Bella somehow managed to push him away even though she wanted to yank him back for a repeat performance. With a little lift of her chin, she picked up her purse and turned on her heel. She dearly wanted to stomp away, but it was damned difficult when her legs felt weak and rubbery. And of course stomping away was moot, since they were headed for the same condo. *Wow, can my life be any more screwed up?* "Well you're sure out of my system. No, wait. You were never in my system!" Bella punched the elevator button with her thumb so hard that it hurt, and she gave a little yelp of pain.

"You okay?"

"I think I just broke my thumb, but other than that, I'm just fine and dandy." Of course, she was far from fine, and she wasn't quite sure what *dandy* meant. The events of the past week were catching up to her, and she was dangerously close to crying.

They stepped onto the elevator and the doors closed with a *whoosh*. Bella wished for piped-in music, but there was only silence. What was it about elevators that felt so doggone intimate?

"Let me see it," Logan requested.

"See what?" She refused to look at him and kept her gaze on the climbing numbers.

"Your thumb."

"I'll live," Bella responded, even though her thumb was really throbbing.

"Come on. I've hurt my hands a million times over the years. Let me see if it's jammed or sprained but not broken. But if it's stoved, I'll need to pull it out of the socket."

"No!" She widened her eyes and cradled her hand protectively away from him. Luckily, the elevator doors opened and she rushed out into the hallway. Although she was tough in so many big-city ways and could hold her own against anybody, when it came to blood or bodily injury, she was a complete and total wimp. "I told you, I'm fine," she said, but the quaver in her voice totally betrayed her. To add insult to injury, when she tried to twist the key in the lock, pain shot up her arm and the key fell to the hardwood floor with a soft *clink*. "Oh, damn!"

"Bella, let me do it," Logan offered in a gentle voice, and stood there, all blond, blue-eyed, and caring. He almost made her forget why she was pissed at him. *Right. Because he's a guy or something.*

"Okay," she said in a small voice, and stepped aside. "But once we're inside, you're not coming anywhere near me or my hand. Got that, buster?"

# 15

## *Terms of Endearment*

"*B*USTER?" LOGAN STRAIGHTENED UP FROM PICKING UP THE key and her purse and gave Bella an amused look. "Really?"

"Pain is shooting from my thumb and short-circuiting my brain. Give me a break . . . buster."

Logan's smile faded and he stepped back for her to enter, and then walked in and flicked on a light. "Does it really hurt that much?" As an athlete, Logan was no stranger to injury, especially his damned elbow, and he was used to sucking it up. But he couldn't stand the thought of Bella hurting. She stood there so tiny and so gorgeous, and he wanted to pick her up and carry her, for some insane reason.

She shrugged her slim shoulders but cradled her hand, and it bothered him. "Look, I am, admittedly, a complete wimp when it comes to pain." She rolled her eyes. "I'll live," she insisted, but swallowed hard. "I'm acting like a damned drama queen. My poor mother used to work a full day and then come home and create her jewelry. I used to play up anything remotely painful to get her attention. I'd wail at a simple paper cut or a stubbed toe. Old habits die hard."

"Well, at least let me make you an ice pack." Logan sighed as he walked over to the kitchen counter. Luckily, he located a plastic grocery bag. He filled the bottom with ice and tied it shut. "Have a seat," he said, and he was relieved when she sat down without protest.

"I'm sure it's nothing. I'm just being a big old baby."

"Well, let's see." He knew her admission was meant to minimize her injury, but damned if he didn't picture her as a little girl craving the attention of an overworked single mom. Logan's heart went out to her even though he couldn't exactly relate. His father was on him like white on rice, wanting to know his every move from what he ate to when he went to bed each night and everything in between. All Logan ever wanted was to escape and play some Nintendo with the other kids in the neighborhood.

And pain? Pain was supposed to be overcome. Logan wished he had a dime for every time he had been told to walk it off, suck it up, and get back in the game. And the irony of it all was that doing just that might have ruined his career and his father's dream of seeing his son pitching in the major leagues. Instead, here he was in Cricket Creek, Kentucky, tending to a woman he barely knew yet who managed to bring out protective, tender feelings that he didn't even know he was capable of having. And the even crazier part about it was that he was beginning to like it way too much.

Logan sat down and scooted his chair around to face Bella. "May I take a look?"

"You promise not to yank on it or anything?"

"I promise."

"Really?" She looked at him with wary brown eyes.

"Your opinion of me might not be high, but my word is always good."

She gave him a jerky nod. "Okay."

"Thank you. . . . I think." Logan gently picked her hand up and placed it in his palm. The base of her thumb did appear slightly swollen. "Can you move it?"

She tucked her bottom lip between her teeth and oh, so slightly wiggled her thumb. "Ouch!"

"Hurt?"

She nodded, causing a lock of her sexy-as-hell hair to fall across her face. "A little."

"I'm sorry that I pissed you off, Bella. This was my fault." Without thinking, Logan reached over and tucked the silky softness behind her ear. His knuckles brushed against her cheek, and damned if he didn't long to lean over and kiss her.

"I overreacted. Like I said, I'm in a dark and twisty place where men are concerned. David was cheating right under my nose, and your dismissive comment sent me over the edge. I guess I'm feeling pretty low right now."

"Don't let that ass clown do that to you."

Bella pressed her lips together and nodded. "I know. I just can't get past it."

"Bella, you seem like there's more fire in you than that."

"You must think I'm a wimpy little drama queen. I assure you that I'm not." She gave him small smile. "Well, at least the drama-queen part."

"I don't think that at all." Logan inhaled a deep breath to clear his head, but her subtle floral scent made him want to moan. Her small hand looked so feminine resting in his big palm, and he dearly wanted to bring her injured thumb to his mouth and kiss it. He almost laughed, thinking there wasn't an inch of her small but luscious body that he didn't want to explore with his mouth. "Bella, I'm going to look at it a little bit closer, okay?"

She groaned. "I guess so."

Logan gently examined her thumb, hating it when she winced. "It looks to me like you've probably just strained some ligaments. If you ice it down and take an ibuprofen for the inflammation, you should be good to go." He draped the bag over her hand. "It might be sore for a couple of days."

"Oh, that's cold!"

"I know, but keep it there."

Bella glanced up at him. "I guess you've had countless injuries like this, only worse, especially your elbow." She reached over and traced the scar on his forearm. "And you played with pain."

"I was taught at an early age that it's part of the game," he said with a shrug. "No pain, no gain, as my dad used to say."

"When you were a little kid?" She blinked at him in disbelief.

"Yep."

"That's awful! You needed your boo-boos kissed!" she sputtered, and dislodged the ice pack.

Logan laughed and put the ice back.

"I'm serious."

The compassion in her eyes was genuine, and Logan felt a pull of emotion that he didn't expect. "I know, but *boo-boo* sounded funny," he said, though he was glad to see her feisty nature return. But when she frowned and traced the scar once again, his smile faded. Her gentle touch and sympathy were things he rarely got and always craved.

"What about your mother? Surely she showered you with kisses?"

Logan hesitated. Bella was hitting on sore spots that he never talked about. He shrugged as though it didn't matter. He had often hidden tears of pain on his pillow when he had wanted his mother rubbing his head and soothing him with tender words. "I knew she wanted to. I could see it in her eyes."

"Wanted to? But you were her little boy . . ."

"Standing up to my father caused huge arguments, and so after a while she stopped trying." He shrugged again. "I guess it made me tough."

"I hope that Ty doesn't let you pitch until you're healed," she said.

"He won't."

"As long as you're honest about the pain," she said, and then looked up from his arm. "Promise me you will be."

"I've learned from my mistakes—believe me," Logan answered, and then sighed.

"Me too," Bella said with a sad smile. "Hey, I'm sorry about the kiss of anger."

"I asked for it, remember?"

"Yeah, you did," she accused, but it lacked her earlier heat. "Jerk," she added, but it was said softly, and damned if she didn't look at his mouth as if wanting to kiss him again.

"Guilty," he said gruffly, and put the ice back when she moved it. "Look, Bella. We're both putting our lives back on track. This is a kick-ass condo that neither of us can afford on our own, and if we stay out of each other's way, we can make this arrangement work. I promise not to get out of line again. But I will be looking out for you."

She rolled her eyes. "Whatever."

"But I'll keep my hands to myself."

"Thanks. I think I'm okay to go to bed now," she said with a soft smile.

"Sleep well," he said in what he hoped was a matter-of-fact tone. He watched her walk out of the room and then sighed. Keeping his hands off Bella was going to be damned difficult, but guarding his heart was going to be even harder.

# 16

## *Forever Young*

"**Y**OU MAKE ME FEEL LIKE I'M EIGHTEEN AGAIN, JESSICA. I swear I could make love to you all night long." Ty eased her back against the mound of pillows and began nuzzling her neck.

"*Mmm,*" Jessica groaned, and slid her hands up his bare back and then down to cup his ass. "Don't make promises you don't intend to keep."

"Oh, don't worry. I won't," he assured her with a low chuckle. He loved her boldness and hoped it was a sign that she was feeling more comfortable with him and continuing to let down her guard.

"And thank you for the wonderful back rub. You turned my tense muscles into warm jelly. I don't think I've ever been so relaxed in all my born days."

"Hmm. I was just at your fortieth birthday party. That's a lot of born days ago," he teased.

"Oh, well. You're no spring chicken either, Mr. Triple Threat."

"I know, but I wasn't kidding. I don't feel like it when I'm with you," he said, and meant it. "You've put the zing back in my step."

Jessica blushed and covered her face with her hands.

"Hey," he said, and gently pried her fingers from her cheeks. "There's no need to be embarrassed." Ty leaned back on one elbow and cupped her chin. "You work hard and deserve to be pampered. And I love doing it. All you have to do is ask."

"Now, that's an offer I can't refuse," Jessica said with a wide smile that lit up the room.

"Oh, baby. Damn, I just want . . ." Ty began, and then paused to shake his head. "Wow," he said, and gave her a lopsided grin.

"Wow . . . what?"

"Noah said something to me at your birthday party," he began again, but then had to get his emotions under control before going on.

"What did he say, Ty?" she gently prodded.

His grin faded and he gazed at her with serious eyes. "Noah said that it made him happy to make Olivia smile. I flippantly told him that he was whipped." Ty shook his head and rubbed the pad of his thumb over her bottom lip. "Ah, but I absolutely get it now," he said softly, and then swallowed hard. "Jessica, I'd do anything to keep that smile on your face."

"Oh, Ty." She reached up and held his cheek in the palm of her hand. "My God . . ." She closed her eyes and pressed her lips together, but emotion that she was always so good at controlling escaped, allowing two fat tears to leak out of the corners of her eyes.

"I think you missed my point. I said, *smile* . . ."

"I'm sorry. I seem to be overcome lately. I don't really understand it myself. How's this?" She complied with a trembling lift of the corners of her mouth that simply tore him up. "Better?" she asked, and when she opened those amber eyes, he was lost.

Unable to answer, he dipped his head and kissed her softly, tenderly. When he tasted a warm, salty tear, he was completely consumed with emotion. These intense feelings were foreign territory, frightening and yet exciting. He wanted to tell her that he loved her, but he worried that it was too soon and so he refrained, but just barely. Damn, but he wanted to go over to the balcony and shout it to the rooftops. Ty knew that Jessica was coming around and slowly letting him in, but the tremble in her lips beneath his told him that she was still vulnerable and that he needed to be patient and wait for the right time to declare his feelings.

So instead, he kissed a moist trail down her neck and over the soft swell of her breast. When he swirled his tongue over a dusky pink nipple, she gasped and threaded her fingers through his hair. Ty licked and sucked until she arched her back, pushing her breast deeper into his mouth.

"God!" When Jessica gasped, Ty caressed her other breast, tweaking her nipple between his finger and thumb. "Your mouth is . . . mmm . . . is . . . God . . . magic!"

"Jessica, I can't get enough of the way you taste . . . the way you smell. Mmmm, I want to explore every inch of you."

"Then be my guest and do it," she offered in that husky voice that drove him nuts.

"I do believe I will take you up on your kind invitation," he said with a grin. He loved that she was being playful, but he wanted to tell her that he didn't want to be her guest. He wanted her permanently.

He loved her natural approach to sex. No toys, lotions, or potions—well, unless you counted being tied to the bed. Just . . . skin. And, oh, how he loved her body. Her curves were meant for sliding his hands and tongue over. They had just made love, but she was getting him aroused all over again.

Amazing.

Ty slid one hand oh, so lightly down Jessica's torso to her inner thigh and then back up again until she shivered beneath his touch. Gooseflesh rose on her skin, and her nipple puckered beneath his tongue. He repeated the action, coming closer and closer to her mound, teasing and exciting them both.

"Ty, you are driving me wild," she whispered, and arched her hips.

"Is this what you want?" he asked, and then sank his middle finger into her silky, warm heat.

"Yes!"

"You are so wet."

"For you. Again. Kiss me!" she pleaded, and so he raised his head and captured her mouth with a long, hot kiss. He savored the feel of her breasts pressed against his chest, and she caressed his back, his shoulders, and shoved her fingers into his hair as if she couldn't get close enough or ever stop touching him. Ty had never felt this kind of earthy passion and he knew why. He loved her. The thought exploded like confetti in his head, and he had to bite his tongue in an effort not to tell her. With a groan, he withdrew his finger and parted her legs. "I need to be inside of you," he said, and then thrust deeply into her sweet heat with one long stroke.

"Ty . . ." she said, but when he thrust again, she hooked her legs around him. "Oh, God . . ." she moaned, and matched his rhythm, loving him, kissing him wildly. And when she arched her back and cried out, it sent him over the edge with a hot rush of intense pleasure that ripped through him and shook him to the core.

"Jessica . . ." Ty stayed there, buried deep, with his forehead resting against hers. His heart pounded and his body throbbed and he couldn't find the words to express how he felt. He wrapped her in his arms and held her tightly, wanting the night to last forever. Neither of them spoke. It was as if words couldn't capture the moment.

Ty eased from inside her body and kissed the top of her head. It suddenly occurred to him that in his fit of passion, he had forgotten to slide on a condom, and he swallowed hard. He thought about saying something, but didn't want to ruin the moment or alarm her. Besides, at her age, what were the odds that she would become pregnant? But truth be known, the image of her carrying his child brought on a shot of fear, and then an excited rush that made his heart beat faster. Still, he should say something. "Hey," he said softly, "in the heat of the moment, I forgot to wear a condom."

"Oh . . ." He felt her tense slightly.

"I'll be more careful, but I'm not worried." His answer seemed to relax her, and he rubbed her shoulders until the tension melted away. Ty smiled, thinking that if Jessica was pregnant, it was meant to be and he would marry her without a qualm. In fact, he had paused by the jewelry store at the mall just yesterday, thinking he might buy a bracelet or necklace, but found himself glancing at engagement rings. It was just a glance, but still. . . .

When Jessica moved, snuggled closer, and sighed, Ty realized that she was sound asleep. He shook his head. It was no wonder. They had been making love for more than two hours, and she had worked a full day on her feet. She had to be exhausted. The thought had him cradling her close and wondering what he could do to pamper her the way she deserved.

Opening day was right around the corner, and they were both busy as hell, but there had to be something he could do to give her a much-needed break. Ty closed his eyes and vowed that when the baseball season was over, he was going to take a beach vacation and whisk her away with him, even if he had to kidnap her sweet little butt. He grinned, thinking that Madison would surely be his partner in crime.

Her warm breath tickled his skin, and although the lovemaking had been incredible, there wasn't anything better than having Jessica sleeping in his bed with her legs tangled with his and her cheek resting on his chest. He kissed her head once more before tugging the covers up over them. His lips curved up into another silly, sleepy smile. Nothing could match this feeling. He felt goofy and giddy, and yet a warm sense of peace settled over him as his eyes got heavy with sleep. *This,* he thought, *is what life is all about.*

Ty woke up to something tickling his face. He frowned and brushed at his cheek and encountered something soft and silky. He opened his eyes and then smiled. Golden blond hair clung to his pillow and to the stubble on his cheek. He picked up a lock and brought it to his nose and inhaled the light floral fragrance.

Hot damn . . .

The sheet and covers were pooled at Jessica's waist, and Ty thought the delicate slope of her shoulder was beautiful. When she moved, the sheet slipped farther, exposing the feminine curve of her waist and flair of her hip, making him want to pull her close and bury his face in her hair while he caressed her bare skin. The thought made him instantly hard.

And then he sneezed.

*"Eeek!"* Jessica squealed and rolled to her back.

"Sorry," Ty said, but he really wasn't, since her breasts were now exposed for his warm, appreciative gaze.

"Wait." Jessica blinked at him in wonder. "Is it really morning?"

Ty nodded toward the window, where fingers of sunlight were reaching through the small gap between the drapes. "It's fairly early so the sun is just coming up, but yes, a new day has dawned. Are you surprised?" Ty asked and ran a fingertip gently down her cheek.

"Yes . . ." She nodded slowly. "I can't remember the last time I slept all the way through the night."

"Really?"

She tugged the sheet up and played with the edge. "Yeah."

"I'm sorry to hear that." Unable to not somehow touch her, Ty reached over and wound his finger around a lock of her sleep-tousled hair. "Why do you think you suffer from insomnia?"

"It's not insomnia exactly. Oh, I crash after a hard day's work, but I've become such a light sleeper." Jessica was quiet for a second and then said, "It started after Madison was born. All she had to do was whimper and I'd wake up." She plucked at the edge of the sheet. "I was so young and so scared that something would happen to her in the dead of the night that any little movement or noise would wake me." She shuddered, but then smiled. "Sometimes I'd just stand there by her crib."

"I bet you never let her cry."

"No," Jessica admitted softly. "I wanted my sweet baby to know how much I loved her and that we would be okay, even though I was scared out of my skin. Love for your child should be unconditional," she stated firmly, but with an emotional tremble that had Ty leaning over and kissing her forehead.

"You are absolutely right, Jessica." Ty looked down at her lovely face and couldn't understand how anyone could abandon her. Oddly enough, he could identify with her pain. Ty had often felt neglected by his cheating father, who cared more about his career and personal pleasures than his wife and son. "I couldn't agree more." He wanted to ask more about her parents. Who in the hell could be so cold-hearted that they would turn their backs on their only child and grandchild?

"I was so afraid and yet so determined to somehow, some way, make a good life for Madison. Of course, Aunt Myra helped a great deal. I couldn't have done it without her. Oh, boy, I was still a child myself." She shook her head. "It's hard for me to believe that she and my father are siblings."

He waited for her to continue, and when she fell silent, he said, "Well, from what I can see, you both did a magnificent job. Madison is a lovely, bright, talented young lady. She lights up a room when she walks in."

"Thank you. She's always been my top priority."

"But now you need to take some time for *you*, Jessica. And your daughter agrees wholeheartedly." He lightly tapped her cheek. "You have earned it."

"I have been," she protested. "After all, I'm here," she added with a shy smile.

"It took some major-league doing."

"Old habits die hard," she answered with a sigh. "And the restaurant business is killer. You have to love food to even think of staying in it. But that being said, I really do understand what you're getting at. Madison is an adult engaged to be married. Aunt Myra has moved in with Owen, and she says she is happy living in blissful sin, but I just bet they up and tie the knot. As you already know, Olivia and Noah are gag-me happy, and while I am so thrilled for them all, I fully admit that I have bouts of loneliness here and there."

Ty brushed a golden lock of hair from her face. "Believe me, I understand. When your life is dedicated to one particular thing, it's difficult to change your focus."

"You mean baseball?"

Ty hesitated but then gave her a wry grin. "In some ways, but not really. I was actually talking about myself." He tapped his bare chest. "Me, myself, and I were pretty much all I had to worry or be concerned about. I didn't realize how good it felt to care about something other than my own success or well-being until I ended up here in this little town. Waking up with a sense of purpose sure feels good. I know Noah feels the same way, but he grew up here. I didn't expect to care so much, but I do," he said, and he wasn't talking only about the town.

"I'm glad," Jessica told him, but then angled her head. "I'm sorry that I misjudged you, Ty. And I certainly try not to be judgmental for any reason. I know that Olivia did much of the same with Noah. I guess we think of celebrities as being something other than human beings. You seem so bigger than life that I guess people are envious of the piles of money you make."

"Hey, my reputation was of my own doing. I don't blame you, but thanks. It means a lot to hear you say that," Ty said, but then shrugged. "I got paid way too much for the ability to hit and catch a baseball and to have my mug on boxes of cereal and bottles of sports drinks—that's for damn sure. And I'm certain at times it went straight to my big old head. But, in truth, I never cared much about the money." He shook his head sadly. "It sure never made me or my mother happy. We didn't give a rat's ass about the huge house we lived in or the luxury car we rode in. All we ever wanted was my father's love and devotion." He inhaled deeply. "Sorry. I didn't mean to get so fired up."

"Hey, you're preaching to the choir. My aunt Myra struggled all her life to keep the diner going, and yet she always had a joke to tell and a smile on her face. My parents had all the money in the world and were flat-out miserable."

Ty shifted his weight on the mattress. "Well, I *can* tell you this: I loved playing over in the middle-class neighborhoods with my friends more than in the gated community where we never even knew our neighbors. At my house everything was quiet, and over at my friends' there was . . . life going on. You know?" He looked at her, and she nodded. "Families grilled outside and kids played games. The pools were aboveground, but everyone splashed and had fun. The music was loud and the laughter louder. Perhaps that's also what convinced me to settle down here in Cricket Creek. I simply like it here."

"We're glad that you did," Jessica said, and while Ty would have preferred that she had said *I* instead of *we*, he was touched by her admission. "I thought you might be bored in a small town," she added casually, but her eyes were serious. "And leave as soon as your investment was secure."

Ty leaned over and kissed her. "I've been anything but bored, both on a personal and professional level. I'm really excited about this ball team, Jessica. I'm taking my role as general manager to heart."

She lowered her gaze. "I apologize. I shouldn't have said that."

"Hey, don't be sorry. I want you to feel as if you can tell me or ask me anything. Okay?" When he tucked a finger beneath her chin, she nodded.

"I'll try."

"Good."

She reached over and placed her palm on his chest. "I know you'll be a great coach and the players will respect and look up to you."

"Thank you," he said, and meant it. He really wanted her to believe in him, and her comment felt good. "One of the things Noah and I have talked about was bringing some pride and integrity back to the game. We've told these kids that they're representing the Cougars and this town and should carry themselves as examples to this community."

"Good for you, Ty."

"And as much as we want to have a winning season, we won't do it at the expense of the health of any player." He inhaled and blew out a slow breath. "There are some parents and coaches who don't get that concept. Look, I want to win as much as the next guy, but it blows my mind when coaches or even parents put a kid at risk."

"I guess Logan Lannigan is a prime example."

"You're right, Jessica. And to me he's still just a kid. I hope we can bring him back even better than he was before his surgery. I just hope he can keep his head screwed on straight. I did have a good talk with him, and I was impressed. He might act all big, bad, and cocky, but I've got his number."

She gave him a slow smile. "Ah. I bet he reminds you of yourself."

Ty chuckled. "You got that right." He was pleased that she was beginning to know him so well. "But, hey, you know as well as I do that success at this level doesn't come without cost. Most restaurants don't survive. Most players never make it to the big leagues. But to have a shot, you have to work your tail off." He smiled. "And you certainly do."

"Yes, but most of the time I love it." She got a faraway look in her eye and then added, "Funny, but my mother loved to cook."

"Did you learn from her?" Ty asked casually, listening closely. This was the first time Jessica had ever mentioned anything this personal about her mother.

"Yes, a little bit." Jessica lowered her eyes and toyed with the sheet once again. "My mother didn't get the chance to cook very often, since we had a chef on staff at the house." She paused, and a small smile tugged at the corners of her mouth. "But every little once in a while, when my father would be out of town on business, Mom would send Chef James home, and together we'd make something simple but fun, like grilled cheese, a BLT, or meat loaf. Those foods became a comfort to me, and I treasured those nights."

"I understand. It was an altogether different atmosphere when my dad was out of town or at spring training. My mom and I had nights just like those when I was a little kid. Those meals we shared in easy companionship were special to me too." He smiled at the memory. "Wow, I never thought about it until now that my love of food stemmed from those happy nights. Jessica, we have a lot more in common than I realized."

"Yeah, I guess we do."

Ty nodded. "We were both only children that were meant to feel as if we had to be perfect by overbearing fathers. God, I would never be that way to my own kid." He shuddered. "Ugh. I hate to admit it, but I'm glad that my mother finally had the courage to leave the jackass. Hearing her cry was the worst." He looked at Jessica and thought to himself that he couldn't imagine ever doing or saying anything that would bring her to tears. He'd rather chew glass. "So, when did you decide you wanted to go to culinary school?" he asked, and unable to keep his hands off her, he picked up a lock of her hair and rubbed the softness between his fingers.

"I used to sit at the kitchen table and do my homework when I was a kid. I loved watching Chef James prepare meals. After I begged and pouted, he started letting me help. First it was simple stuff like tearing lettuce and snapping beans, but then suddenly I was learning to whisk sauces and season soups. I was hooked. And then it all came together at Aunt Myra's diner. I combined Chef James's sophistication with my mother's down-home cooking. Aunt Myra recognized my talent and pushed me to go on."

"So Wine and Diner is the perfect combination."

"It was a big risk in this economy, but Cricket Creek embraced Madison and me when we needed it the most. I'm happy to be living here and giving back. Not only was it the right decision, but it has given my beloved aunt the ability to enjoy Owen and still keep the diner open. She has worked so hard."

"And so have you."

"I'm not the only one." Jessica smoothed a hand over his shoulder and down his arm. "Cricket Creek needed the stadium to revive downtown. Noah has gotten some well-deserved props, Ty, but you deserve lots of credit too. And give that silent partner a hug from me when you see him."

"Thanks. I will," Ty promised. Mitch Monroe was going to come to town for opening day, but his investment in the venture was going to be kept a secret. Ty wasn't quite sure why, but he and Noah were told to keep it on the down low. "I admit that I can't wait for the season to begin."

"Me too." Jessica moved her hand back and forth over his chest, and he had to swallow a groan. Her touch wasn't meant to be sexual, but comforting, and damn if it didn't make it all the more enticing. She could be a little spitfire, but Jessica was a loving, caring woman. Ty wondered if she knew what her gentle touch was doing to him.

"Will you go away with me when the season is over? The beach . . . or anywhere you want to go. Hell, I don't care as long as you're with me." When her eyes widened slightly, Ty could have kicked himself in the ass. He was going too damned fast!

"I would love that," she floored him by saying. "Madison has been bugging me to get out of the kitchen more often and to stop hovering over the staff. It's hard for me to do, but I'm determined to try."

"Smart girl," Ty said causally, even though his heart was pounding. "And she loves you. That goes without question. But even better, Madison appreciates and respects you. That tells me again that you've been an amazing mother."

"There might have been some divine intervention, because I sure prayed for help. Like I said, I was terrified!" Jessica shook her head slowly. "Aunt Myra had never had children either, and we both found out that babies don't come with instructions."

Although Jessica smiled, she couldn't hide the pain in her amber eyes. "I'm surprised your parents didn't come after you and drag you back home," Ty said.

"Ha!" Jessica chuckled without real mirth. "My father was glad to be ride of his shameful daughter, and my mother was afraid to stand up for me."

"Oh, baby, I'm so sorry."

"Thank you," Jessica said with a little catch in her voice. "I gave up hope that my mother would one day just show up on my doorstep. We haven't spoken since the day I called to tell them I was moving in with Aunt Myra."

"Such a sad loss for everyone." Ty traced a fingertip over

her bare shoulder. "So, I'm guessing that your father and Myra don't speak?"

Jessica nodded. "Aunt Myra said that they had grown up poor and that my father was always obsessed with making money. They lost their own parents in a car accident, so you would think that my father would want to remain close to his only sister. But he didn't approve of Aunt Myra. And when Aunt Myra and my mother became close, my father suddenly cut all ties with her. But I always remembered her visits, and I just knew that she would take me in."

Ty could feel the tension in her shoulder and gave her a reassuring squeeze.

"At any rate, Madison was raised on love and determination by a town full of people who watched over her while I worked in the diner. I told her that the saying *It takes a village* was coined for her. I think she still believes it."

Ty leaned back against the pillows and laughed. "Like I said, Madison lights up a room. I understand why Jason fell head over heels for your daughter. Even though, I have to say, that boy has his hands full."

"Ya think?" Jessica asked with raised eyebrows, and then chuckled softly. "So does poor Owen with Aunt Myra."

"Believe me, I don't think either of them minds one bit. And they're both good, hard workers. The landscaping at the stadium is amazing, and Jason sure has some talent." Ty could tell she was getting emotional and wanted to change the subject. Still, he was so glad that she had opened up and shared some of her past with him.

"Oh, I know. And they work well together. The patio at the diner is going to be gorgeous." She glanced at the digital clock on the nightstand. "I'd better get over there soon." She put her fingertips back to her cheeks. "I'm going to have to sneak up the back way to my apartment over the diner. Oh, the walk of shame . . ."

While her tone was teasing, Ty had to ask, "Are you worried about that?"

Jessica scooted up to a sitting position and lifted one shoulder slightly, a shoulder that he wanted to lean over and kiss. "It's a small town, so you have to get used to everyone knowing your business," she said, but Ty suddenly understood. She had learned to weather guilt and shame at a tender age. The wound might have healed, but there were still deep scars. "I just hate gossip."

"Believe me, I know what you mean."

"Really?" She angled her head in question. "Care to elaborate?"

"Actually, I do. Listen, do you have a little while so we can share a pot of coffee and maybe some breakfast?"

"I'm not really needed for the breakfast crowd. I have a capable cook for that," she admitted.

"Hot damn!" Ty leaned over and gave her a high five. "Now, was that so hard?"

"No." Jessica nibbled on the inside of her lip. "Maybe a little," she acknowledged, and then her eyebrows shot up. "Hey, so are *you* doing the cooking?"

Ty winced. "I'm a little intimidated to prepare a meal for you, but, yeah, I'll do the cooking and clean up too. How's that?"

"You keep making me offers I can't refuse."

"Good. And I intend to continue doing it."

"Wow! See, there you go again." She laughed, and her smile was suddenly back.

And he fully intended to keep it there.

Ty scooted from the bed before he ended up pulling her into his arms again. He reached down and tugged on his sweatpants. "I'll go get breakfast started. You're welcome to shower or whatever you want to do."

"Thanks." The smile remained, but rosy color blossomed in her cheeks.

"You're more than welcome to anything you need." Ty reminded himself that she was unsure, vulnerable, and he should tread softly, but, damn, it was difficult, especially seeing her sleep tousled and tangled in his bedsheets. He took a deep breath and paused at the doorway. "Oh, and if you want to lounge in one of my shirts, feel free to grab anything you want."

"Grab anything I want? Those offers just keep right on coming," she said, and gave him a throaty giggle. "I can't believe I just said that." She put a hand over her mouth and shook her head slowly. Her cheeks flushed a deeper rose, making Ty take long strides back to the bed.

He sat down on the mattress and gently pulled her hand from her mouth. "Quit hiding your beautiful face from me."

"You're bringing out a side of me I never knew I possessed. Maybe there is more of Aunt Myra in me than I ever realized."

"Whatever you're afraid of that's making you hold back . . . let it go and set yourself free."

"It's not easy, but I'm trying."

"That's all I can ask." He leaned over and kissed her cheek and then stood up. "Do you have any special requests for breakfast?"

"Eggs Benedict?"

"You've got to me kidding me," he said in a low voice.

"Yeah, I was. How about cooking some good, old-fashioned scrambled eggs?"

He pointed at her and snapped his fingers. "Now you're talking. Scrambling eggs and grilling are about the extent of my abilities."

"Maybe you need some lessons."

"I would love that."

"Good. I can teach both you and Madison. . . . Oh, my goodness." She looked at him with a big smile and bright eyes. "Cooking classes at the diner. Wine tasting too! This could be so much fun in the dead winter season."

"Excellent idea!" He shook his head. "You are amazing." His eyes met hers and locked. He didn't know how much longer he could keep from telling her how much he loved her. He swallowed the words on his tongue. "Okay, I'm off to scramble eggs."

"Don't overcook them!" she called after him. "And make the coffee strong!"

"Oh, God. The pressure is on!" He smiled when he heard her laughter, but then had to pause at the kitchen counter to catch his breath. He could really get used to waking up to Jessica in his bed, but more important, in his life.

# 17

## *Fair Game*

JESSICA CAUGHT HER BOTTOM LIP BETWEEN HER TEETH AS she scooted from the bed. It suddenly felt deliciously wicked to be naked, but for some reason she felt the need to tiptoe over to his walk-in closet. She flipped on the light and then put her fingertips to her lips when she spotted the rack of neckties. "Oh, my God," she whispered in a high-pitched squeak. Had she really tied the man to his bed? When that vision popped into Jessica's head, a delicious, hot shiver snaked down her spine. Yes, she certainly had! She stared at the ties and tilted her head. "And guess what. I loved it," she whispered with a sense of wonder.

Jessica stood there for a long moment, but then she smiled. For such a long time, she had suppressed her true self. Her father's stern disapproval and her mother's nervous fear had sucked her personality right out of her body, leaving her an empty shell. As an adult, she had come to the realization that sex at such a young age had been her way of seeking love and attention, and an act of rebellion. But the hot shame of the pregnancy had been crushing, causing Jessica to walk a straight line from that day forward, never giving anyone the least little reason to attach any kind of scandal or gossip to her name.

And she was sick and tired of walking on eggshells. Ty was right. She needed to let go — give herself the freedom to live, love, and laugh! "It's about damned time," she said, and then looked around the big closet for a T-shirt. She tugged a black baseball-cut shirt from a hanger and smiled at the Cougars logo in the center. She thought about searching for her bra and panties, but shook her head. "Who needs 'em?" she said brazenly, and when the soft cotton shirt slid against her bare skin, she closed her eyes and inhaled deeply. The masculine scent of leather, starched shirts, and spicy aftershave filled her head and curled her toes. She suddenly wanted a long, hot kiss but first she needed to brush her teeth.

"Oh, my God!" Jessica muttered when she viewed her reflection in the mirror. Her usual, carefully brushed hair was in wild disarray around her shoulders. Except for a trace of smudged mascara, her makeup was gone, and yet there was a glow in her cheeks and a sparkle in her eyes. She smiled and knew the reason why.

She was happy.

With the smile intact, she tamed her hair with Ty's brush and then located a toothbrush still in the package. A few minutes later, her face was scrubbed and her breath was fresh. Now she was ready to claim a kiss from the cook.

Jessica padded on bare feet down the hallway and almost groaned at the aroma of brewing coffee. But when she stepped into the doorway of the kitchen, her newfound bravery took a hike and she swallowed hard. She stood there uncertainly and was considering heading back to the bedroom for her own clothes, but watching Ty putter around in the kitchen captured her attention, and she was suddenly rooted to the spot.

Since when was cracking eggs into a bowl so very sexy? *Right. Since it's Ty McKenna doing the cracking.* The act of whisking was even better. Muscles bunched and flexed, and when he reached up into the upper cabinet for plates,

his low-slung sweatpants slid even farther down on his hips.
One little tug and she could have them at his ankles, press
him up against the counter, and . . .

Ty turned around. "Hey, there you are! Hungry?"

"Oh, you have no idea."

"I . . . uh . . ." His mouth opened and closed at her comment. "C-coffee?"

"Yes, but go back to what you're doing. I can help myself. Do you have cream?"

Instead of answering, he simply blinked at her.

"Ty?"

"Y-Yes?"

"Do you have cream?" Jessica asked slowly.

"Cream?"

"For my coffee." She pointed to the coffeemaker, but his
gaze remained on her.

He gave her a lopsided grin. "I'm sorry. I'm trying to
focus, but I can't get past you standing there in my shirt. I
swear, I think it is the sexiest damn thing I've ever seen. . . ."

The intensity of his gaze made her melt like hot fudge
sliding down a scoop of vanilla ice cream. She no longer
cared about coffee or scrambled eggs. All she could think
about was her hands on his bare skin. And the evidence of
his desire for her made her feel sexy and bold. "Come
here," he requested in a whiskey-rough voice that had her
legs moving before her brain had a chance to react. His
gaze was like a magnet drawing her forward, and she was
powerless to resist. Or perhaps it was because her resistance was gone and she was embracing feelings that were
growing stronger every minute she spent with him.

Ty leaned against the counter in open invitation, and
Jessica understood. He needed her to make this move. He
wanted her to show him that her walls were coming
down . . . and so she did. Jessica walked toward him without
hesitation, but slowly. Deliberately. When she stood before
him, he didn't move or say a word, but the look in his eyes

was enough. Jessica reached up and put her hands on his bare chest. The feel of his warm, smooth skin over hard muscle made her breath catch. The steady beat of his heart thudding beneath her palm made this seem so real and solid.

Lasting.

And yet Jessica stood very still and waited for the fear, the uncertainty, to chase away the happiness blossoming in her heart. But all she felt was love radiating between them. Jessica wanted to tell him how she felt, but she held back, oddly feeling that saying the words would somehow shatter the foundation that had been building for the past year. Saying those three little words might bring back the fear that had haunted her childhood like ghosts, and she wanted those demons to be gone forever.

Jessica felt it, strong and sturdy like the beat of Ty's heart, but she wouldn't say it until she was ready to do so without reservation or hesitation. She could tell by his white-knuckled grip on the edge of the countertop that he wanted to touch her, and she smoothed her hands down his chest and reached for his hands. After rubbing her fingers gently over his, she leaned in and placed a tender kiss in the middle of his chest. She felt his quick intake of breath and was amazed that a single kiss could bring this big, strong athlete to his knees.

This must be love. It had to be love.

*Finally!* Jessica soaked up the feeling like a plant needing water, but she couldn't raise her head, for fear that he would certainly see the stark reality shining in her eyes. And so she leaned her forehead against his chest, wanting his strong arms around her and him telling her it would be okay.

But the fear that she had chased away suddenly sensed her weakness and pounced. She felt the sharp talons digging in and clawing away her happiness. "I can't do this," she whispered, but when she would have backed away, Ty put his arms around her. "Let me go!" She pushed at his chest.

"No!" He held her tightly, as if he understood her erratic behavior. She was embarrassed and wished the floor would swallow her up. "I won't let you go."

"Yes, damn you!" She pushed harder, but she was no match for his strength. She kicked at his shin and connected. He grunted but didn't release her. She felt like a child having a temper tantrum, and yet she couldn't control her emotions. "Let me go," she croaked.

"Not in this lifetime." His hold was strong but gentle, and when he kissed the top of her head, she started to cry. Fear and anger that had been bottled up for years spilled down her cheeks. "I'm so s-sorry. Just let . . . m-me go."

*"Shhh!"*

"I don't want this!"

"Bullshit!"

She titled her face upward. "It's not b-bullshit. I hate this feeling of . . . weakness. That's what love does. Hurts! Release me."

"Say it again, Jessica."

"It hurts."

"What hurts?"

She had fallen into his trap and would not say it.

"Love," he prodded softly.

She tried to push away, but he wouldn't allow it. "If you don't let me go, I'm going to bite your . . . your nipple off!"

"Go ahead. Do it."

Jessica pushed, but his arms were like steel bands. "I'm serious," she growled.

"So am I. I'm not going to let you go. Ever."

"Then say good-bye to your nipple."

"You're not going to hurt me." He released his hold just enough to give her access to do whatever damage she wanted to inflict.

"I'm giving you one last chance to keep your nipple attached to your body." Of course, her threat was laughable, but he didn't chuckle. He didn't plead, and simply stood there trusting her. *Well, I'll show him!* Love and trust were going to make him a one-nipple man.

"This is gonna hurt!"

"Go for it."

"Don't say I didn't warn you!" Jessica stalled, but when he stood firm, she put her mouth over his nipple. Dear God, she tried to ignore her traitorous body's reaction. She clamped her teeth on him and waited for his muscles to tense up, but he stood there all relaxed and confident. She bit down a little just to scare him and to prove her point, but he didn't even flinch! Jessica ordered her brain to bite harder, but her mouth wouldn't obey. *Damn!* She didn't want to draw blood, but she wanted to prove the very valid point that you can't trust anyone with your heart or you'll be so very sorry.

But she simply could not cause the man any real pain.

She opened her mouth and let go. "You win," she said gruffly.

"This isn't about winning or losing. I knew you wouldn't hurt me. Even though my shin might be bruised."

"Right. It was my bare foot. And, yeah, well, I didn't want your stupid nipple hanging out of my mouth, so you got lucky. *Ew*."

"You're a crappy liar."

"And this is the craziest conversation I've ever had. We both know I wasn't going to bite your nipple off! Just let me go. Ty, I've tried to let my guard down. I want to. I simply can't."

"Can't?"

"Oh, don't go all Madison on me!"

"What?"

"Nothing." She inhaled a deep breath. "Now would you *please* allow me to exit with just a tiny bit of my pride intact?" She tugged and struggled. Damn, he was strong. "This brute strength you're using isn't playing fair."

"I'm not playing fair. I'm playing to win."

"Win what?" she sputtered.

"Your love," he replied, and then abruptly set her free.

When Ty turned back to the stove, Jessica stood there uncertainly. She shifted her weight from one bare foot to the other and absently watched him open a loaf of bread.

"Toast?" he asked in a brisk but not unfriendly tone.

"Uh, yes." Was she supposed to share a casual breakfast after what just went down?

"I hope wheat is okay."

"Yes. Uh, can I do anything to help?"

Ty shook his head without turning around. "No. Just help yourself to some coffee and have a seat. I'll handle the rest."

"Okay," Jessica answered with a slight hesitation. Her body was still pumping with fight-or-flight adrenaline, but she forced her feet to move. After pouring a mug of coffee, she sat down at the kitchen table and watched him prepare breakfast with surprising efficiency for someone who claimed not to know his way around the kitchen. A few minutes later, he presented her with a plate of fluffy eggs, crisp bacon, and golden brown toast. "Thank you."

"You're welcome. More coffee?"

"Please."

"Orange juice?" he asked with a polite smile.

"Yes, thank you." She took a sip of the cold, pulpy juice after he set the glass down in front of her.

"Can I get you anything else?" Ty asked before he sat his down across from her.

"No. This is lovely." She picked up the bacon and took a crunchy bite.

"Hope the eggs aren't overcooked," he said with a slight grin.

Jessica popped a forkful into her mouth and shook her head. "Perfect."

"Thank goodness." When Ty made a show of wiping sweat from his brow, Jessica managed to chuckle.

"Seriously, if you ever decide to quit coaching baseball, head on over to the diner and you can be a line cook."

Ty inclined his head. "Good to know."

Jessica smiled and they ate in companionship, carefully avoiding any mention of their previous encounter. They chatted about opening day, the weather, and countless other subjects, and ignored the white elephant in the room. And it worked . . . until they both reached for the strawberry jelly at the same time. When their fingers brushed, it was like an electric current, and when Ty's eyes widened, Jessica knew he felt it too. But when Jessica tried to withdraw her hand, Ty held on to her fingers.

"Hey," he said gently. "I've put myself out there and told you how I feel. I love you." He paused and swallowed hard. "But I won't push. I'm going to back off and give you the space you need to decide what you want to do."

"Okay."

He squeezed her hand. "We've got something good here, Jessica, and we've both waited a long time to find it. I hope you can see that." He paused and took a deep breath. "But if you decide otherwise, I will reluctantly and regretfully let . . . you go."

Jessica didn't trust her voice, so she simply nodded. A voice in her head screamed that she was crazy . . . that she should scoot back from the table and slide into his willing arms. But she remained rooted to the spot. "Thank you," she finally managed to whisper.

"Hey, I'm just protecting my body parts," he said with a slight grin.

Jessica closed her eyes. "My God, you must think I'm crazy."

"No." He squeezed her hand once more. "I watched my father hurt my mother. I know how destructive betrayal can be, so I understand your pain, your fear. But I can promise you this: I would never, ever intentionally hurt you. I'd cut off both of my damned nipples before I'd do that."

Jessica opened her eyes. She knew he was telling her the truth. "I believe you."

"Well, I'm putting the ball back in your court. It's gonna kill me, but I'll leave you alone and let you come to me when and if you're ready."

"I appreciate your patience, Ty."

He gave her a slow, sexy smile. "Just keep in mind that I am very ready and more than willing."

Jessica moaned. "There you go again, not playing fair."

"Sorry, but the stakes are pretty big," he tried to joke, but Jessica saw the emotion in his eyes. He scooted back from the table and turned away. "As promised, I'll clean up. I know you need to get over to the diner."

It was all Jessica could do not to walk over and slide her arms around his waist. But it suddenly hit her hard that her heart wasn't the only one at risk. She had the power to hurt him as well. He was giving her the space she needed, and when she knew she could keep the demons of her past at bay for good, she was going to come to him with open arms and never look back.

# 18

## Sweet Southern Comfort

"LOGAN, SERIOUSLY, YOU'VE GOT TO PUT SOME CLOTHES on."

"What do you mean? I'm wearing clothes," Logan protested innocently when he was anything but. For the past week he had been parading around in nothing but gym shorts in an effort to get Bella's attention. This whole platonic agreement they had going on wasn't really working out for him. He stretched his legs onto the coffee table and crossed them at the ankles before pointing the remote at the television.

"I mean it."

Logan slid his gaze over to Bella and sighed. "Maybe if you wouldn't keep the heat turned way up, I'd wear a shirt."

"The heat isn't turned on!" Bella tapped her bare foot on the hardwood floor and folded her arms over her chest. She was wearing black leggings and a sweatshirt that covered way too much of her body for his liking.

"Oh . . . well, it's hot in here," he protested.

"Then open a window!"

And have her bundle up even more? *No, thank you.* Of course, it was probably that he simply got hot every time he looked in her direction. In fact, he might just have to grab a sofa pillow to hide what she was doing to him right now. "Look, I'm probably just overheated from another long-ass workout today. Coach McKenna has been running us like dogs, getting ready for opening day Saturday. The man has been in a pissed-off mood lately. I think he needs to get laid."

"Logan!" She fisted her hands on her hips, looking all feisty and flustered, and damn if he didn't want to kiss her.

He shrugged. "I'm just sayin'. I thought Ty was all into Jessica, but I haven't seen them together lately. Do you know anything about that?"

"Some."

"Has Jessica been in a pissed-off mood too?"

"Not pissed off. Jessica doesn't really get that way. Just, I don't know . . . sad." She looked down at the floor and sighed.

"You're worried about Jessica, aren't you?" Logan clicked MUTE on the remote and gave her his full attention.

"Yeah." Bella looked across the room at him with stormy eyes. "I know she wants to be with Ty and she just won't give in. It's driving Madison nuts too."

"I can tell that you care," he said quietly.

"Jess has been like a mother to me. I want to see her happy."

"What do you think is holding her back?"

"Fear. She's been hurt. I can relate," Bella said darkly. "Oh, and speaking of mothers—mine is coming in for the game Saturday."

Logan raised his eyebrows. "Will she be staying here?"

"Yes." Bella nibbled on her bottom lip.

"Bella, you have told her about me, right?"

"She knows I have a roommate."

"A guy roommate?"

Bella lifted one shoulder slightly. "Not so much."

"Bella! Don't you think that's a detail you should have told her?"

"It just never came up in the conversation, okay?"

Logan slammed his feet down onto the floor. "No, it is definitely not okay."

"She's my mother. I will handle it."

Logan narrowed his eyes.

"Are you ever going to put a shirt on?"

He arched one eyebrow. "Does it turn you on?"

"No!" she sputtered.

"Then why do you care?"

Her chin came up. "I don't. Forget I mentioned it."

Logan grinned. "I think you do."

She stomped her foot. "I don't! You could be naked, for all I care."

"Really?" He stood up and put his hands on the waistband of his shorts.

"Oh, stop! What are you—twelve?"

"Inches?"

"Oh, in your dreams!" She gave him a head bop.

"In *your* dreams . . ." He arched one eyebrow.

"Yeah, right! You are getting under my skin something fierce!"

"Oh, I bet you'd like me under your skin."

"You are so . . . *cocky*!" she said between clenched teeth.

"Wanna see?"

"Oh, my God!" She raised her palms upward. "I've got to get out of here." She turned and marched out of the room.

"Where are you going?" he called after her.

"Away from your adolescent crap."

Logan plopped back down onto the sofa and sighed. "Well, that little plan sure didn't work," he muttered. He sat there for a minute and frowned down at his stomach when it rumbled. *Maybe Bella will go with me for a bite to eat,* he thought. But when she failed to reappear, he figured she must have had a change of heart. With another dejected sigh, Logan picked up the remote and was about to turn the sound up when Bella walked into the room.

"Holy shit," Logan whispered when he got a look at what she was wearing. He was used to seeing her in her all-black hostess uniform or in sweats around the condo. And he had seen her in the hot little dress at Jessica's birthday party. But seeing her in low-slung, tight jeans and a body-hugging blue sweater had him all but swallowing his tongue. The V-neck showed off the soft swell of her breasts, and a delicate silver necklace shimmered against her skin. To top it off, she wore some sexy-ass black heels that made him want to groan.

"Why are you groaning? No more *South Park* on tonight?"

*Oh, shit. I really did groan.* "Very funny," he replied sullenly. "Where are you going dressed like that?" he demanded.

"Jeans and a sweater?"

He pointed to her shoes. "And those ridiculous heels! And your boobs are hanging out."

"These are Kate Spade shoes and my *boobs* are not hanging out!"

"Where are you going?" he asked again.

"Who are you, my mother?"

Logan didn't think he was capable of blushing, but damned if he didn't feel heat creep up his neck. "You're just a barrel of laughs tonight."

"Well, you're sure not. I'm going over to Sully's, if you must know."

"Sully's? Oh no, you're not."

"Excuse me?" She put her hand on one jutted-out hip.

"Dressed like that?"

"Jeans and a sweater?" she repeated and shook her head up at the ceiling. "And here I thought my mother wasn't coming until this weekend."

"Bella, this isn't a birthday party at Sully's. This time of night there will be lots of local dudes playing pool and getting their drink on. At Noah's insistence, Coach McKenna gave us the day off tomorrow, so there will be lots of ball-players there, whooping it up." *And hitting on you,* Logan thought with a grimace. "It's not like happy hour in a martini bar in Chicago. Things can get a little rough."

"Pete keeps an eye on things. Come on, Logan. You're being unreasonable," she accused, but he saw a little flash of uncertainty in her eyes and he knew she wasn't as confident as she wanted him to believe. And while he might be a bit overprotective, he wasn't all that out of line. Sully's was a honky-tonk bar, and on a typical Thursday night it could indeed get rough. Not a place for high heels and French nails.

"Fine, but I'm going with you."

"The hell you say!" she sputtered, and then she grinned. "Wow. I'm already starting to sound like I'm from here."

"But you're not."

"I'm outta here," she said with a flip of her hair.

"Wait for me!" Logan jumped to his feet.

"No, Logan. I don't . . . Hey, what's wrong?" she asked when Logan grimaced and grabbed his thigh.

"Nothing," he lied through gritted teeth. He had a sudden charley horse that was killing him. But Logan was so conditioned to ignore pain that it was still difficult for him to admit the agony the hard knot was causing. Giving in to pain was considered weakness by his father. "I'm fine," he tried to say in a normal voice, but it came out gruff with suppressed pain. "It's just a little cramp. It'll pass." He waved her off. "Go on to Sully's. I'll be over there in a little while."

"Logan, sit your butt down."

"I'm fine."

"Would you stop! You're in obvious pain. Sit down and tell me what to do to make it go away."

"Go on! You're hell-bent on getting out of here. It'll pass," he said, but had to grit his teeth to keep from moaning. Damn, this was a bad one. "Just too much of a workout. When I stood up so quick, my leg cramped up."

"Damn you, Logan!" Bella's heels clicked on the hardwood floor as she hurried over to him. "Sit down." She gave his chest a gentle shove and he gratefully complied. "Prop your leg up and tell me what you need to make it better," she added in a gentle tone.

Logan leaned back against the cushion when a muscle spasm caused white-hot pain to shoot up his leg. He closed his eyes and swallowed hard.

"Oh, my God," Bella said when she felt the hard knot in his thigh. "Will massaging it help?"

"Yeah," he admitted with a choppy nod.

Bella knelt down on the floor, but when she started massaging the knotted muscle, he jerked and couldn't suppress a low moan. "Oh, God, I'm hurting you!"

"Not your fault," he managed, and tried to grin but failed. A bead of sweat rolled from his temple. He felt queasy and had to clench his jaw in an effort not to moan.

"Please tell how to make it better. Heat? Ice?" she asked, and the slight tremble in her voice went straight to his heart. Logan had plenty of trainers tend to his injuries, but the caring tone of her voice helped him to relax like a shot of sweet Southern Comfort. "Heat," he said, but then a sudden spasm cut off the rest of his sentence. "*Ahh*, shit!" he growled, and pushed his shoulders against the cushions.

"Oh, Logan!" The distress in her voice had him opening his eyes and looking at her.

"Sorry. I'm being a puss."

"Shut up! I'd be crying like a baby," she said, but her tone was tender. "There's a fucking knot the size of a golf ball in your thigh. Give yourself a break! Do you have a heating pad?"

He nodded. "In my bedroom beneath the bed. I'm—" He had to pause to catch his breath. "I'm probably low in potassium. It got warm this afternoon and I most likely—*ahh*—sweated out too much fluid. There are sports drinks in the fridge."

Bella pushed up to her feet. "I'm on it."

"Thank you." When she hurried off, he managed to admire her shapely butt in the tight jeans, even through the haze of pain. While he detested this show of weakness, he had to admit that her concern felt damned good. It might not be the best time in either of their lives to fall in love, but something was happening between them. They could fight it all they wanted, but the more he was around Bella, the stronger the feelings got, and he knew she felt the same way. These feelings went deeper than mere sexual attraction. He liked Bella's company. She made him laugh but she had a serious side that made for lively debate and conversation. She was feisty and tough but had a soft side that made him want to protect her at any cost. He might have known her for only a few weeks, but it sure didn't feel that way. In fact, he didn't think he could handle not having her in his life.

Holy shit, he just might be falling for her.

*Okay,* he admitted to himself, *not might.* He was. And he hadn't even slept with her. Damn, the image of Bella in his bed had him groaning—and not in pain.

"Oh, here I come." Bella heard Logan's moan and hurried toward the sofa, almost tripping in her heels. With a curse she toed off the shoes and handed him the Gatorade.

"Thanks." He untwisted the lid and took a long swig.

"Drink it all." When he put the bottle on the coffee table, she picked it up and handed it back to him.

"Bella, I'll try, but my stomach is doing flip-flops."

"Oh!" She gave him a sympathetic grimace and still managed to look beautiful. "Okay, but try to sip it, then." She knelt down and plugged in the heating pad, then gently placed it on his thigh. "I sure hope this helps."

"It's already easing up. The fluids and the heat will do the trick. If you want to leave, I'll be fine," he offered, but hoped she wouldn't.

Bella gave him a firm shake of her head. "No. I'm not leaving you like this! What do you take me for?"

"A warmhearted, caring person," he said, and meant it.

She looked from the dial she was adjusting, and he had trouble figuring out how damned David could ever cheat on someone as amazing as Bella. "Thank you, Logan."

They were so used to bantering back and forth that this unexpected serious moment took them both by surprise. Although neither of them verbally acknowledged it, their gazes locked briefly and something shifted between them.

"I'm only speaking the truth," he said, and the pain started to subside. Logan knew the Gatorade and heat were helping, but her gentle concern eased a hurt that wasn't physical. The two of them were bruised and battered in more ways than one, but Logan felt a sense of peace settle over him. Yes, he wanted to make it back to the major leagues, but for the first time in his life, baseball, winning . . . they were taking a backseat to something more meaningful and lasting. He felt some of the constant pressure ease up, and he smiled.

"Better?" Bella asked.

"Yeah, it's gonna be all right," Logan said, but he wasn't really talking about the knot in his leg. "You can head on over to Sully's now."

She looked at him for a second, and his heart thudded in his chest. "No, I'll wait for you."

He grinned. "Good."

"Not that I need you for protection or anything. I can take care of myself. You owe me dinner after all this waiting-on-you-hand-and-foot stuff." She gave him one of her hair flips, but he wasn't buying it. She busied herself slipping on her sandals.

"You need to get ya some cowboy boots instead of those silly-ass shoes," he said with a shake of his head.

"Oh, would you just shut up about my shoes and put on some clothes? I'm hungry."

"Are you seriously going to walk all the way to Sully's in those things? They've got to hurt your feet."

Bella looked down at her feet. The shoes were gorgeous but pinched her toes. She thought about it for a second. "I'll be fine."

Logan raised his eyebrows. "Okay, but don't ask me to carry you home when your feet are killing you," he warned, but his threat was empty. In fact, he hoped her cute little dogs would be barking so loud that she begged him to carry her.

And he would. Gladly.

# 19

## All or Nothing

"Here," Madison said, and shoved a bottle of Midol in Jessica's hand.

"What's this for?"

Madison raised her eyebrows. "You mean you're not PMSing?"

"No!" Jessica answered, and leaned one hip against the counter. The diner was closed, but she couldn't bring herself to head upstairs to her silent, lonely apartment.

"*Hmm . . .*" Madison tapped the side of her cheek. "I wonder what your problem could be. I wonder if it could be the same thing that's been making Ty a total grump."

Jessica stopped straightening up the already pristine counter. "He's been grumpy?" she asked casually, but flicked Madison a glance.

"Mom, that's an understatement. Jason said that Ty bit his head off yesterday, and then, of course, apologized. Ty's not usually a grumpy sort." Madison sighed and gave Jessica a pointed look.

"I'm sure it's just pre–opening day nerves."

"Just who are you trying to fool? Yourself? Because you're not fooling me."

Jessica remained silent since she didn't have a reply that made any sense.

"Mom, why are you fighting this?" Madison persisted. "It's making you miserable, and that's just not your personality either. That's got to tell you something. What in the world are you waiting for?"

"I'm waiting until I'm ready to take that step."

"Waiting?" Madison sputtered. "That's just stupid."

"I have too much going on right now to have a serious relationship. The time has to be right, Madison."

"You are so full of it."

"Ma-di-son!"

"Oh no, I don't deserve a *Ma-di-son* for that one. You deserve a *Jess-i-ca*! Quit being such a chickenshit."

"Don't talk to me that way."

"Well, you're pissing me off! Mom, seriously, this is stupid. There is no other word for it."

"Don't judge someone until you've walked in their shoes."

"Okay, then. I will." She bent over and slipped her sandals off. Hand me your shoes."

"Um, that was a figure of speech."

"No. I'm going to give you my cute sandals and I'm going to put on your sensible flats. Then I'm going to tell Jason that we can't see each other because he's too busy at the stadium, and I have to concentrate on the new play I'm working on and on preparing to teach fall classes. We'll just have to wait until the time is right for us to be in a serious relationship."

"Stop mocking me," Jessica tried to say firmly, but her voice quavered.

"Mom, I would never do that. I'm making a point." She inhaled a deep breath and blew it out. "Okay, look. At least get out of here," she suggested in a gentle tone. "I'm meeting Jason over at Sully's. Come on over with me."

Jessica shook her head.

"What? Come on. Why the hell not?"

"I'm not in the mood."

"Really? Or is it because you're afraid you might see Ty? He sure hasn't been in here, and I just bet he's been eating over at Sully's. I guess he's being just as stupidly stubborn as you are."

"No, he's respecting my wishes and giving me some space."

Madison placed her palms on the counter and leaned forward. "Wait. You told him to stay away from you?"

"Yes," Jessica admitted.

"Mom, you do know that if you keep pushing him away, eventually it's going to work."

Jessica's heart hammered at the thought.

"The man can only take so much rejection."

"I'm not rejecting him!"

"Then what do you call it?"

"Being sure! This is a big step for me."

"I agree." Madison nodded firmly. "A big step backward. Mom, you had this whole fear thing conquered. What happened?"

"I don't know," she answered softly, and traced circles on the counter with her fingertip.

"It was the intensity of the feelings, wasn't it?"

Jessica looked up in surprise.

Madison gave her a knowing nod. "Scary, I know. There is so much power behind the emotion of love."

Jessica inhaled a deep breath. "Madison, I hate to ask this, but how did you gather up the courage to say yes to marrying Jason when more than half of all marriages fail?"

"Really, Mom?" Madison shook her head in disbelief. "You've got to be kidding me."

"Sweetie, I'm sorry. I shouldn't have asked that question. I don't mean to put indecision in your head."

"You haven't," Madison assured her. She gave Jessica a level look. "Okay, let me ask you this. What made you sink your life savings into this diner, knowing full well the state of the economy and the fact that restaurants have such a high failure rate?"

"It was my dream."

"Worth the risk?"

Jessica closed her eyes and nodded her agreement.

"I rest my case."

Jessica opened her eyes and looked at her daughter. "I've got to go all in, don't I?"

"Finally!" Madison raised her hands upward and shook them. "Praise the Lord! You finally get it. Wow. Is teaching going to be this difficult?"

Jessica gave her a wobbly smile. "For your sake, I hope not. But, then again, I'm a slow learner."

"Oh, Mom!" Madison walked over and wrapped her arms around Jessica. "I love you so much. It hurts me to see you sad. Let the past go once and for all."

"No."

Madison pulled back and looked at her. "Come again?"

"Madison, I don't need to let go of the past. It's made me who I am today. I just need to stop fighting it. My past has taught me some valuable lessons." She pressed her lips together and gathered her emotions. "I know what love is and what love isn't."

"And it certainly isn't deserting your child in her time of need," Madison said with an edge to her voice that Jessica rarely heard. "But . . ." Madison began, and then stopped.

"What aren't you telling me?" They rarely spoke of her parents, and Jessica's heart pounded with anticipation. When Madison hesitated, Jessica prompted, "Madison?"

Madison scooted up to a sitting position on the countertop. "One evening not long after we had moved back here, Aunt Myra and I were washing dishes, and she turned to me and suddenly shook her head. When she got teary-eyed, something she almost never does, I asked her what was wrong." It was Madison's turn to press her lips together.

Jessica scooted onto the counter with her and looped her arm around her daughter's shoulder. "You can tell me anything. You know that, right?"

Madison sniffed and gave her a jerky nod. "Aunt Myra said that she almost called me . . . Molly. That I looked so much like her . . ." Madison trailed off and swallowed hard. "Do I look like her, Mom?"

"Yes," Jessica answered softly. "You have my mother's eyes, her hair. You are pretty much the spitting image." She hesitated, "And her laugh, although I rarely heard it."

"That has to be hard for you."

"Sometimes. And then other times it was like it was all I had of my mother . . . the good in her anyway."

Madison angled her head.

"What, sweetie?"

Madison looked down at the countertop for a long moment and then looked back up. "I asked Aunt Myra how she thought that her brother could have abandoned you and let her help raise me. I asked what kind of monster could do such a thing. And I wanted to know how she thought that Molly—I am sorry, but I can't call her my grandmother—could leave raising her grandchild up to her sister-in-law?"

Jessica's heart thudded and she pushed back to get a look at Madison. "What did Aunt Myra say?"

"She said that William Robinson was a bully, a tyrant." Madison put a gentle hand on Jessica's leg. "Mom, Aunt Myra said that Molly thought it was best for you to be away from him and that she was making the ultimate sacrifice by giving up her child and grandchild."

Jessica felt a hot flash of anger.

"Oh, I'm sorry. I've upset you!" Madison put her hand

over Jessica's white-knuckled grip on the edge of the counter.

"No, don't be upset. These are things you have every right to ask."

"You don't believe that, do you?"

Jessica looked at the sweet face of her daughter, the face that looked so much like her mother's. "She loved to cook but wasn't allowed," Jessica finally said, and then shook her head. "He hated everything from her unruly hair to the name Molly, which he called common. It was as if he wanted to purge everything connected with his impoverished childhood from his life, including his only sister."

Madison slapped the countertop so hard that saltshakers jumped. "Why didn't she just come with you? She could have lived with us! Cooked here in the diner!" Madison's eyes filled with tears. "Why?" she repeated brokenly.

"Fear," Jessica whispered. "Fear can be paralyzing."

"Keep you from doing what you really want to do," Madison added, and gave her a level look. "Mom, don't let that happen to you."

"You're right." She inhaled deeply. "Oh, but it takes so much courage when your heart is at stake."

"Well . . ." Madison raised her eyebrows. "Courage isn't something you're lacking now. Is it?"

"No."

Madison waited in silence.

"Oh, boy, I just fell into some sort of trap, didn't I?"

Madison widened her eyes in innocence, but Jessica wasn't fooled for one second. "Whatever do you mean?"

"You have that something-up-your-sleeve look in those gorgeous eyes of yours. What do you have in your hand?"

"Just my cell phone."

"Who have you been texting?"

"Jason."

"And?"

"Bella, to see if she is going to Sully's, and she's going with Logan."

"Oh . . . how is that whole arrangement holding up?"

Madison rolled her eyes. "It's complicated."

"Is that what is says on her Facebook profile?"

Madison chuckled. "Humor . . . must mean you are in a better mood?"

Jessica narrowed her eyes. "Okay, enough small talk. What have you just cooked up? And, no, that wasn't diner humor."

"Well . . ." Madison slid from the counter and landed on the ground as if ready for flight. I might have asked Ty if he was going to Sully's to grab a late bite."

"Is he?"

"No. Mr. Grumpy said he was tired and staying in, even though I happen to know he has the day off from coaching tomorrow."

"There's more, isn't there?"

"Well, and I might have said that I would bring him some leftovers from here on my way over to Bella's."

"And what does this have to do with me?" Jessica asked, but then shook her head and backed away. "Oh no! I am not taking food over to Ty's!"

"He sounded so hungry. And I'm heading straight to Sully's. It would be out of my way, and I did promise. Could you do this little thing for me?" She put her thumb and index finger an inch apart.

"No!" Madison gave her the pout that always worked. "Oh, come on. Are you really bringing out the pout?"

"Works on Jason."

"Bless his heart."

"Mom, this is your chance. Be brave! Thought you were all in—or are you all talk?"

"I'm all talk."

"Well, start walking the talk!"

Jessica closed her eyes and inhaled a deep breath. "I

can't throw myself at him again with food in my hands. Especially after I asked the man for space."

"Ty gave you your space. Now it's time to close the gap. Do you seriously think he won't be thrilled to see you?"

"Maybe he's moved on." *Oh . . .* That thought sent a shiver down her spine.

"He is pining for you."

"Pining? Really?"

"Panting?"

"Madison!"

"Mom, march your tushie into the kitchen and make the man some food. You know all of his favorites by now." She pointed toward the double doors.

"You're pretty darned good at giving orders."

Madison smiled. "I know. It's a gift." She looked down at her phone and then sent a message at superfast speed.

"Jason?"

"Nope. Ty, asking where his care package was." She shooed her hands toward the kitchen. "Go take care of his package. You know you want to," she said in a singsong voice. And when Jessica opened her mouth, Madison said, "I know—Ma-di-son!"

Jessica looked at the kitchen doors and felt a little surge of excitement.

"I'm leaving. I am trusting you not to wuss out."

"I'm on it," Jessica promised.

"Good! Okay, I'm going to bounce. Jason is headed over to Sully's," she said, but then closed the distance between them and gave Jessica a big hug. "I love you, Mom." After a quick peck on the cheek, she hurried out the door.

"Oh, boy," Jessica said under her breath, and then headed into the kitchen and flicked on the light. She blinked in the bright glare for a moment and smiled. She was admittedly nervous at Madison's latest scheme, but her blood was pumping and the zing of excitement was so much better than the dull ache that had plagued her since she stopped seeing Ty. It had been less than two weeks, but it seemed like a lifetime. Of course, by *seeing Ty*, she meant in the flesh. The man was never far from her thoughts. And the dreams . . . ? Oh, dear *Lord*.

Jessica hummed as she put together a very nice variety of all of Ty's favorites. She added a slice of apple pie that had been baked fresh that morning. She had set it aside for her breakfast, and now she just might be having apple pie in bed . . .

# 20

## Food for Thought

WHEN TY'S STOMACH RUMBLED IN ANGRY PROTEST, HE patted his abdomen. "Hey, buddy. I know you miss Wine and Diner," he mumbled as he started clicking through the more than seventy channels yet again. Nothing captured his interest, not even sports or the Food Network. Pausing on *South Park* couldn't squeeze a laugh out of him. Then again, lately all he had been doing was going through the motions. Not good, when opening day was just a few days away. Noah had finally suggested a day off for everyone, and Ty had reluctantly agreed. He needed to get his damned head screwed on straight! These kids were depending upon him, and although he tried to stay focused, constant thoughts of Jessica kept interrupting his concentration.

And he did miss her food, but he just couldn't bring himself to go in Wine and Diner, not even for takeout. Thinking about Jessica was bad enough, but seeing her would just about do him in. So many times in the past few days he had picked up his cell phone and scrolled down to her number just to hear her voice, but always aborted the call. Ty sighed. He had promised to give Jessica her space and he wasn't about to go back on his word. He wanted her to come to him. . . .

But, damn, it was killing him.

Ty didn't know it was possible to miss a woman this much. It was like a dull, throbbing ache that only Jessica's touch could cure. Sleep couldn't even bring relief, since his slumber was filled with sensual dreams about making love to her. He couldn't eat, he couldn't sleep, and it was taking its toll on him big-time. He was starting to snap at people for no real reason, and he hated doing that.

Noah had tried to get him to head over to Sully's to grab a bite and play some pool, but Olivia was joining him and Jason was meeting Madison. Ty didn't think he could stand being there without Jessica at his side, and so he had begged off. He should have gone just to keep an eye on his players, who were sure to show up there in droves. Bella had tried her best to get him over there, and although blowing off steam would have been a good thing, he just didn't feel up to socializing. And so here he sat in sweatpants for yet another night on his couch, surfing through channels with a frown on his face.

It sucked.

Ty inhaled deeply and scratched his chest. Oh, well. At least Madison was bringing him some food, although he wasn't quite sure he could eat Jessica's cooking and not go crazy with the need to see her. He thought about calling Madison and telling her not to bother when the doorbell chimed. "Too late," he mumbled, and padded on bare feet over to retrieve his sad little care package.

Ty swung open the door and stood there dumbfounded. "You're not Madison," he said, and then felt like a complete dork.

"Well, she did have this plan about switching identities, but, yeah, I'm not Madison."

"So what brings you here?" he tried to ask casually, even though his heart was beating like a bass drum.

She raised the bag. "To bring you this food."

"But . . ."

"Ty, this is the part where you invite me in," Jessica said, and she pointed with her free hand to the shopping bag. "There is some good stuff in here."

"Madison was supposed to bring that," Ty repeated with a hint of embarrassment, but stepped back for Jessica to enter. As he caught a whiff of her perfume and the aroma of diner food, his body immediately responded. His stomach grumbled and his dick stood at attention. He smiled at this unexpected pleasure, but then the truth hit him. "Wait. Let me guess. . . . You were coerced into lugging this over here," he said as he followed Jessica into the kitchen. Damn, she made jeans and a casual green sweater look amazing. Her hair was pulled back in a sensible ponytail, and her makeup was minimal, and she had never looked better. "I'm really sorry."

"I can leave."

"No, I mean I'm sorry that you were coerced into coming here. Not that you're, you know . . . *here*. I don't want you to be here if you don't want to be. . . . Damn, I'm bumbling like an idiot," he rambled, while she took plastic containers from the brown shopping bag. "Sorry. Must be from lack of rest and nourishment."

"You can quit apologizing." Jessica paused and looked over at him with concern. "Have you been sick?"

"Yes, in a manner of speaking." Ty decided to lay it on the line. "Jessica, I can't eat. I can't sleep. I'm a total train wreck."

"Opening-day nerves?"

"Hell, no."

She looked across the table at him as if daring him to say what was on his mind. "Then what?"

"Apparently, I can't function without you. So no pressure or anything, but you have my health and the future of the Cricket Creek Cougars resting on your shoulders." He reached up and raked his fingers through his hair. "I'm really trying to give you your space or whatever, but I have to tell ya that it isn't really working out for me."

"It isn't really working out for me either."

"Really?" he asked in a voice chock-full of hope. "How so?"

"Well, today Madison handed me a bottle of Midol."

"Oh, so that's the problem?"

She blushed, but then gave him a wry smile. "No . . . not that time of the month for me."

"Oh . . ."

"Apparently, I've been, well . . ."

"A little cranky?"

"A lot cranky. That's a polite way of putting it."

"So, this whole space thing isn't what you needed?"

"Not at all."

Ty felt a warm wave of happiness wash over him. "Any suggestions?"

Jessica nodded. "A few," she replied, and pulled a bottle of wine out of the bag. "I thought we might start with some Shiraz and some chicken-liver pâté. Oh, and hmm, I have some artichoke dip and a block of Havarti cheese. Oh, look!" She pulled a plate of dark chocolate truffles out of the bag, along with a generous slice of apple pie. "Imagine that."

"You have no idea the things I have been imagining."

"So, you've missed my cooking?" Her smile widened.

"Yes." Ty's neglected stomach rumbled loudly in appreciation, making Jessica laugh. "Oh, damn. I sure love it."

She looked at him with a soft expression in those lovely amber eyes. "Madison reminded me that I know all of your favorites."

"I was referring to your smile." He closed the gap between them. "Screw more space. I want to get as close to you as I possibly can." He reached down and tilted her face up. "I missed you beyond belief. Jessica, my sorry ass simply can't live without you in my life." He chuckled. "I feel like I should burst into song or something, but I really suck at singing."

"Then why don't you just shut up and kiss me?" she demanded, but there was a quaver in her voice that went straight to Ty's heart.

"That was my next option," he said with another low chuckle, and then dipped his head and captured her mouth with his. The mere touch of his lips on hers sent a jolt of pure desire surging through him. He groaned and deepened the kiss. God, he loved the way she smelled, the way she tasted, and it felt so damned good to have Jessica warm and willing in his arms. While the food smelled amazing, he didn't know if he could stop kissing her long enough to eat. A few minutes ago he had felt depressed and drained, and now he was full of energy. Ty didn't just *want* Jessica in his life.

He needed her.

When his stomach betrayed other body parts and growled, Jessica pushed at his shoulders. "You need to eat."

Ty shook his head. "That means I have to stop touching you."

She arched one delicate eyebrow. "Not necessarily."

"What do you have in mind?"

Jessica put her palms on his chest and moved her hands suggestively. "How would you like a picnic in bed?"

"I would like that a lot!" he answered with so much enthusiasm that Jessica chuckled.

"Good. I brought mostly finger foods."

"Ah, finger foods." Ty tapped his temple. "Smart thinking. We could multitask."

"Why don't you head into the bedroom, put on some music, light some candles, and turn down the bed? I'll fix a tray and be in to join you shortly."

"Anything you say, as long as you're on the menu."

Jessica tipped her head back and laughed.

Ty put his thumb and index finger on the bridge of his nose. "Sorry. That was pretty corny."

"Maybe . . ." Jessica said, and then pulled a can of whipped cream from the bag. "But accurate. I hope I'll be the main course."

"Oh, dear God," Ty said when a mental image of Jessica naked and slathered in whipped cream and drizzled with chocolate popped into his head.

She pulled out a tray of plump red strawberries. "Something to dip with." She shooed him with her hands. "Go on and get ready."

Ty looked down at the big bulge in his pants. "I am ready."

"Ty!"

"Okay, I'm on it. Just don't take too long," he pleaded.

"I won't. I'll just be a few minutes." She pointed to the wine. "Just take the bottle and glasses for me and I'll be right in."

Ty nodded and hurried to his bedroom. His heart thudded and his poor dick was hard enough to hit a baseball out of the park. Still, he took extra pains to light candles that, luckily, Jessica had brought over weeks ago. He put on some soft jazz to set the mood and then turned down the bed. He uncorked the wine and poured two glasses before climbing into bed.

Ty sat there sipping his wine and thinking that he had never felt such heightened anticipation. This was worse than waiting on deck in the bottom of the ninth with two outs and down by one run. His heart pounded and his blood hummed.

And then she entered the room.

"Hungry?" she asked as she set the artfully arranged tray of food down on the bed.

"I am a starving man," he said in a husky voice. "The food looks delicious, but you look even better."

"Do you mind if I slip into one of your shirts? These

jeans and this sweater aren't meant for lounging around in."

"Help yourself to anything you want," he offered, and nodded toward the closet.

"The ties?"

"Hell, no. I want my hands free to touch you, Jessica. Hurry. You're killing me."

She chuckled as she disappeared into the walk-in closet. Ty loved hearing her laughter, loved hearing her moan. . . . Hell, he simply loved her. She seemed different, more relaxed, confident and ready. He only hoped that fear didn't rear its ugly head once more and chase her away, but if it did, Ty wasn't going to retreat and give her any more damned space. He was going to stay the course. Giving up on Jessica Robinson wasn't an option.

He looked down at the array of food and was trying to decide what to try when Jessica entered the room, and he knew just what to sample first. Damn, she looked good in his faded flannel shirt. She had rolled up the sleeves, and the tail hit her at midthigh. He wanted to know if she had shed her bra and panties. Her ponytail swayed back and forth as she made her way across the room, and he couldn't wait to tug the band free and slide his fingers through her hair. "How come you look so good in my shirt and I'd look silly in yours?"

She stopped in her tracks and laughed. "Well, now. I prefer you in no shirt at all."

"Get over here, woman!"

"Your wish is my command."

"Oh, that's a dangerous offer."

"I'm feeling dangerous." The flickering light of the candles made her complexion appear golden, and he couldn't wait to slide his tongue all over her warm, smooth skin. "Bring it on."

"Oh, don't get me started."

"What do you mean?" she asked as she climbed up onto

the bed. "I intend to get you started, and I don't plan on stopping anytime soon. At least, that's the plan."

Ty handed her a glass of Shiraz. "I like it when a plan comes together."

"Me too," Jessica said, and sat cross-legged on the bed. She took a sip of the wine and then unfolded a cloth napkin over her lap. "Hmm, I wonder what to sample first?" she pondered, and then picked up a deep red strawberry and dipped it in a dark chocolate sauce in a dainty little dish. But instead of putting it in her mouth, she cupped her hand beneath the berry to keep the sauce from dripping and said, "Open wide."

The chocolate was thick, rich, and warm, but the strawberry was refreshingly cold on his tongue. The flesh was firm and sweet but slightly tart, and the two flavors together were a party in his mouth. *"Mmm,"* he moaned, and licked the sauce from the corner of his bottom lip. "Did you make that sauce?"

"Yes. Do you like it?"

"Love it."

"Good. It's going to be part of my fondue night at the lounge. I wanted the texture to be creamy and thick enough not to drip too much, and a semisweet flavor to complement the strawberry." She dipped a smaller strawberry into the sauce and popped it into her mouth. "Yeah, I think this is pretty much perfect."

"Me too," Ty agreed, but he wasn't referring to the strawberry. He watched her tongue lick across her full bottom lip and almost groaned. He was having a difficult time not pushing the food aside and pressing Jessica into the bed, but she had put so much work into the buffet that he didn't want any of it to go to waste. Still, you could cut the sexual tension with a knife. He took a sip of the wine that tasted tannic on his tongue after the sweet fruit. He picked up a round cracker and spread some pâté on it, but took Jessica's lead and reached over to feed her. After she took a bite, he ate the other half. "Mmm, good stuff." He looked at the smear on his thumb, and when he lifted it to his mouth, she reached over and took his hand.

"Allow me," she said in her sultry voice, and when she licked the dab from his thumb, Ty thought he was going to melt into the mattress. She fed him a slice of creamy Havarti cheese, letting her fingers trail down his chin, and when he leaned closer for a kiss, she popped a green grape into his mouth. The juicy sweetness squirted over his tongue, and, God, he needed to kiss her, but she tipped up her glass, preventing him access to her luscious lips.

Ty decided that two could play this game. He picked up a thick slice of banana and dipped it in the chocolate, deliberately soaking his fingers in the sauce. He ate the banana but frowned at his fingers and then arched an eyebrow at her.

"Wow, you're a mess," she cooed, and slowly licked the sweetness from his thumb. She leaned forward, allowing her shirt to gape enough for him to see the soft swell of her breasts . . . and no bra was in sight. She shifted on the bed and the tail of the shirt rode up her thigh, barely covering her bottom. "Another strawberry?" she asked. When he nodded, she dipped it into a bowl of whipped cream. She leaned over and let the cream slide from the strawberry onto his chest. "Silly me!" Jessica said with fake innocence, and proceeded to come up to her knees and lick the fluffy cream from his chest. The pleasure of having her warm, wet tongue on his skin had Ty trying to swallow a moan, but he didn't succeed. "Sorry," she said with the lift of one shoulder. "I'll try to be more careful."

"No problem," Ty replied gruffly, and decided he was a point behind in this very fun game of trying to drive each other crazy. He slathered a slice of apple with a dark golden sauce. "Is this caramel?" he asked, and then accidently-on-purpose dropped the fruit onto her shirt. "Oh, look what I've done." He clicked his tongue. "Guess that shirt is going to have to come off." He popped the apple into his mouth and shrugged.

"I think you're right," Jessica agreed, and reached for the buttons.

Ty watched as each button revealed tantalizing glimpses of her bare skin. The mellow wail of a saxophone seemed to set the sultry mood, and the candlelight flickered off the walls, making shadows dance as if swaying to the music. Jessica took her sweet time, and when she was finished, she turned her back to him and shrugged the shirt off, letting the flannel pool at her waist.

The gentle slope of her shoulders and delicate curve of her back were so damned sexy that it took his breath like he had been hit with a solid punch to his gut. He tossed the shirt onto the floor, not wanting anything in his way. "My God, Jessica, you are one lovely woman." He then gently tugged the rubber band from her ponytail and watched her golden tresses cascade down her back. "I love having my hands in your hair." When he massaged her scalp, she moaned and tilted her head into his hands.

"That feels amazing." Her voice was a low purr that sent a hot shiver down his spine. *Wow . . .*

Jessica was naked. In his bed.

He moved the tray out of his way to his nightstand. "Jessica, lean back against the pillows. I want to feast my eyes on you." When he felt her stiffen slightly, he put his hands on her shoulders. "Why did you hesitate?" Ty didn't want any doubt on her part. He wanted her to come to him with all of her heart and with no regret. No fear.

"Ty, I'm forty years old. The bloom of youth is long gone."

Ty was so relieved that he almost laughed, but the seriousness in her tone gave him pause. "That's your concern—your body?"

She nodded slowly. "The women I saw you with . . ."

"Have got nothing on you," he said firmly. "Jessica, I've

seen your body from head to toe. You're physically beautiful."

She snorted. "For my age?"

"For any age," he said with conviction. "But even better yet, you are gorgeous from the inside out." He brushed her hair to the side and kissed her bare shoulder.

"You make me feel beautiful," she said with a breathy sigh, and tilted her head to the side.

"Because you are." Ty kissed the tender inside of her exposed neck and then pulled back and said, "You know the night of your birthday, when Logan was all over you? Well, I was having those same insecure feelings."

"What? You've got to be kidding me."

"Come on, he's a young stud. I have gray in my hair and crow's-feet around my eyes."

"That's crazy."

"Ah, so I'm still ruggedly handsome?" he asked low in her ear, but he was making a point.

"Of course . . ." she sputtered, and then shook her head. "You have to know that you are incredibly handsome."

"I'm past my prime, and for an athlete, it's hard to take. Seeing these young kids working out every day only reinforces that fact." He shrugged. "Oh, but, Jessica, you have no worries there. You have a natural sensuality about you that just blows me away. Why would you even begin to think otherwise?"

She toyed with the edge of the sheet. "I guess I started feeling self-conscious about my body when I was sixteen and pregnant. It seemed like everybody was staring at my growing belly. And then my young body changed in ways that I never expected." She sighed. "I'm sorry. I'm ruining the moment."

Ty shook his head. "No. I want to know everything about you, Jessica. I'm glad that you're opening up and telling me things that bother you." He trailed a fingertip over her shoulder. "I want to be your shoulder to lean on. Your soft place to land at the end of a tough day. To wrap you in my arms and make all of your troubles disappear."

Her shoulders rose and a sigh escaped her. "I've never had that in my life," she admitted.

"Me neither. And I want that." When he wrapped his arms around her from behind, she leaned back into his embrace. Hot emotion welled up in his throat and he had to pause before he could continue. "Jessica, I want to always be your friend first and then your lover." He tightened his arms around her. "Hey, I know you're still a flight risk, and that puts my own heart on the line. But I am willing to take that chance," he said and then felt her shoulders tense up. "You've thought of that, haven't you?"

She nodded.

"I understand. Jessica, I never wanted a lasting relationship for those very reasons. I never, ever wanted to hurt someone. I have seen firsthand the destruction it can cause. . . ."

"But?"

Ty put his hands on her shoulders and gave her a gentle squeeze. He knew what he was about to confirm would be a risk, but he decided to go for broke. "But I fell in love with you." There . . . he'd said it, and now he held his breath waiting for her response. "Now that I know what it feels like, I can't live happily without you by my side." When she remained silent, he added, "Again, no pressure or anything. Just, you know, my happiness is on the line," he added, trying for humor. But instead of laughter, her shoulders started to shake.

*Oh, dear God, is she crying?* "Oh, Jessica. Damn, I was joking! Well, not really joking, because I really am good for nothing without ya. . . . Well, damn I'm blowing this all to hell." When her shoulders shook harder and he saw her swipe at her eyes, it tore him up. "Aw, Jessica, stop. Baby, look at me. Please! I didn't mean to upset you! I never meant to make you cry. I take it back."

"That you love me?"

"No, not that . . . Hell, I don't know. Just stop crying!"

# 21

## The Heat Is On

JESSICA NEVER UNDERSTOOD WHAT *tears of joy* MEANT until now. She attempted but could not contain her emotion. "I'm . . . okay," she tried to assure him with a sniff, but then her shoulders shook with laughter and she had to swipe at the tears leaking out of the corner of her eyes.

"You're not okay," Ty insisted, and tried to turn her around so that he could see her face. "Jessica, what did I say to make you cry?"

"Oh, Ty . . ." She turned and put her hands on his cheeks. "You were just so cute, the way you declared your feelings, and it hit me straight in my heart. But then when you started bumbling around with your speech, it struck me as sweet and endearingly funny, and I just started laughing and crying at the same time." She smiled and had to blink back more moisture. "These are happy tears. I just can't contain myself. I don't want to contain myself, and it feels amazing!"

"Thank God," he said with such conviction that she giggled again.

"I'm sorry. You are just so cute!" she said.

"Damn, I'm supposed to be a tough-as-nails coach. Don't let anyone know my cute, cuddly side. Okay?"

Jessica grinned.

"This is where you're supposed to say that my secret is safe with you."

"I promise not to tell anyone that Mr. Triple Threat is really just a softy," she assured him, and then laughed again.

Ty leaned in and kissed her tenderly. "I'm a super softy where you're concerned. Damn, girl, when I thought I'd made you cry, it tore me up. Seeing you cry brings me to my knees." He kissed her again and then said, "I really do love you, Jessica. I know this sounds trite, but life feels empty without you in it."

"Oh, Ty." Her laughter died in her throat, and she searched his face for any sign of insincerity but saw only honesty in the depths of his eyes. Tears welled up once again.

"Please tell me those are still happy tears."

Her laughter gurgled in her throat. "Yes. Oh yes!" Jessica's heart pounded and she closed her eyes for a long moment. Finally, she inhaled a deep breath and said, "Ty, I love you too. I've known it for a long time now, but this little break we took solidified it. I am miserable without you." She leaned forward and kissed him softly, soundly, but then a hot, sultry feeling of desire started at her mouth and slowly sank south. When Ty groaned, Jessica smiled against his lips and then boldly caressed between his legs. He was hard and ready. "Oh, and that part about you being a softy . . . mmm, not true. At least not here."

He chuckled but jerked when she wrapped her hand around his erection. "Never for long when you're around," he readily admitted, but then pulled back and looked at her. "But you do have me wrapped around your finger. There's no sense in denying it. I haven't felt this good in days, Jessica, and it's all because of being with you."

Jessica gave him a slow smile. "And you're about to feel even better."

"God . . ." Ty breathed when she leaned back against the

pillows. She allowed him to look his fill. While her breasts weren't as firm as they once were and she had stretch marks here and there, Jessica had never felt sexier. The heat of his gaze melted away every last inhibition, and when he cupped her breast in his big, warm hand, Jessica arched up into his palm. He caressed her flesh, and when he rubbed his thumb over her sensitive nipple, she didn't even try to hold back the moan of pure desire. "Oh, God!" she breathed when he leaned over and sucked her nipple into the silky, wet heat of his mouth. When he licked her in small circles, Jessica threaded her fingers through his hair and urged him on. He sucked and nipped lightly, sending sharp needles of longing shooting through her body.

A moment later, he shucked his sweatpants and they were skin to skin.

Jessica moved against him and was unable to get close enough. She loved this man. Absolutely loved him. "I've waited so long for this," she said as she slid her hands down his back to his very nice ass.

"Almost two weeks," Ty said.

"No," she said with a catch in her voice, and he pulled back and looked into her eyes.

"All our lives," he finished with the uncanny understanding that was beginning to come naturally to them.

"Yes."

"Ah . . . Jessica," Ty said, and wrapped his strong arms around her. "This is how much space you get from now on," he told her, and gave her a hard squeeze. "So you had better get used to it."

Jessica laughed and hugged him back. "I'll get used to it, but I'll never take you for granted."

"I love your sweet honesty," he said, and then kissed her hotly, deeply, before leaning to the side on his elbow. "I know. Believe me, I really know. I've seen too much deception and heartache not to appreciate what we have. It's a gift, and I will treasure it always."

Jessica started to blink back tears, but then gave in to her emotion and let the hot moisture leak from the corners of her eyes. "Me too."

"Ah . . . damn, sweetheart." When he kissed the wetness away from her cheeks, something beautiful broke open inside her. "I do love you." He kissed her again, and she could taste the salt of her tears on his tongue. It blew her away that this big, strong, tough athlete could be so gentle and so very tender. In turn, she wanted to ease any pain, any ache that he would ever have. And when she kissed him back, it wasn't just with her heart, but with her soul.

"And I love you." After waiting so long to say those words to him, Jessica found that she couldn't say them enough. She moved against him, loving the way their bodies fit. Smooth, warm skin slid deliciously, sensuously back and forth. Her nipples grazed his chest, sending hot tingles through her body until her toes curled. She wanted him like she had never wanted anyone else. Ever.

"I want you," Ty whispered in her ear, echoing her thoughts once more. He rolled away briefly to slide on protection and then was back in her arms. He kissed her with wild abandon and caressed her everywhere. Jessica matched his passion kiss for kiss and moved her hands over his back, into his thick hair. When he entered her with one deep stroke, she welcomed him with a deep sigh and wrapped her legs around his waist. She wanted him closer, deeper. . . . And when tenderness turned to pure heat, Jessica let herself go. . . .

More than an hour later, they had used every inch of the king-sized bed. Pillows had been tossed to the floor, and the comforter was a heap at one corner of the mattress. Chocolate and caramel sauce had become finger paint, and Jessica would never again look at a strawberry the same way. "Oh, dear God."

Ty chuckled. "Worn-out?"

"Mmm, yes," she admitted, and then rested her head on

his chest. "I need a shower," she said in a weary voice, but couldn't resist kissing his warm skin.

"Me too," Ty agreed in the same tired tone.

"But I would have to move."

"I know. It won't be easy. Baby, that was some workout."

Jessica's low giggle seemed to give him energy. And when he rolled over and licked her caramel-flavored breast, she felt another long pull of desire. "We couldn't possibly..." she protested, but when his hand moved between her thighs and he caressed her mound, a sweet ache rolled over her. She was bone-tired and tender and yet she couldn't begin to tell him to stop. He nuzzled her neck and slid his finger over her in leisurely circles until her breath started to come in short gasps. "I can't believe you can make me feel this way . . . again."

"Believe it."

"God . . . Ty!" Jessica didn't think he could make her come yet again, but she felt the tight curl of desire start to unravel. She arched her back. . . . It was almost too much and yet achingly sweet, falling just short of pain. When he dipped his finger into her tender, wet heat, she moaned and jerked with the shock of sharp pleasure that she didn't think she had left in her. His low rumble of laughter felt like silk sliding over her skin, and when he touched her swollen bud once more, Jessica climaxed as if in slow motion. The deep, exquisite pleasure tore a moan from her throat.

"Oh . . ." Jessica gripped Ty's shoulder. When she whimpered, he chuckled again. "Dear God!" She felt as if she were made of warm honey, slowly melting into the mattress.

"Ready for that hot shower now?"

"Oh, right. Like I could stand. My body has gone from solid to liquid."

Ty laughed. "How about if I fill up that big garden bath with some steaming-hot water? I'll even carry you into the bathroom."

"Now you're talking."

"It's big enough for two," he said suggestively.

"Even better."

Her eyes were closed, but she managed a smile.

"Ah, baby, don't ever stop doing that."

"Stop what?" She tried to raise her eyebrows in question, but even they were weary.

"Smiling." He traced the outline of her mouth with his fingertip.

"Well, you put it there."

Ty groaned. "Now the pressure is on *me*."

Jessica's smile widened. "Can you handle it?"

"Absolutely. I perform well under pressure," he said in a teasing tone, but then fell silent.

Jessica opened her eyes and looked at Ty. All traces of humor were gone.

"Hey." He grasped her chin gently. "I want to make you happy, Jessica."

"You already have made me happy," she said, and it was true. She needed this big, strong, sexy man like a thirsty plant needed water. The intensity of her feelings made her hands tremble and her throat constrict. But Jessica suddenly felt exposed, shaken, and she would have looked away if Ty hadn't had a firm grip on her chin . . . and a vise grip on her heart.

"I'm going to chase that haunting doubt right out of those amazing eyes of yours." He sighed and dropped his hand. "I'm sorry. I am trying really hard to go slow with you, Jessica, but I just can't stop myself. The last thing I want to do is screw this up. But I can tell you one thing for sure. You can put your faith and trust in me, and I won't ever let you down."

"I believe you."

"Good. Never stop," he said, and then scooted off the bed and scooped her up in his arms.

Jessica laughed as she looped her arms around his neck. "Where in the world are you getting your energy?"

"I'm getting my second wind. I guess after all of the moping around I did, I'm just ready to go. Think you can hang with me, girlie?"

Jessica laughed with pure delight. "I'm going to give it the old college try."

Ty let her slide slowly down his body until her feet reached the tile floor, but instead of releasing her, he held her close. "It feels great to have you back in my arms once again."

"There's no place on earth I'd rather be."

# 22

## Truth or Dare!

BELLA INHALED THE PUNGENT SCENT OF DARK-ROAST COF-fee as she scooped it into the paper cone. She usually liked to sleep in on her day off, but she wanted to cook Logan a big breakfast in honor of opening day. Plus, her mother would be arriving later for the game, and she needed all the energy she could get to deal with Nicolina Diamante. Her mother still didn't know that Logan was a guy, but Bella shoved that little detail from her brain and concentrated on gathering together the ingredients for a big, old, country-style breakfast feast.

While humming to herself, she opened the refrigerator and located a carton of eggs and a package of sausage links. After fishing a bag of frozen hash browns from the freezer, Bella found the skillets she needed. She cooked as silently as she could in an effort not to wake Logan before he needed to rise. Once the sausage links and hash browns were popping and sizzling in the skillets, she paused to pour a big mug of strong coffee. After adding cream and sugar, she took a bracing sip and sighed.

"Something sure smells amazing."

"Oh, my God! You scared the daylights out of me!" Bella squeaked, and almost sloshed her coffee over the rim of the mug. She turned to give Logan an accusing glare, but the sight of him in nothing but blue shorts made her eyes widen instead.

"Sorry," he said with a sheepish grin, and headed over to the cabinet to grab a coffee mug. His blond hair was bed-head messy, and he nonchalantly scratched his bare chest while yawning. How could a person look so good after just waking up?

"Well, you shouldn't sneak up like that." Logan made her feel frumpy in her leggings and oversized T-shirt. Her face was washed free of makeup, and her hair was a mass of messy waves tumbling over her shoulders.

"Okay . . . but I do live here, you know."

Boy, did she ever. "Yeah, but you aren't usually awake this early, and I was sort of in a zone."

"Couldn't sleep," he admitted while pouring the steaming brew into his mug. After replacing the carafe on the warmer, he looked her way.

"Oh, sorry to hear that," Bella said, and tried not to stare at his near nakedness. She wondered if he paraded around like that just to turn her on. Not that she was about to let him know how much she wanted to grab him and do something crazy like lick his nipples or squeeze his butt . . . or both. She felt her face grow warm at the image, and hoped Logan thought it was from the heat of the stove. "Opening-day jitters?"

Logan took a long sip of his coffee but gazed at her over the rim of his mug. After lowering his arm, he examined the contents. "Not really."

"What, then?"

He paused for a second and then lifted one shoulder, causing muscle to ripple. "Just . . . stuff," he finally replied, but his gaze lingered on her long enough to send a hot shiver down her spine.

Were thoughts of her keeping him awake?

*Don't even go there,* she sternly reminded herself, but it

was getting more and more difficult each and every day she spent under the same roof with him. And it wasn't just that he made her heart race every time he entered the room. She simply enjoyed his company and looked forward to the time they spent together. Bella felt more at ease with Logan than she ever had with David, and already knew much more about him. Conversation with Logan came easy, and she found herself thinking about him during the day. "Would you like some breakfast?"

"Sure. Whatever you're making would be great. Thanks," he said with one of those smiles that turned her inside out.

But it suddenly pissed her off that he could make her feel this way! Bella had overheard Noah talking on the phone about Logan just yesterday. He had said that Logan's elbow was healed and his arm was coming back stronger than ever. It wouldn't take long for a major-league franchise to sit up and take notice. Why get involved with someone who would be leaving town as soon as he could?

"Wow, and hash browns too?" Logan commented with another smile. "Thanks for cooking such an amazing breakfast, Bella."

Bella shrugged. "I was bored and hungry," she mumbled, and took a sip of her coffee.

"Oh." His smile faltered, making her feel like an ass. "Well, lucky me, I guess."

"Yeah," she said as she lowered the temperature on the links and potatoes. "I overheard Noah say that your arm is stronger than ever." She flicked a glance his way.

Logan nodded. "I've got the green light to pitch in relief."

"Are you excited?"

"Sure." He took another sip of his coffee but averted his gaze.

"You don't seem like it."

"I am," he insisted, but without much conviction. She knew that she had hurt his feelings and it bothered her.

"Do you want your eggs over easy?" she asked, even though she knew damned well that he did. She knew everything from his favorite ice cream to how he liked his steak prepared.

"Scrambled like yours, if it's easier."

"No, I don't mind fixing them the way you prefer."

"I don't want you to go to any trouble, even though you're bored."

Bella felt tears well up in her eyes, turned back to the stove, and started flipping the golden hash browns. A moment later she put down the spatula with more force than necessary.

"Bella, I don't get it. Did I do something to piss you off?"

Bella whirled around to face him. "Yes!"

"What the hell did I do?"

She stomped her foot so hard that the sausages rolled around in the skillet as if in surprise. "You . . . you're almost *naked*!"

"That's *it*?" He set his coffee mug down on the kitchen table with a *thump* and angled his head in question. "Do you want me to put on a shirt?"

"Yes!"

"Okay! Geez . . ." he grumbled and turned to leave.

"Wait. Oh, Logan, I lied."

He came to an immediate stop and then slowly turned around to face her. His blond brows came together. "So you *don't* want me to put a shirt on?" he asked slowly.

"Yes . . . no." She shook her head and gazed up at the ceiling. "Oh, God." After taking a deep breath, she decided to come clean. "Okay, here goes. I lied about fixing breakfast because I was bored. I was making this big spread for you."

Logan's frown remained. "So you went to all of this trouble, and I pissed you off by walking around in my gym shorts? I walk around in them all the time. Bella, we've been through this, and you insisted that it didn't bother you."

"I lied about that too."

He gave her a lopsided grin.

"This isn't funny, Lo-gan!"

"Okay." When he took a step closer, Bella backed away and came up against the counter. "So, is this confession time?"

"No!" she said, but then realized he was talking about himself. "Okay, maybe."

"What else have you lied about, Bella?" he asked softly.

Her chin came up. "It's your turn," she tossed back at him.

"Oh, really?" He arched one eyebrow. "How about a little game of truth or dare?"

"I hate that silly game," she scoffed.

"Really?" He took a step closer, crowding her space. "Well, how about I let you go first?"

Bella narrowed her eyes, but then said, "Okay. Truth or dare?"

"Truth."

"Do you parade around half-naked to try to get me . . . excited?"

"Truth."

"I knew it!" She stomped her foot, forgetting that she was braless. Her breasts jiggled and she folded her arms over her chest. "My turn."

"What?"

"You have to let me have my turn. It's only fair."

"Whatever." Her pulse pounded, but she shrugged as if it were no big deal. "Dare." She wasn't about to tell him any more of her secrets.

"Touch me with both hands for one minute."

Bella snorted. "That's it?" She did a little head bop and put both index fingers on his chest.

"With your *hands*, Bella. Not just your fingertips."

Bella rolled her eyes and sighed. "Whatever," she repeated, but when she splayed her hands on his warm skin, she had to swallow a moan.

"One minute," he reminded her when she would have snatched her hands away. He knew her all too well.

"Right . . ." She tilted her head to the side and shrugged. "One minute."

"I know . . . *whatever*."

They stood there silently, and she started ticking off the seconds in her head. But when she got to thirty, she lost count, since all her brain could handle was her hands on his bare skin. Just when she was about to give in and pull his head down for a long-awaited kiss, he said, "Okay, time's up."

Bella wanted to snatch her hands away, but that would be a dead giveaway, so she leisurely slid her palms down his torso and trailed her fingertips over his skin before breaking contact. She had the satisfaction of feeling his ab muscles contract.

"Your turn."

*Oh no.* "I need to finish making breakfast."

"It can wait," he said, and flicked off the burners. "Unless that was too much for you," he challenged.

"*Pfft*. Okay, Logan. Truth or dare?"

"Dare," he responded easily.

Bella decided to get even. "Put *your* hands on *me* for one minute."

"Okay," he said, and slid both hands up her big T-shirt.

"What are you doing?" Perhaps this wasn't such a good idea after all.

"It had to be bare skin, right?"

"Oh . . . right," she said, shrugging to hide the hot shiver caused by his big, warm hands on her back. She tapped her toe as if bored, but in reality, her pulse pounded. She wanted so badly for his hands to roam over her body, but he stood very still. At about thirty seconds, his fingertips dug just slightly into her skin, and she knew he was having the same thoughts. Each second ticked in tandem with the slow *thud* of her heart. Heat radiated from his chest, and if Bella moved forward just an inch, she would be flush against his body. "Are you ready to end this stupid game?" Bella tried for a tight tone, but her voice came out breathy. She looked up at him and angled her head in question.

"No." His eyes locked with hers. "Truth or dare?" he challenged.

"Truth!" If she had to put her hands on him again, she knew just where they would land.

"Do you want to kiss me?"

"No!"

"Tell the truth, Bella!"

"I did!"

"I don't believe you."

"I don't want to kiss you because I wouldn't be able to stop there. How's that for the truth? Are you happy that you've humiliated me?" She reached up and pushed at his chest, but he grabbed her wrists and held her firmly.

"Humiliated you?"

"Yeah! Why do guys like to do that?"

"Just how am I doing that, Bella? Huh?"

"I'm falling for you, and all you want is a piece of ass!" she sputtered.

"Really?" He dropped her hands and then took a step backward. "Wow. That's what you take me for?" The look of hurt on his face went straight to her heart and squeezed. He looked at her for a long, measuring moment, but then shook his head. "You're full of crap. You don't really believe all I want is to bed you. How could you fall for a guy like that?"

Her chin came up, but she remained silent.

"You want to believe that, Bella. It's your armor."

"You'll be leaving as soon as you get picked up by a minor-league team."

"That's a factor, but that's not it either."

"Really? So tell me, then. What exactly is my problem, Logan?"

"You said it before. David humiliated you. Hurt you. You're not willing to risk it again. Pride and fear are getting in your way." He shrugged. "Until you let go, you can't move forward. Oh, believe me, I know that drill backward and forward." He turned on his heel and started to walk away.

Bella blinked at his back. He was right. And she was letting him slip away because of it. She had to stop him! "Truth or dare?" she asked softly.

Logan stopped and balled his fists but didn't turn around. When his feet finally moved, she thought he was going to keep on walking out of the kitchen and out of her life. Her heart pounded with sheer terror, and she knew now that she had never felt about David the way she felt about Logan. He was her friend, and she didn't want to lose him. If he got called to the minor leagues, she would just have to follow him!

But instead of walking away, he pivoted to face her. "Truth," he said firmly.

Bella pressed her lips together, swallowed hard, and then asked, "Do you care about me?"

"Yes. More and more each day."

When he didn't even hesitate, she put her hand to her mouth.

"Truth or dare?" he asked gruffly.

She removed her hand and gave him a trembling smile. "Dare . . ."

"Kiss . . ." Before he could get the rest out, she ran forward and jumped up into his arms. With a surprised grunt, he grabbed her and stumbled back against the wall. Bella wrapped her legs around his waist and shoved her fingers through his shaggy hair and kissed him. She kissed him soundly, deeply . . . *wildly* until they were breathless and laughing. He cupped her bottom in his big, capable hands.

"You didn't let me finish my dare. "I was going to say kiss my ass."

She shoved his shoulder. "You were not."

"Kiss my . . ." he began, but was interrupted by the door-bell chiming.

Bella's eyes widened. "Oh, my God!"

"Who could it be?"

"I just bet that's my mother!"

"Holy crap," Logan said with wide eyes.

"Yeah!" Bella scrambled to the floor. "Get some clothes on." She looked down at his erection. "Oh . . . sorry. Hold that thought!"

He shook his head sadly. "Why is it that I have both the best and worst of luck?"

Bella giggled, but then nibbled on her bottom lip.

"Bella, she does know that I'm a guy, right?"

"Not exactly."

He rolled his eyes. "Should I wear a wig and talk in a high-pitched voice?"

"Hey, my mother is a modern woman. She'll be fine with this," Bella assured him with a smile and a firm nod. She only hoped she was right.

When the doorbell chimed again, Logan hurried into his bedroom and Bella headed to the front door. *Maybe it won't be my mother, after all,* she thought, but when she opened the door, Nicolina Diamante stood on the other side.

"Bella!" she said with a big smile, and dropped the han-dle of her huge suitcase. "Sweetie, it is so wonderful to see your beautiful face." She reached up and pinched Bella's cheeks. "I have missed you so!"

"Me too," Bella admitted, and felt moisture well up in her eyes. Her mother could be a force to be reckoned with, but she loved her dearly. "Come on in and see my place." She stood back and then reached over and picked up the handle of the bulging suitcase.

"It's lovely," Nicolina said, and spun in a slow circle. "You were lucky to have it furnished for you."

"Yes, it's perfect," Bella agreed.

Nicolina reached over and put her hands on Bella's shoulders and squeezed. Her mother was a tiny little thing, but made up for her small stature with her bigger-than-life personality. They shared the same wide mouth, petite nose, and deep brown eyes, but Nicolina's hair was auburn and cut chin length and angled toward her face. "So, how have you been?"

"Good," Bella said. "Busy."

Nicolina angled her head and studied Bella. "There's something different about you." She rested a French-tipped fingernail to her cheek and tapped. "A . . . glow."

Bella swallowed hard. "Um, I was in the kitchen, cooking." She fanned her face. "I'm just flushed from the heat."

"Mmm . . . no. I'm not buying that," she said, and then her eyes opened wide when they heard the unmistakable sound of the shower starting. "Who is that?"

"My roommate," Bella said nonchalantly, but she could feel heat creep up her neck.

"What is *his* name?" Nicolina asked.

"How did you guess?"

"You're as nervous as a cat on a hot tin roof. I sort of had an inkling when you failed to mention a name to me. I can always tell when something is up. So enlighten me about this roommate of yours."

"His name is Logan Lannigan, and he plays baseball for the Cricket Creek Cougars."

"Are you sleeping with him?" she asked in true Nicolina Diamante blunt form.

"Mother!" Bella protested in a stage whisper, and glanced down the hallway.

"Well?"

"No! We're roommates for convenience's sake. Sharing expenses and the rent . . ." She recalled what her mother

almost walked in on, and willed herself not to blush.
"That's it."

"Really? Then why do I feel as if I walked in on something?"

"I was cooking breakfast! Follow me into the kitchen
and see for yourself." Bella used the opportunity to turn
away from her mother and head down the hallway.

"Quite a feast you're cooking up for your so-called
roommate of convenience."

"It's opening day. I wanted Logan to have a big breakfast," she said, and then realized how intimate it sounded.
"Help yourself to some coffee, Mother," she offered, and
turned the burners back on. "Are you hungry?"

"Famished," Nicolina admitted. "It's been a long time
since I've eaten a big breakfast like this."

"The mugs are in the top cabinet," Bella said as she
opened up the carton of eggs. Her gaze darted to the doorway, and she wondered when Logan would make his appearance.

"Thank you." She stood up on tiptoe and reached for a
mug. "So, do you like living in this small town?"

Bella paused, but then gave her an affirmative nod. "Yes,
I do. Mother, you'll just love Wine and Diner. Jessica has
done a fabulous job combining down-home cooking and an
elegant flair."

"And Madison? How is she doing?"

"She's helping out at the diner until she starts teaching
creative writing at a local liberal-arts college. Oh, and she is
engaged to be married!"

"So you told me. To a local boy?" Nicolina asked, and
arched one auburn eyebrow as if it were hard to believe.

"Mother, don't be a snob. Jason is a wonderful man."

"I'm not a snob!" she protested, looking a bit put out. "I
will admit that having you suddenly moving to this little
town has been a shock to my system, but I have an open
mind. In fact, I'm looking forward to the baseball game.

You know how we loved going to Cubs games." Her smile was a little wistful, and it hit Bella hard that her mother must miss her only daughter living in Chicago. After all, it was only the two of them plus a handful of relatives that they saw on holidays and at funerals. A sudden flash of guilt washed over her.

Bella flipped the sausage links over and then turned to her mother. "Mother, Madison had a suggestion that I think you might want to consider."

"The look on your face suggests that I should sit down for this." She carried her mug over to the table and sat down.

Bella leaned one hip against the counter and said, "There are some lovely storefronts almost finished near the new stadium. As a matter of fact, one of them is going to be a bridal shop."

Nicolina cradled her hands around her coffee mug. "And?"

"You design lots of jewelry for weddings."

"Bella, are you suggesting that I open Designs by Diamante here in Cricket Creek, Kentucky?"

"A big portion of your business could still be online. But this location would be perfect. Grammar's, a wonderful local bakery, is going to open a small store specializing in wedding cakes in the same shopping center, and I think a florist is going in there as well." Bella felt a shot of excitement. "The more I think about it, the more it could work. Mother, I don't have to stay hostess at Wine and Diner forever. I could help you. . . ." She lifted one shoulder and decided not to press too hard, too soon. "It's just a suggestion, but this weekend while you're in town, you should check it out and at least consider it. This little town used to be quite a tourist attraction, and when the economy comes back, it's going to break loose. I know you had your sights set on Chicago, but this just might be the ticket."

Nicolina pursed her lips and nodded slowly. "I'll take a

look and give it some thought," she answered in an even tone, but Bella could see a spark of excitement in her mother's eyes.

"Great." Bella smiled and was about to expand on the idea when Logan walked into the room. He wore designer jeans and a black golf shirt with a Cricket Creek logo stitched in gold. His hair was slightly damp but neatly combed, and as usual, her heart skipped a beat at the mere sight of him. Logan was simply gorgeous, and Bella felt a sense of pride. She wanted to tell her mother that he was becoming more than just a roommate, but the suddenly more serious tone of their relationship was still too new. She was worried that her mother would think that Logan was a rebound relationship after David and that it was too quick, too soon. But in her heart, Bella knew it wasn't so.

"Good morning," Logan announced in his deep, sexy voice. His teeth flashed white against his golden tan.

"Good morning." Bella felt her cheeks grow warm when their eyes met. "Logan! I'd like you to meet my mother, Nicolina Diamante." She swung her hand in an arc toward the kitchen table. "Mother, this is my . . . roommate, Logan Lannigan."

Logan walked over to the table and extended his hand. "Nice to meet you, Ms. Diamante. I hope you'll enjoy the game today."

"It is nice to meet you as well, Logan. I'm quite the baseball fan, so I'm looking forward to the game. I understand we have amazing seats behind home plate."

"We'll try to bring you a win."

"And what position do you play?"

"I'm a pitcher. I'm coming off Tommy John elbow surgery, so I will only pitch in relief until my arm is ready."

"Well, the best of luck. I'll be cheering for you."

"Thanks," he said politely, and then headed over to the

coffeepot. "Breakfast looks amazing," he said to Bella. He looked so nervous that she wished she could give him a hug.

"Thanks. Have a seat. It's almost ready."

"Want your coffee heated up?" Logan asked, and held up the pot.

"Yes, thanks." Bella had to admit that she was enjoying this domestic feeling. She was relieved that her mother seemed to have taken the news of Logan being a male roommate so well, but, then again, her mother was a liberal thinker. Nicolina Diamante could be smothering at times, but Bella suddenly hoped that her mother would give real consideration to moving to Cricket Creek.

"Do you need any help, Bella?" her mother asked.

"Thanks, but I've got it," Bella replied as she cracked eggs into a bowl. She flicked Logan a shy, reassuring glance. His gorgeous male presence seemed to fill the small room, and once again Bella wished she could wrap her arms around him. Her body still hummed with passion interrupted by the arrival of her mother, and she had to wonder when they would get the chance to finish what they had started.

"Logan, come and have a seat," Nicolina said. "Save your energy for the baseball game."

As she popped English muffins into the toaster, Bella could feel her mother's gaze on her, even as she made small talk with Logan. Bella was certain that her mother could feel the vibe between her and Logan, and Bella knew she would probably be grilled about it later. But for now she wanted to enjoy breakfast with the two people in the world who mattered the most to her.

As she retrieved a carton of orange juice from the refrigerator, Bella had to marvel at the crazy turn of events her life had taken in such a short amount of time. Just a month ago, if anyone had told her she would be living with a man in Cricket Creek, Kentucky, she would have laughed. And yet here she was . . . and happier than she had been in a long time. Logan was right. It was high time that she let go of pride and fear and went full speed ahead with confidence.

# 23
## Game On!

JESSICA FLIPPED THE SIGN AROUND IN THE WINDOW OF Wine and Diner to read CLOSED and headed outside to watch the opening-day parade march down Main Street. Since just about everyone in town would be attending the baseball game, it was pointless to keep the diner open. Plus, Jessica wanted her employees to have the opportunity to watch as well. So after the lunch rush, she opted to close the doors and head out to take in the opening-day festivities.

Cricket Creek had been blessed with an unseasonably warm spring day and a cornflower blue sky. Bright sunshine sparkled off squeaky-clean storefront windows and glossy painted signs. Excitement crackled in the air, and spectators sat on curbs and lined the sidewalks, waiting for the parade to begin.

Jessica smiled when she heard the enthusiastic sound of the Cricket Creek High School marching band playing "Take Me Out to the Ballgame." Honking horns and the wailing siren of fire trucks mixed with lively chatter and laughter. The streets of Cricket Creek hadn't been this packed in years, and it sent a thrill of hope shooting through Jessica's body. She weaved her way through the crowd until she spotted Madison, Jason, Aunt Myra, and Owen in a perfect location on the corner of Main and Second streets.

"Hey there," Jessica called with a wave, and then squeezed in next to Madison.

"It's about time," Madison complained with a good-natured shove to Jessica's shoulder.

"How are you doin', little mama?" Jason asked with a big smile. He and Madison looked cute in their Cougar baseball caps. They were holding hands, and it just warmed Jessica's heart to see her daughter so happy. And Jason was a fine young man!

"Better now that I'm finally here."

"Mom, you should have let us help you close up," Madison protested.

"Then you wouldn't have gotten this premier spot," Jessica replied with a shake of her head. "Isn't this just so exciting? And what a beautiful day we have here!"

"I've been guarding this here corner with my very life," Aunt Myra said with a flip of her long braid over her shoulder. "I had to karate chop two little kids and shove an elderly lady who tried to get past me with her walker."

Jessica laughed. "Thanks, Aunt Myra."

Owen shook his head. "And you think she's joking?"

Jessica laughed harder. She thought it was simply amazing how much Aunt Myra had brought shy Owen out of his shell. "I guess Olivia is riding in the parade with Noah?"

"No." Owen shook his head. "Olivia's on a big float that the drama club and glee club helped her build. But she'll catch up with us over at the ballpark."

"I know Olivia has been waiting for this day with such anticipation," Jessica said, and gave Owen a huge hug. When she pulled away, she wasn't surprised to see him grow misty-eyed.

"It's so wonderful to see my Livie so happy. She deserves the best," Owen said.

"It's crazy how far we've all come in the past year, isn't it?"

Aunt Myra nodded. "Noah Falcon sure did shake things up when he roared back here last spring in that red Corvette of his." She smacked her thigh. "Sure is funny how Olivia was his high school tutor, he bein' the football star right here in Cricket Creek. And after all these years, they ended up together. Who would have thought?"

Owen smiled at Myra. "Yep, funny how love can be right under your danged nose and you don't even know it."

Jessica was delighted to see Aunt Myra blush. Those two were proof positive that opposites attract and yet could bring out the best in each other.

"And then again, some people are just a bit hardheaded," Jason commented, and got a shove from Madison.

"Hey, what made you think I was talking about you?" Jason asked with raised eyebrows, only to be rewarded with another shove.

"Were you?"

"Yeah." His comment got him another shove, followed by a giggle. The sunlight caught the diamonds in Madison's engagement ring and tugged a smile from Jessica. They had all come such a long way in a year's time, and today was shaping up to be just perfect. This parade was a celebration of more than just opening day. It was a new beginning for the entire town. Their lives seemed to be coming together like scattered pieces of a big jigsaw puzzle, and it was going to be interesting to see how everything fit together as time moved on.

"Bella and Nicolina better get here soon, or we won't be able to watch together," Madison commented, and got up on tiptoe to look around. "I texted Bella where we'd be watching."

"Yes, I'm looking forward to seeing them," Jessica commented. As if on cue, Bella and Nicolina hurried across the street just before the police closed off the intersection from traffic.

"Jessica!" Nicolina shouted, and gave Jessica a big squeeze. "It's so nice to see you. And don't you just look amazing."

"Thank you, Nicolina. So do you," Jessica said, and it was true. Like her daughter, Nicolina Diamante was movie-star gorgeous and had the attitude to match. She was drawing stares from the crowd but didn't seem to notice.

"I'm looking forward to a tour of Wine and Diner. Bella says it's lovely and has your special touch."

"Why, thank you, Bella," Jessica said, and turned toward her. "Are you ready for some baseball?"

"Yeah, baby!" Bella replied, and Jessica thought there was something different about her young friend. The cloud of depression had dissipated and was replaced with a bright smile and a spring in her step. Jessica had to wonder if Bella had been bitten by the love bug as well. Jessica looked at matchmaker Madison and arched a questioning eyebrow, and she immediately caught her drift.

Madison shot Jessica a discreet, I-knew-it nod before giving Nicolina a hug. "You are as gorgeous as ever. You and Mom are such cougars!"

"Oh stop," Nicolina said, but Jessica could tell that she was pleased at Madison's comment. Like her, Nicolina had dedicated her life to her daughter and work. Jessica had never known her to be in a steady relationship and had to wonder if she was willing to give it any consideration now that Bella was an adult. "Now introduce me to this handsome young man of yours."

Madison took a step back and gestured toward Jason. "Nicolina, I'd like you to meet my fiancé, Jason Craig. Jason, this is Nicolina Diamante."

"Nice to meet ya, Ms. Diamante," Jason said, and politely shook her offered hand.

"Same here. Congratulations, Jason. Madison is a lovely,

talented young woman." She took a step back and smiled. "My best to you both!"

"Thank you," Madison and Jason responded.

Nicolina grabbed Madison's hand and squeezed. "You must be having such fun planning the wedding!"

Madison shrugged and then glanced up at Jason. "We've been so busy that it's been put on the back burner."

"I would love to help," Nicolina offered.

"Mom!" Bella said brightly. "That's an excellent idea."

Jessica nodded. "Oh yes, we would love that. Wouldn't we, Madison?"

"Absolutely," Madison agreed.

Jessica motioned toward Aunt Myra and Owen. "I'd like you to meet my aunt Myra Robinson and our friend Owen Lawson."

"Lovely to meet you too," Nicolina said, and extended her hand. "Such a friendly atmosphere," she said, and turned to Bella. "No wonder you love it here."

"We'll give you the grand tour tomorrow," Madison said.

"And of course you'll have to eat at Wine and Diner!" Jessica said.

"I can't wait!" Nicolina raised her voice over the sound of the approaching marching band. "I am sure the food is amazing."

"Thank you, Nicolina. We still have all of Aunt Myra's classics on the menu, but we've added a modern flair. And Jason did an amazing job on the remodeling." She nodded toward Owen. "Owen and Jason created an outdoor patio that is fabulous. It opens tomorrow."

Nicolina smiled and took a step closer so that only Jessica could hear. "And I wanted to thank you for giving Bella a job. I sure do miss her, but she needed this change of atmosphere."

"Oh, it was my pleasure hiring her. She is a hard worker, and I look after her as if she is my own daughter. It's been nice for Madison too. They get along like sisters." She placed a hand on Nicolina's arm. "But I can understand how it must be hard for her to have moved here. I would miss Madison."

"It's been tough," Nicolina admitted. "Bella wants to show me a storefront located by the stadium."

"To open your own jewelry store?" Jessica felt a surge of excitement and smiled brightly.

"It's just a thought, but yes."

"Oh, that would be wonderful!" Jessica felt like jumping up and down with childlike joy. Could this day get any better?

"I would ask you if you're content living here in this small town, but happiness is radiating from you, Jessica." She sighed. "I just don't know if I could make the adjustment. I've lived in Chicago all my life." She glanced over at Bella, who was laughing at something Aunt Myra said, and shook her head. "But it seems like Bella is embracing life here, so I should at least give it some serious consideration. It's a big decision."

Jessica put her arm around Nicolina and gave her narrow shoulders a quick squeeze. "We have more in common than I ever realized. I would enjoy having you around." She removed her arm and then shrugged. "Sometimes we make some decisions more difficult than they need to be. Madison has told me a number of times that I'm the queen of overthinking. Just go with your gut. That's what I did with Wine and Diner."

"Thanks. That's sound advice."

Jessica grinned. "Oh yeah, and you have to work your ever-loving tail off."

Nicolina laughed. "Well, we were both single moms. I'm no stranger to hard work." She looked in the direction of Bella and Madison and then turned her gaze back to Jessica with misty eyes. "We did a good job, didn't we?"

"Yes, we did." Jessica reached up with her palm. "Give me a high five, girlfriend!"

Nicolina smacked her hand hard, drawing the attention of their daughters.

"Mom, here come Noah and Ty!" Madison shouted just as Noah's red Corvette convertible turned onto Main Street. A handsome silver-haired man she didn't know was driving, and Noah and Ty were perched up on the back of the shiny car, waving to the cheering crowd. When they reached the corner, Ty turned and tipped his cap directly at Jessica, who in turn blew him a kiss. They were tossing out wrapped candy from a bucket and showered the crowd with Tootsie Rolls.

Nicolina accepted a piece of candy from Jessica. "Oh, so Bella was right. There is something going on between you and Ty McKenna."

Jessica felt herself blush, but gave Nicolina a nod. "Who would have thought, huh?"

Nicolina wiggled delicate auburn eyebrows. "He is one fine-looking man," she commented, just as the driver of the Corvette looked their way. He was wearing aviator sunglasses, but it was obvious that his gaze lingered on Nicolina. "Who is he?" she asked casually, but Jessica noticed the feminine interest.

"To tell you the truth, I don't know. I'm guessing he must be a baseball friend of Noah and Ty's. She tipped her head sideways. "But, you know, Ty did mention that there would be someone sitting in the section we're sitting in. . . . Hmm . . ."

"What?"

"He looks so familiar. I know I've seen him in Chicago Blue many times. . . . Oh!" Her eyes widened and she suddenly knew.

"Do you know him?"

Jessica nodded slowly and then leaned close to Nicolina's ear. "If I'm not mistaken, that's Mitch Monroe. He's a big-business tycoon from Chicago. I knew there was a silent investor in the baseball complex, and keep it on the down low, but I just bet it's him."

"Oh . . ." Nicolina nodded thoughtfully and then shrugged slightly as if she weren't all that interested, but Jessica made a mental note to make sure the two of them were seated next to each other. After the parade ended, they followed the boisterous crowd over to the baseball park. Although the league that the Cougars competed in was a step below actual minor-league baseball, the stadium was state-of-the-art. The complex hugged the banks of the Ohio River, and new developments were springing up everywhere, including the strip of shops Nicolina had been referring to earlier as a potential location for Designs by Diamante. Future plans included several shops and maybe even a hotel connected to a small-scale convention center. Jessica smiled at the transformation that was putting Cricket Creek back on the map.

Bright sunshine glinted off the river, and for the first time in a long while, there were lots of boats out on the water. The marina had also been spruced up in hopes of a good season, and Jessica's smile widened. Good things were yet to come. She could feel it!

"Owen, the landscaping is lovely!" Jessica commented, and noticed that Aunt Myra beamed up at him. Jessica knew the feeling. She was proud that Ty was not only manager of the team, but part owner as well. He and Noah had certainly outdone themselves. The Cricket Creek Baseball Complex was stunning.

"Thank you, Jessica," Owen replied. "It sure was a labor of love."

"And to top it off, it is such a gorgeous day!" Bella gushed, and linked her arm with her mother's. "It's so great that you could make it, Mom."

"Thank you, sweetie! I am having so much fun."

"Now all we need is a win!" Jason declared, and they all agreed.

"Anybody hungry?" Aunt Myra asked, and got nods all around. They headed for one of the many long lines for the concession stands, but the time went fast since they were chatting with everyone in sight.

After a round of hot dogs, they made their way toward their seats just before the Cricket Creek High School band marched onto the baseball diamond to play the national anthem. They all paused and proudly sang along with the standing-room-only crowd.

Their seats were directly behind home plate. Rows were staggered in a *V* behind the backstop, and Jessica made sure that she and Nicolina sat in the first row of only four seats. "Nicolina, let's you and I sit here in the middle and keep the outside seats vacant for Olivia and Mitch Monroe. It will be easier that way."

"Okay." If Nicolina was on to her little matchmaking scheme, she didn't let on, and nodded.

Jessica put her jacket over the seat next to her so that Mitch would have to take the seat next to Nicolina. She had no idea if anything would come of this, but something in her gut told her to do so. "Besides, we don't want to be sitting next to Aunt Myra, since she yells at the umpires." Jessica turned and winced at Owen. "Sorry about your luck," she said, but he only laughed. Madison shot her a what-are-you-up-to look, but when she spotted the silver fox Mitch coming their way, she gave Jessica a discreet, oh-I-know-where-you're-going-with-this thumbs-up.

Jessica watched Mitch look at his ticket stub and up at the occupied seat where he should have been sitting. "Would you mind taking this seat?" She gestured next to Nicolina. "We're trying to keep the couples seated next to each other, if you don't mind."

"Not at all," he said in a smooth-as-silk voice, and then smiled at Jessica before giving his attention to Nicolina. "I'm Mitch Monroe."

"Nicolina Diamante," she said coolly, and extended her hand.

"What a bracelet," he said, and she beamed.

"Thank you."

After shaking her hand, he turned to Jessica.

"It's one of her designs," Jessica felt compelled to inform him. "I'm Jessica Robinson."

"Ah yes, Ty's friend and owner of Wine and Diner. He raves about your inventive cuisine. I used to be a frequent patron of Chicago Blue Bistro. It hasn't been the same since you departed."

"Why, thank you. I thought I recognized you. I'd like you to meet the rest of my crew." When he complied, she introduced everyone, and then they all sat down to witness the first pitch. They were on the second batter when Olivia finally showed up. She waved to everyone and sat down with a long sigh. "Where have you been?" Jessica asked.

"We had to take the float back to the high school. The parking lot looked packed, so I decided to hoof it over here." She fanned her face. "*Shew!* I was kickin' up some dust."

"Well, you've only missed one ground out," Jessica told her. "Isn't this just so exciting?"

Olivia's head bobbed up and down, and she put a hand to her chest. "Yes! I can't believe this day is finally here."

Jessica leaned back in her seat and gestured to Nicolina. "Olivia, I'd like you to meet Bella's mother, Nicolina Diamante."

"Oh, so you're the jewelry designer? It's a pleasure to meet you."

"Likewise. Bella seems to just love it here."

"And to her left is Mitch Monroe. He's a friend of Noah and Ty and is in town for the game."

Mitch stood up and shook Olivia's hand. "Olivia, it is so nice to finally meet you. Noah speaks very highly of you."

"Welcome to Cricket Creek, and thank you for your kind words. Noah sure has given back to his hometown, and we couldn't be more proud of this gorgeous complex."

"Olivia, I've known Noah for a long time, and I've never

seen the man so happy," Mitch added before sitting back down.

At the crack of the bat, all eyes were back on the game. The Richmond Rockets suddenly had a man on second with only one out. Next was a sky-high pop-up to the shortstop and local boy Reed Wilson. The crowd collectively held their breath and then cheered like crazy when Reed caught the ball. An easy fly ball to left field ended the first half of the inning.

For the next four innings, the game was a pitcher's duel, and with only two singles from the Cougars, the crowd was getting restless. Jessica noted that Mitch and Nicolina watched the game with interest but also had eyes for each other. She overheard them discussing Nicolina's jewelry, and said a silent prayer that Bella's mother would decide to open a shop in Cricket Creek.

"I hope we start hitting," Jessica said to Olivia. "I'd love to win this opening game. My stomach is in knots."

"Me too." Olivia nodded, but another inning went by with three quick outs from each team.

"I'm headed to the concession stand," Mitch announced when they stood up for the seventh-inning stretch. "Would anyone like anything?"

Jessica put her hand to her stomach, which was a bit upset. "I'd love a Sprite, if you wouldn't mind." *Perhaps a cold, fizzy drink will help me,* she thought, but had to mask her grimace with a smile.

When Olivia requested a bottle of water, Nicolina asked, "Mitch, would you like me to go with you to help carry things?"

"Why, thank you. That would be nice," Mitch replied with a charming smile. His teeth flashed white against a deep tan, and although his silver hair gleamed in the bright sunlight, Jessica guessed him to be only in his mid- to upper fifties, nearly the same age as Nicolina. Jessica made a mental note to ask Ty more about his intriguing friend.

As soon as Nicolina and Mitch walked away, Jessica turned to Bella, Madison, and Aunt Myra, who were elbowing one another and grinning. "Interesting," Jessica commented to Bella. "I do believe you mother has an admirer."

Bella nodded. "Mom has had men all over her for as long as I can remember. I think she must have been burned so badly that she's not ever going down that path again."

"Maybe it just takes the right man," Aunt Myra said, and got a hug from Owen.

Olivia smiled at her father and Aunt Myra. "Yes, indeed," she agreed, and then winked at Jason as well.

Jessica thought again that this would be such a perfect day if only she didn't suddenly feel so rotten. She thought it could have been the hot dog that she ate earlier, but everyone else seemed fine, and she had eaten only a pastry and coffee earlier. She inhaled a deep breath and hoped that the Sprite would do the trick.

"Are you feeling okay, Mom?" Madison asked. She still had an uncanny way of sensing that something was wrong, no matter how hard Jessica tried to hide it.

"I'm fine. Just a little tummy upset. It must be the sun and the excitement."

"You do look a little pale," Aunt Myra chimed in.

"I'll be okay as soon as I get the cold drink." She wasn't about to leave the game.

When Mitch and Nicolina returned, she took a grateful sip of the soft drink. The cold fizz helped. "Thank you," she said to Mitch. "I was parched."

"No problem," he answered. Jessica tried to remember more details about him, but nothing other than his messy divorce and flamboyant daughter came to mind. At the top of the eighth inning, the Richmond Rockets' bats suddenly got hot and Logan Lannigan started warming up in the bull pen. After only one out, the Rockets had the bases loaded, with their cleanup hitter waiting on deck.

Ty emerged from the dugout and motioned to the umpire for time. Jessica felt her heart skip a beat at the sight of him in his baseball uniform, and suddenly wished she had seen him play back in his Triple Threat days. After a minute of chatting with the pitcher, he motioned for Logan to come in as relief.

Jessica put down her drink and turned to Bella, and had to hide a smile when she noticed that Bella had a death grip on the arms of her seat.

"He's coming in to put out the fire," Jason commented.

"Put out the fire?" Madison asked. "Oh, you mean to stop the hitting."

Jason patted Madison's arm. "You're learning the lingo, baby."

"Oh, I sure hope he does," Bella said, and inhaled a deep breath.

"He will," Jessica assured her, and hoped that she was right. There was no doubt in her mind that Bella and Logan were becoming more than mere roommates.

Madison reached over and put her hand over Bella's. "We're pulling for Logan."

"I'm so nervous for him," Bella admitted, and this drew a curious look from Nicolina.

Jessica smiled inwardly. Madison's matchmaking mojo was spot-on once again. She turned around and watched Logan throw a few warm-up pitches. The crowd watched with rapt attention, knowing that Logan Lannigan was a former minor-league player trying to make a comeback.

"I'm anxious to see what the kid can do," Owen said, and they all waited for the batter to step back into the box.

Jessica was so intent on watching that for a moment she forgot about her unsettled stomach. But when she leaned back in her seat, she was hit with another wave of nausea. She reached for her drink and hoped that she could make it through the rest of the game. She took a deep breath, praying it would make her feel better, but the smell of hot dogs and popcorn made her stomach reel. She closed her eyes and gripped the armrest and tried to focus on the game.

"Are you okay?" Olivia asked with a frown.

"Just nervous," Jessica replied.

"I understand. This is a big day for us all in more ways than one." Olivia patted Jessica's hand. "Everything is finally coming together, isn't it?"

Jessica nodded, and knew she was referring to much more than the baseball complex. When Logan wound up and threw his first pitch, they all turned their attention back to the baseball diamond. The fastball hit the catcher's glove with a hard *smack* for strike one, and the crowd cheered. When the next pitch was fouled off, Logan had the Rockets' batter at two strikes. The crowd grumbled when he stepped out of the box and took a practice swing. Logan picked up the rosin bag and shook it in his hand, and Jessica's heart pounded with anticipation.

Olivia leaned over and said, "I can't imagine what it must feel like to be in Logan's shoes right now."

"Me neither," Jessica agreed. "My heart feels as if it's going to beat right out of my chest."

The batter stepped back into the box, tapped the dirt, and then stood there, waiting for the next pitch. Logan leaned over, nodded to the catcher, and went into his windup. The batter took the next pitch that was low and outside and then fouled the next throw off deep into left field.

"Don't give him anything to hit," Jessica mumbled, and held her breath when the next pitch was again low and away.

"Full count with the bases loaded," Mitch said to Nicolina.

"I'd smoke him with a fastball," Jessica heard Owen say, but wasn't quite sure she agreed. The crowd seemed to be collectively holding its breath when Logan stared the batter down, nodded to the catcher, and then went into his windup. The batter swung . . . and missed the ninety-five-mile-per-hour fastball that sounded like a gunshot hitting the catcher's mitt.

The crowd went nuts but then quieted down. The bases were still loaded. Jessica looked over at the dugout and saw Ty and Noah with their heads bent together. She would have loved to have heard their conversation. The next batter stepped into the box and took the first pitch for ball one.

"Swing at the ball," Jason shouted, but the batter didn't and took the next pitch for another ball.

"He's got to come at him with a strike," Olivia said, and Jessica nodded.

Logan wound up and brought another smoking fastball, but the umpire called it a ball.

"That caught the outside corner!" Nicolina leaned forward and shouted. Jessica looked at her in surprise, but then she remembered that she and Bella were big baseball fans and went to many Chicago Cubs games.

"I thought so too," Mitch agreed, and gave Nicolina a grin. "Let's see what he comes back with."

"I'd challenge him with another fastball," Nicolina told him. "A fly ball would end the inning."

"And we don't want to walk a batter in," Mitch added.

Logan shook off the catcher and then nodded. He challenged the batter with another fastball down the middle this time. *Crack!* Jessica watched with wide eyes as the baseball went sailing into center field. The fielder backed up and up until he was at the warning track, but at the last second reached up and snagged the ball.

The crowd came to its feet and roared its approval. Olivia turned and gave Jessica a high five. "*Shew*, that was close!"

"It's just a long fly ball," Nicolina said. "No harm done."

"Now we need some hits!" Olivia said. "This nothing-to-nothing pitcher's duel has been exciting, but now it's time to score."

"Yes, we do!" Jessica nodded. Her stomach gave a little lurch, but she inhaled a deep breath.

The Rockets' pitcher was also showing some fatigue, but while the Cougars were able to get the first two batters on base, they ended up leaving them stranded.

"I guess Ty is going to leave Logan in," Jessica said to Olivia, and she was right. She turned around and said to Madison, "Wow. This is about to kill me."

Madison nodded down at her. "I am on the edge of my seat! But Logan is doing a fantastic job. Ty and Noah must have confidence in him."

"My fingers are crossed," Jessica showed them her hands and then turned back around in her seat.

When Logan stepped up onto the mound, Olivia said, "Okay, here we go!"

Logan struck out the first two batters, much to the approval of the crowd. The Rockets brought in a pinch hitter for the pitcher, but Logan didn't seem one bit rattled and gave him a curve ball that the batter missed by a mile. The next ball was fouled off, and then a grounder to Reed at shortstop ended the first half of the ninth inning.

Jessica kept her fingers crossed that the Cougars scored and ended the inning. Her stomach was still on the fritz, and she sure didn't want to endure extra innings.

"Well, we're at the top of the order and have a new pitcher," Jessica heard Aunt Myra comment.

"Yep," Owen said, "this should be interesting."

"I'd love a walk-off home run," Jason said.

"Oh, boy. More lingo," Madison said. "I need a *Baseball for Dummies* book," she said with a chuckle. "But I can tell you one thing: I never knew sports could be this exciting."

"Oh, my little nerd," Jason chided, and Jessica would have laughed if she hadn't been in so much discomfort. When the batter came up to the plate, the conversation ceased and all eyes were back to the baseball field.

The lead-off batter walked.

"We'll take it," Nicolina said.

"A walk is as good as a hit," Mitch agreed.

The next batter went down swinging, much to Jessica's dismay. She took a swallow of her drink and crunched on some ice. A long fly ball moved the runner into scoring position, but the Cougars were down to one last out.

"All we need is a single," Jason said. "Reed has some speed. He would score easily."

After two swings and two misses, Jessica feared extra innings, and she wasn't sure she could make it. The Sprite was no longer helping. She swallowed hard and barely refrained from putting her hands to her stomach. If it wasn't food poisoning, she wondered if she had picked up a bug of some sort.

And then it happened—a line drive straight up the middle scored Reed and the game was over! Fireworks went off and the crowd came to its feet to give the Cougars a standing ovation. High fives, chest bumps, and hugs were going on all over the stadium. Jessica turned to Olivia and wasn't surprised to see tears swimming in her friend's eyes.

"Wow, that was nerve-racking, but fun," Olivia said. "Noah and Ty are going to meet us for an aftergame celebration at Sully's. You're going, right?"

Jessica nodded. "I want to, but my stomach seems to be upset. I'm going to head home and take something. Hopefully it's just my body reacting to the excitement. I'll head over there as soon as I get this under control."

Olivia frowned. "Do you want me to come with you?"

"Thanks, but no. I should be fine in a little while." She turned to tell Madison and Aunt Myra. "Honey, I seem to have a bit of indigestion. I'm going to head home and rest up a bit before heading over to Sully's. If Ty gets there before me, let him know, okay? I don't want to call and interrupt anything going on in the clubhouse." When they both offered to come with her, she waved them off. "I'm sure I'll be fine in a little bit. Just save me a seat."

Madison gave her a concerned frown, but nodded. "Okay, but call if you need me."

"Will do."

Once she was home, Jessica took an antacid tablet and decided to lie down on the sofa, hoping to feel better. This was odd, since she usually had a stomach of iron and rarely felt sick. "I think it's just a twenty-four-hour bug," she mumbled, but suddenly her heart beat double time. "Ohmigod."

"Wait!" Jessica sat up straight. After thinking for a minute, she shook her head slowly. "I'm late . . ." She put her hand to her stomach, and her heart thumped hard. "We used protection." She thought for a moment but then closed her eyes. Oh . . . there was that *one* time. "Dear God," Jessica whispered. She might not have a twenty-four-hour bug after all . . . but rather a nine-month pregnancy!

She fell weakly back against the cushions. For a moment she was too stunned to even begin to process her feelings. And then hot shame mixed with cold, hard fear washed over her. Finally, a single tear leaked out of the corner of her eye, and she angrily swiped it from her cheek.

"This can't be happening again," she whispered, and then burst into tears.

# 24
## Why Wait?

WHEN TY AND NOAH WALKED INTO SULLY'S, THEY WERE met with a standing ovation and wild cheers. Players were also drifting in and getting a round of cheers. A beer was pressed into each of their hands as Ty and Noah made their way over to a big table near the bar. Olivia rushed forward and hugged Noah, and then gave Ty a big hug as well.

"That was an amazing game," Olivia gushed.

"Thanks," Ty said, and tipped his baseball cap to the rest of the party sitting at the table. He had showered and changed into jeans and a black Cougars-logo golf shirt, but had left his baseball cap on. "Where's Jessica?" he asked with a frown.

"Mom wasn't feeling well," Madison explained.

Ty felt a rush of concern. "What's wrong with her?"

"Upset stomach," Madison replied. "She wanted to go home and rest for a while but I hope she'll be here soon."

"I should go and check on her," Ty said, but Madison shook her head.

"Mom wouldn't want you to leave the celebration."

"I don't care," he said. "I want to make sure she's okay." The thought of Jessica being sick had Ty's own stomach in sudden turmoil.

"Ty, you know Mom." Madison shook her head firmly. "That would upset her even more. I'll go outside and call to see how she's doing. You go ahead and enjoy the celebration."

Ty reluctantly nodded. "Okay, but I want to know what's going on with her. Let me know."

Madison patted his arm. "I will. Mom is one of those people who rarely gets sick, so I'm sure it was either something she ate or the excitement of the game, or perhaps a little of both."

Ty nodded again, but his gut was telling him that something just wasn't right. It wasn't like Jessica not to contact him, but then again, perhaps she was resting or even asleep. He decided to let Madison call and then go from there. He took a long swallow of beer and went about socializing.

Ty talked baseball and put on a good show of laughing, but in the back of his mind he was worried about Jessica. He kept looking at the doorway, hoping she'd come in, but after a good thirty minutes, Madison still hadn't returned and he was about ready to pull his hair out. When he noticed that Aunt Myra was gone as well, he knew that something had to be really wrong.

He could just feel it.

After excusing himself from the party, he went outside and dialed Madison's number. "Come on, Madison . . . answer." When she didn't pick up, he sent her a text message and then waited. Finally, just when he was ready to head over to Jessica's apartment, his phone beeped. With a hammering heart he opened up the text message. It read: *Mom is still having some stomach troubles, but she said for you to have a good time and not to worry.*

"Right . . . not to worry." Ty shook his head and read the message three times, looking for some hidden message. Something didn't feel right about the whole situation. He looked over at his car and then back at Sully's, trying to decide just what to do. After a couple of minutes, Owen came outside. "Hey, Owen. Have you heard from Myra? Is Jessica really okay? I'm worried."

"Myra just called and told me she was going to stay with Jessica for a while, so I'm going to head on home."

"Do you have a bead on what's wrong? I'm really concerned and I don't know what to do."

Owen clamped a hand onto Ty's shoulder. "Jessica is in good hands, so you don't need to worry on that score."

Ty took off his cap and scratched his head. "Yeah, but I want to be with her."

"Son, believe me, I understand."

"So what should I do?"

"It's not my call, but I know how strong-headed those three are, so my advice is to do as they're askin'."

Ty inhaled a deep breath and blew it out. "Okay, but do me a favor. If you hear anything, would you give me a call?"

Owen squeezed Ty's shoulder. "Sure I will. Look, I do know this—if it was something serious, Myra would have let me know." He smiled. "I know you're worried about your woman. But this is your night and I know she wants you to enjoy it. So get back in there and whoop it up a bit. Maybe Jessica will show up here in a little while anyway."

"I hope you're right."

"Me too," he said. "I'm plumb tuckered out. But that sure was a helluva game. I'm looking forward to the rest of the season."

"Thanks, Owen." Ty watched him walk over to his truck, but was reluctant to go back inside. He didn't know how much longer he could wait before calling Jessica's number and hearing her voice for reassurance. After another moment of hesitation, Ty decided to go back to the party. He was greeted once again with high fives and slaps on the back, but the beer suddenly didn't taste so great and he no longer had an appetite when just a little while ago he had felt famished. Celebrating without Jessica by his side just didn't feel the way it should, and it only reiterated what he already knew: He loved her deeply.

He wanted to marry her.

The thought slammed into his brain and made his hands shake. The thought had randomly crossed his mind in a pleasant *what if* kind of way before, and he had paused more than once to look at engagement rings, but he now knew without a doubt that he wanted Jessica Robinson to be his wife. A win didn't feel so great without her with him. He was forty years old and had waited a lifetime for this to happen. . . . Didn't ever really think it would. But, damn, he didn't like being on the outside, waiting to hear if she felt okay. He didn't want Madison or Aunt Myra taking care of her. Ty wanted to be the man in her life in every sense of the word. He smiled. Tomorrow he was going to buy an engagement ring. He loved Jessica Robinson and wanted her by his side not as his girlfriend, but as his wife.

Why wait?

"Madison, go on back to Sully's," Jessica pleaded. "I'll be fine in a little while."

Madison shook her head firmly. "Do you think I believe that for one minute, Mom? My God, you've been crying!"

"It's only hormones. I've been crying at Hallmark commercials lately." *Perhaps after years of holding back, the dam has finally broken,* she thought wryly.

"Bull," Madison protested, and sat down in the easy chair across from the sofa.

"Aunt Myra, please explain aging to Madison," Jessica said, and sighed.

Aunt Myra looked across the room from her perch on the armrest of the sofa. "Madison, she's right. Hormones can play havoc with your emotions."

"See?" Jessica raised her palms upward. "You should go back to the party with Jason. I'm sure Bella and Nicolina want you there too. Owen is heading home so Aunt Myra can stay with me for a while."

"Mom, Ty is really worried. He wants to come over."

"No!" Jessica sat up straighter and tried to calm her pounding heart. "I don't want him to miss anything. I'll be fine." She made shooing motions with her fingers. "Go."

Madison looked as if she wanted to protest, but surprised Jessica by standing up. "Okay, but if you want me to come back later, I will."

"Thank you, sweetie." She forced a smile. "Tell Ty I'll call him . . . later."

Madison gave her a curious look. "Why don't you call him now?"

Jessica lifted one shoulder. "I don't feel up to it just this minute," she replied, and tried to keep her voice steady. "Just let him know that I'm fine. . . . I think everything has caught up with me and my forty-year-old body is responding."

"Okay," Madison said, but looked at Aunt Myra. "Call me, okay?"

Aunt Myra nodded. "I will," she promised, and walked Madison to the front door. As soon as it was closed, she turned to Jessica. "So . . . are you pregnant?"

Jessica felt emotion well up in her throat.

"How did you guess?"

"It wasn't all that difficult. I'm surprised that Madison didn't suspect, but I suppose young kids don't think old people actually have sex, much less procreate."

Jessica tried to laugh, but her sense of humor failed her.

"Oh, Aunt Myra, I felt terrible the entire game and didn't really think it was anything more than indigestion. But I suddenly realized that I'm . . . *late*."

Aunt Myra came over and sat down next to Jessica. "Oh, sweetie . . . don't fret. Something tells me this is meant to be." She drew her into her arms and hugged her hard.

"Aunt Myra . . ." Jessica started crying. "How in the

world could I allow this to happen? I'm no longer a young girl!" She pulled back and looked at her aunt. "This . . . this is terrible."

"Is it?"

"Yes! I'm so embarrassed. Ashamed! And how in the world can I tell Ty?" She held her head in her hands. All of the emotions from years ago came flooding back in giant waves. "Aunt Myra . . . my *God*!"

Aunt Myra tilted Jessica's chin up. "You listen here, missy! You've *never* had anything to feel ashamed about! While teenage pregnancy isn't anything we want to see happen, you handled yourself with flying colors. You should feel proud of yourself and your life, not ashamed," she said hotly.

"Oh, but I don't want Madison to know. . . . I don't want anyone to know!"

"Maybe you're not, Jessica."

"Oh, Aunt Myra, I feel sick and I'm late." She sniffed hard and shook her head. "What else could it be?"

"Well . . ." Aunt Myra shrugged. "You *are* forty. Your body will start to really give you fits."

Jessica sighed. "Well, I will know soon enough." She tried to smile, but failed. "Please don't tell anyone about this, especially not Madison. I know that she suspects that something isn't as it seems, but she also sensed that I wanted to be alone."

"You know I won't breathe a word of this, not even to Owen. Honey, do you want me to stay here tonight?"

"No, that would just make everyone suspicious. Go home to Owen. I'll be fine. But I would really appreciate if you would run Wine and Diner tomorrow. I need to take a pregnancy test to be sure."

"Sweetie, I don't want to leave you."

"I will be fine. Truly."

Aunt Myra gave her a measuring look, but then patted Jessica's leg and stood up. "All right. But I am a phone call and a short drive away. Don't you dare hesitate to call."

"Thanks, Aunt Myra. I don't know what I'd do without you. You have been such a blessing in my life."

"I will always be here for you," Aunt Myra said in a firm voice that shook with emotion. "And I do know that Ty McKenna loves you. Keep that in mind, Jessica. If you are with child, that man will do right by you."

Jessica nodded and waved. "I will keep that in mind," she promised, but as soon as Aunt Myra closed the door, she leaned back against the cushions and felt emotion well up in her throat once again. She thought of all of the people who had deserted her in her time of need when she'd discovered she was pregnant with Madison, and she shivered with apprehension. And the last thing she wanted was for Ty to do the *right thing*. Pregnancy wasn't a reason for marriage.

Love was.

*And Ty loves you* went through her head, but she put a hand over her tummy and shut her eyes. "Yeah, everybody loves me until I mess up."

But then Jessica suddenly thought of her mother making the decision not to follow her to Cricket Creek or demand that she come home. "Oh, my . . ." Her hand remained protectively over her stomach, and even if she wasn't sure if she was pregnant, she knew that giving up her child would be a sacrifice she could never make. And her mother had done it . . . for her. All at once, she believed this with absolute clarity: Her mother had given Jessica the ticket to freedom and happiness and had paid the ultimate price. She folded her arms across her chest and ached for her mother's gentle touch, and prayed that someday, somehow, she would find a way to see her mother again. "Oh, Mom!" The thought made her so sad but lifted the weight of anger from her shoulders.

Jessica sighed. Tomorrow couldn't come soon enough.

# 25

## Sweet Dreams

"GOOD MORNING!" BELLA POURED A STEAMING MUG OF coffee for her mother and then one for herself.

"Good morning, Bella. I hope you slept well on the sofa. I still feel bad about taking your bed. You could have slept with me, you know."

"Mom, I don't mind the sofa. I'm a restless sleeper and didn't want to keep you up." Logan had partied pretty late and was either still asleep or was giving Bella some time to visit with her mother. She was coming to find out that he was much more considerate than she ever dreamed. "Well, you and Mitch Monroe sure were chummy last night." She sat down at the kitchen table and smiled over at her mother.

"He's an interesting man," Nicolina admitted.

"He seemed very into you."

"We were talking business, Bella."

"Right . . ." Bella poured creamer into her coffee and stirred her spoon in slow circles. "Well, he's also a handsome man."

"I suppose," Nicolina said with a casual shrug, but the color in her cheeks told Bella that she was attracted to him.

"So are you going to see Mitch again?"

"He's going to show me the storefronts under construction down by the stadium."

"So, is he an investor in the riverfront project?"

Nicolina pressed her lips together, but then leaned forward and whispered, "Yes, but don't say anything. He wants to remain a silent partner in this venture."

"Mom, he could be quite an asset to you if you decide to open up the jewelry shop. Maybe an investor as well?"

Nicolina stared down at her coffee. "He's expressed interest. I gave him my Web site so he could see more of my product."

"Mom!" Bella felt a tingle of excitement. "This could be the break you've been waiting for."

Nicolina tilted her head sideways. "I trust his expert opinion—that's for sure. If Mitch says this is a good market, I believe him."

"You make a cute couple." She waggled her eyebrows.

"Bella! My relationship with Mitch Monroe is strictly business!" she sputtered.

"Whoa, there. I'm just teasing," Bella said, but in reality she wasn't. They really would make a striking couple.

"Besides, he's only here for a few days and then is going back to Chicago."

"And so are you. At least for the time being. So . . . ?"

"We might meet for cocktails and—"

"I know—discuss *business*," Bella interjected, and rolled her eyes.

Nicolina took a sip of her coffee. "Speaking of cute couples, I suppose Mr. Game Saver is sleeping in after last night?"

"We're not a couple," Bella insisted, but felt heat in her own face this time.

"Right . . ." Nicolina mocked, but then smiled warmly at her. "Arabella, I see the way you two look at each other. And you were a nervous wreck when he came in to pitch. You don't have to keep your feelings a secret from me. I don't know him well, but I like what I've seen so far. I just don't want you rebounding from David."

"I'm not," Bella said, and realized that it was true. She felt more strongly about Logan in this short period of time than she had ever felt about David.

"Ah, so then there is something between you two?"

Bella caught her bottom lip between her teeth.

"I knew it," Nicolina said, and patted Bella's hand. "I wish you happiness, whether I come to live here or not. You know that, right?"

Bella blinked hard. "I never meant to stay here, Mom. It just somehow feels right. I'm really trying to take it slow with Logan. All I know for sure is that I am happier than I've been in a long time."

"Well, then, you should stay here," she answered firmly, but her smile trembled a bit.

"But . . . we've always been a team."

"You're an adult now, Bella. Whether it is with Logan or someone else, if you find true love—*happiness*—grab it and hold on tight. It doesn't come along often," she said with a smile, but her voice was wistful.

"And you should too."

Nicolina shrugged and glanced away.

"Mom! You're right: I am an adult now. Like Jessica, you've dedicated your life to raising a daughter. Now it's your turn to get out there and find a life other than being my mother. You are so talented! Go for it and don't look back." She reached over and grabbed her mother's delicate hand. "It's your time now."

"I'm fifty-two years old, Arabella. The bloom is off the rose."

"Shut up!" Bella narrowed her eyes at her mother. "First of all, you're gorgeous. And second, you can fall in love at any age. Just look at Myra and Owen!" She leaned back in her chair and arched one eyebrow. "And I noticed how Mitch Monroe looked at you!"

"He is out of my league."

"I can't believe you just said that!" Bella's bare feet hit the floor with a *smack*. She thought her mother was one of the most confident women she knew, and this admission stunned Bella. "Why in the world would you say that, Mom?"

"Bella, he's a big-business tycoon. I'm from a poor Italian family and have only a high school education. I'm sure that he is used to a much more educated, sophisticated woman." She wiggled her fingers in the air.

"I've always thought of you as sophisticated. Mom, you are beautiful, have style, and are supremely talented. I'm stunned that you would even say such a thing, much less believe it!"

Nicolina lifted one slim shoulder. "I put on a good show."

"Oh, come on, Mom . . . really?"

"Bella, I was a struggling single mom for years."

"You're a talented jewelry designer!"

"*Pfft*. I sell my jewelry at craft shows!"

"Mom, you've created beautiful designs for how many brides and wedding parties?"

"For friends," she argued.

Bella leaned forward. "It's called referrals. Networking. Sure, it comes from friends and family at first, but then grows. Why are you selling yourself short? We've talked about opening a shop for years. You have a kick-ass Web site. Why are you hedging *now*?"

"Because before it was only talk . . . pipe dreams."

"And now you're facing possible failure."

She nodded.

"So what if you do fail?" Bella asked softly. "Isn't that better than never trying?"

"Bella, if I fail, I will have eaten up the savings that I've worked so hard all of these years to build up."

"Money?" Bella gave her mother a level look. "That's not really the reason, is it?"

"No." Nicolina cupped her hands around the mug as if warming up cold hands. She finally shook her head slowly. "Oh, Bella, if I fail, the dream is gone. And then what do I have?"

Bella remembered her mother's excitement when a new shipment of beads would arrive, or the joy of a finished necklace that turned out beautiful. She would often design late into the night and then have to go to work early the next day. Suddenly, it all made sense. "Oh, Mom, your dream got you through some tough times. Didn't it?"

"I clung to it like a lifeline." She reached over and took one of Bella's hands. "I always hated the sacrifice you had to go through. "We ate lots of tomato soup and grilled-cheese sandwiches so that I could buy my materials. And I could never afford new clothes for you."

"Mom, I never thought of our simple dinners as a sacrifice. I loved sorting through the colorful beads and watching you work. And my clothes?" She laughed. "You would sew trinkets to my jeans and make those amazing beaded headbands! All of my friends loved those headbands. Oh, Mom, my clothes were the coolest in school and nobody else had them."

Nicolina smiled softly. "I had forgotten about those headbands."

Bella tapped her fingers on the table. "You should think of having a children's section in the store! Even little girls are fashion conscious these days. Those headbands would fly off the shelves. And beaded bracelets? Teenagers are wearing them halfway up their arms." She bounced in her chair. "And Jessica is going to add a retail section at Wine and Diner for selling Kentucky-made items. You could start marketing your jewelry there to give yourself some exposure!"

Nicolina tipped her head to the side and her smile widened. "You're getting me excited about this."

"Mom, allow the excitement to melt away the fear factor. Let me tell you something. This little town has some backbone. Instead of becoming another casualty of this economy, the people here have dug in their heels and are fighting back."

Nicolina closed her eyes and inhaled deeply. "Bella, my heart is beating a million miles a minute."

"We're still a team, you know." Bella's voice was gruff with emotion. "I don't have any money to contribute, but I'm still a mean bead sorter."

When Nicolina opened her eyes, they were swimming with unshed tears. "I know I drive you crazy sometimes, but I love you, Arabella. More than anything in this world."

"And I love you. No matter what happens in our lives, that will never change." She had to clear her throat. "Now, can I fix you some breakfast?"

"I'm having brunch with Mitch at Wine and Diner, so I'll just have another cup of coffee." She handed Bella her mug. "Speaking of Wine and Diner, have you heard how Jessica is feeling?"

"No." Bella shook her head as she stood up. "But I plan on calling Madison in a little while."

"I sure hope she's okay," Nicolina said. "She must have felt rotten not to have come over to Sully's last night. Maybe she'll be at the diner later."

"I hope so," Bella agreed. "I'm off today, so I plan on being lazy."

"When I get back, I'll be lazy with you."

"Right . . ." Bella handed her the mug. "You don't know how. But I'll be glad to teach you."

"Well, I think I'll start my lazy day by taking a long, hot bath."

"Excellent! Are you going to the game with me tonight?"

"Yes," she said, and then flushed a little.

"Let me guess. You're heading over there with Mitch?"

"Well, we will be checking out the shops available for

lease, and it simply makes sense to head there together. He, of course, is going to the game too so it's only natural—"

"Mom!" Bella laughed as she cut her off. "You don't have to explain yourself. It's gorgeous out. Enjoy your day and your man."

"He's not *my* man."

"He is for today."

Nicolina smiled. "You know, you're right."

"And one more thing," Bella said, causing her mother to pause at the doorway. "Nobody, and I do mean nobody, is out of Nicolina Diamante's league. You got that, Mama?"

"Got it." Her chin came up and she saluted, but her smile faltered just enough to let Bella know that this was still an issue with her mother.

"Good!" Bella shot her a smile, but it faded as soon as her mother left the room. She had always thought of her sassy mother as one of the strongest, most confident women she knew, and she had been floored by her mother's admission. But after thinking about it, Bella could relate. The feisty attitude she put out there wasn't always what she was feeling beneath the surface, and when David had cheated right under her nose, Bella's self-worth had been shaken to the core. "Well, enough of that nonsense," she muttered as she walked into the living room to tidy up the covers on the couch. It was about time to reclaim her self-confidence!

A little while later, Nicolina walked into the kitchen where Bella was stirring up ingredients for pancakes. "Making silver dollars?" Nicolina asked, bringing a smile to Bella's face. Silver-dollar pancakes had been her most-requested breakfast as a child.

"Yes, with whipped butter and dusted with powdered sugar."

"Sounds delicious." Nicolina spun in a circle. "How do I look?" she asked casually, but looked closely at Bella.

"Mom, you'd look good in a burlap sack, but your tan jeans and tweed jacket are classy. Ralph Lauren?"

"Yes, on sale at an outlet."

"And the chunky turquoise necklace adds a splash of color and a Western flair." She gave her mother a thumbs-up. "When are you leaving for your date—I mean, business venture?"

Nicolina rolled her eyes. "I'm meeting Mitch in the lobby downstairs as soon as he texts me that he's here," she answered, and as if on cue, her cell phone beeped. She glanced down at her phone. "He's here." She put one hand to her chest and then looked up. "I'll see you at the game!"

"Mom, don't be nervous. You look amazing!"

Nicolina blew Bella a kiss and hurried out the door.

"Well . . ." With a smile, Bella turned back to the pancake batter and put it in the refrigerator before creeping down the hallway to see if Logan was awake. Just as she reached the door, it swung open.

*"Eeek!"* Bella bumped into him with a surprised squeak. When her mouth brushed up against his warm chest, she stumbled backward and had to brace her hand against the wall for support. "You scared the daylights out of me!"

"I do live here, you know."

Oh . . . did she ever. "You already know that I get startled easily."

Logan folded his arms across his bare chest and leaned one shoulder against the doorframe. He looked sleep rumpled and delicious in low-slung black sweatpants. "Well, you were creeping up on me. Shouldn't I be the one startled?"

"I wasn't creeping up on you." She pushed away from the wall.

"Sneaking in to kiss me awake?"

"You wish!" she sputtered, but the make-out session in the kitchen hung in the air between them.

"Yeah, I do." He gave her a lazy grin, but then widened his eyes and mouthed *Is your mother here?*

Bella gave him a shake of her head. She wanted to say

more, but the realization suddenly hit her that they were alone. All day . . .

"Oh, then you were coming into my bedroom to have your wicked way with me." His lazy smile widened, and he reached up to scratch the dark gold stubble on his chin. "I get it now."

"Ha! In your dreams."

"As a matter of fact, you were in my dreams."

"You're making that up."

"No, Bella, I'm not." His teasing grin faded and he pushed away from the doorframe. He headed over to her and tucked a finger beneath her chin, tilting her face up. "All I can think about is having you in my damned arms, and last night I dreamed that you were in my bed with me." He sighed. "But I woke up and my arms were empty."

"Well, maybe we should do something about that," she suggested.

"You don't have to ask twice." When he scooped her up into his arms she yelped, causing Logan to laugh. "I really need to have you make noises other than squeaking."

Bella laughed with him, but when he gently placed her in the middle of his bed, she looked up at him with serious eyes. Before, they had been caught up in the moment. This was different.

Logan eased onto the bed beside her and traced a fingertip over her bottom lip. "Hey, if you don't want this . . ."

Bella reached up and cupped his cheek with the palm of her hand. "I'm just afraid of you leaving, Logan. And you know it's going to happen. Now my mother is seriously thinking of moving here and opening a jewelry store. It's been her dream—no, *our* dream—for years."

"Bella, I don't expect you to leave here. Granted, being the girlfriend of a professional athlete isn't easy, but if you truly care for someone, you can give them the freedom to pursue their dream and eventually have a great life together."

Bella's brain tripped over the word *girlfriend*, but she managed to nod. "I agree," she replied softly, and rubbed the pad of her thumb over his cheekbone.

"And it makes coming home so much better." He smiled and then dipped his head and captured her mouth with a sweet kiss. "God, it feels so good having you in my arms. Baby, you have no idea how much I've wanted this."

The sincerity in his eyes had Bella melting against the plump pillows. "Me too," she said, and wrapped her arms around his neck. He kissed her again, but this time with white-hot passion that took her breath away. She moved her hands over his wide shoulders and down to his rock-hard biceps. She arched her back in an effort to get closer.

"These clothes have to go," Logan said, and quickly shed his sweatpants.

Bella swallowed hard when she came up to her elbows and took in the beauty of his naked body. He had the physique of an athlete . . . but whip-cord strength rather than bulk. Watching the ripple of muscle beneath golden, tanned skin when he moved made a hot shiver slide down her spine. "Logan, you are one gorgeous man," she breathed, and then came up to her knees.

"And you are a beautiful, sexy woman, Bella," Logan said, and tugged her shirt over her head in one smooth move. Her breasts were bare, and when he cupped them in his big, strong hands, she sucked in a quick breath. "But as banging as your body is . . . it's *you* that I'm falling for." He looked into her eyes. "And as much as I want to make it back to the big leagues, having you in my life makes me want it even more. But oddly enough, on the other hand, it makes it okay if I fail." He shook his head. "Does that make any sense?"

"Yes." Bella nodded firmly. "It does."

"And I've never felt this strongly about a woman before," he admitted with such emotion that Bella felt tears spring to her eyes. "But enough of that sappy stuff," he said in true Logan form. "Time for some action!" he declared with a grin, then tugged her flannel lounging pants down to her knees. "Dear God," he said when he saw her little pink thong. "That's a picture that's going to haunt me when I'm on the road."

Bella laughed and pulled her pants the rest of the way off and kicked them to the floor before easing back down onto the pillows. When he joined her on the bed, his warm skin slid against hers, making her moan. She shoved her fingers into his shaggy hair that she loved so much and kissed him like there was no tomorrow.

But there was tomorrow, and then the next day and the next . . .

She suddenly knew what it felt like to have somebody in her life who wanted a future together, and it felt amazing. She kissed him deeply, hotly, and with more love than she knew ever existed.

"Do we need protection?" he whispered in her ear.

"No," she answered, and wrapped her legs around his waist. He entered her with one sure stroke, making her cry out with the sheer joy of having him inside her body. He rocked into her with an easy rhythm and murmured words of love in her ear.

"Oh!" Bella's heart thumped harder and her body tingled with sweet heat as her pleasure climbed . . . intensified. She wrapped her arms and legs around him tightly and arched her back, urging him to go faster, deeper, until she exploded with pure pleasure, taking him right along with her.

"Wow," he said, and pressed his forehead to hers. "That was so much better than I even dreamed."

Bella curled her body around his and put her head on his shoulder. While tracing small circles on his chest, she said, "I never would have thought that I'd end up living in Cricket Creek, Kentucky." She chuckled softly and added, "My life has gone from sucky to kickin' in nothing flat. Thank you, Logan Lannigan."

Logan pushed up to one elbow and looked down at her. After a moment, he tenderly tucked a lock of her hair behind her ear and said, "Life can sure be crazy. I saw that ad for tryouts for the Cricket Creek Cougars by chance and almost didn't come. But something compelled me to do it, and I'm sure glad that I did."

Bella nodded. "Madison said that we should always go with our gut. Trust in ourselves."

"I believe it." He smiled again. "And guess what."

"What?"

"Our adventure has just begun."

# 26

## *The Best Day Ever*

TY SNAPPED THE RING BOX SHUT JUST AS NOAH ENTERED his office, and then quickly covered it with his hand. "What's up, Noah?" he asked, wondering if he could discreetly slide the box from the desk without Noah noticing.

"What was that sound?" Noah asked with a frown.

"What sound?" Ty replied, and slowly started to slide his hand toward the edge of the desk.

"That loud snap," Noah persisted as he walked into the room.

"Must have been my World Series ring hitting the wood."

Noah tilted his head. "Funny, you're not wearing your ring. . . . *Ring*?" he suddenly said. He took his cap off and slapped his leg with it. "What's under your hand?"

"Nothin'."

"Oh, really? Show me."

"No." Ty growled, but then uncovered the midnight blue velvet box.

Noah's eyebrows shot up. "Is that what I think it is?"

"If you think it's an engagement ring for Jessica, then yes."

"Holy shit."

"Yeah." Ty looked at up Noah. "Holy shit."

Noah sat down on the edge of the big desk. "So are you going to pop the question?"

"Well . . ." — Ty inhaled a deep breath while toying with the box — "it's kinda hard to do when Jessica won't see me."

"Ty, she's been sick all week. She hasn't even been to any games or work."

"I'm not really buying that bullshit."

"Olivia said that Jessica has strep throat and doesn't want to make anybody ill."

Ty shrugged. "Right."

"It makes sense. She works with food and doesn't want to get anybody on the team sick, including you. We have an important three-game series coming up."

"My gut is telling me otherwise."

"Ty, why the hell else would she stay in her apartment for days? Jason said she's even postponed the opening of the patio until she feels better."

Ty chewed on the inside of his cheek. "Something just isn't right."

"Have you talked to Madison about it?"

"She said the same thing: that Jessica is sick."

"What about Myra? Has she indicated otherwise?"

Ty pointed a finger at Noah. "That was another red flag. Myra was closemouthed and evasive about the whole thing, and she's usually forthcoming."

Noah scratched his head. "I'm sorry. Maybe Olivia could find something out?"

"I don't know," Ty answered, and scrubbed a hand down his face. "Damn. If she doesn't want to see me, then screw it."

"Yeah, right. You have a ring sitting there in front of you."

Ty looked down at the box and swallowed hard. "I just don't fucking get it. Everything was going great. If I did something wrong, then she should tell me, damn it."

"Can I see the ring?" Noah asked in a calm tone.

Ty looked up in surprise. "I guess." He slid the box forward.

"Wow . . ." Noah said when he looked down at the solitaire. The light caught the diamond, making it sparkle. "It's exquisite."

"Yeah." He sighed and then said, "Hey, why haven't you popped the question to Olivia?"

"Oh, we've talked about getting married," Noah admitted. "But she's shied away from the subject. I'm waiting for the right time."

"But you know you want to spend the rest of your life with her, right?"

"No doubt." Noah nodded without hesitation. "But her mother left Owen early in her childhood. I think her painful past still haunts her, so I'm willing to wait for the right time." Noah frowned at Ty. "Um, speaking of *haunt*, you look like you've just seen a ghost. Care to explain?"

"Painful past." Ty's heart thumped. It all made perfect sense. "Holy shit." Could Jessica be pregnant? He waited for dread or fear to wash over him, but all he felt was joy.

"Okay, spill, Ty," Noah prodded, but Jason walked through the open door, grabbing their attention.

"What's up, Jason?" Ty asked, glad to have the interruption. His mind was racing and his hands shook.

"I was about to head out and wondered if there was anything you needed me for before I go," he said, and tucked a sketch pad beneath his arm.

"I think we're good to go," Ty answered, and Noah nodded.

"Cool. Then I'm heading over to Wine and Diner to work on the gazebo."

"Gazebo?" Ty asked.

"Yeah, Madison wants an outdoor wedding, so Jessica is adding a gazebo to the patio. It's a great idea, since she'll be able to rent the space out for weddings after ours."

"Oh yeah. I had forgotten that. How close are you to finishing?"

"Close. Just trim work and a few touches here and there. Why?"

Ty nodded slowly. "Have a seat, Jason. I have something I want you to do for me. And get Madison to help, okay?"

Noah smacked his leg. "Oh, boy. I'm getting the picture. Damn, you're good, Ty."

He grinned. "I know it. Now, if she'll only say yes."

"What's going on?" Jason asked as he scooted a chair up to the desk, and then his gaze took in the ring. "Holy shit."

Noah laughed. "That's been the phrase of the day."

"Keep this on the down low, both of you, and tell Madison not to breathe a word to her mother. We've got some work to do in a short period of time."

Jason nodded. "We will. Now tell me what you want me to do."

Jessica knew that sooner or later she was going to have to venture out of her apartment. Her excuse that she had strep throat was starting to wear thin. Plus, she hated putting the burden of running the diner on Aunt Myra and Madison. Since the article in *Southern Living* magazine, business had been brisk, but the opening of the stadium had kept Wine and Diner packed. She also hated the sad tone of Ty's messages, which were starting to become scarce. Jessica felt tears spring to her eyes. How was she going to tell him that she was pregnant?

Aunt Myra had already guessed, and Jessica was surprised that Madison hadn't picked up on it as well. But, then again, she was forty! "Who in their right mind would think I'm pregnant?" she whispered, and waited once again for the hot shame to send her to the bathroom to toss her cookies.

But this time it didn't happen.

Instead, she put her hand to her still-flat stomach and

felt a sense of peace. This was a life, a child she had created out of love, and anyone who said anything about it could be damned. And if Ty McKenna didn't want this child, then he wasn't the man she thought he was. Plus, she was in a much better position this time around, even though she hadn't done too shabby raising her lovely daughter, Madison. She smiled softly and rubbed her hand in small circles. Funny that she had ended up back in Cricket Creek and was having another child. "Oh, boy . . . or girl," she muttered with dark humor. It was time to come out of hiding and face the music.

A moment later, her phone rang. Jessica looked down and saw that it was Madison and picked up. "Hi, sweetie."

"Oh, good. You sound better."

"I am. I've been popping vitamins and drinking milk."

"Really? Good for you. Wait. You hate milk."

"I've been craving it lately," she admitted, and wondered just how much Madison had already guessed. "But anyway, I'm much better."

"Good, because Jason is having a bit of trouble with the gazebo and wants your opinion."

Jessica frowned. "It's almost dark outside. What's he doing working this late?"

"Oh, Mom, you know how he is. Once he starts a project, he wants it done but done right. So can you come down and take a look?"

"Okay," Jessica replied. "Tell him I'll be down in a few minutes."

"Awesome."

"Okay, bye, sweetie."

Jessica went into her bedroom and slipped out of the hoodie and sweatpants she had been living in for the past several days and tugged on a pair of her favorite jeans and a navy blue blouse. She headed into the bathroom and pulled her hair up into her usual ponytail, and added some makeup before heading down the back stairs to the restaurant. All was quiet and the kitchen was buttoned up for the night.

Jessica inhaled the lingering aroma of food and was thankful that her stomach didn't do flip-flops in protest. A moment later, she walked out the back door. . . .

"Oh, my goodness!" Jessica put her hand to her chest when the patio suddenly came to life with the illumination of hundreds of twinkling lights. She walked toward the gorgeous white gazebo, but instead of Jason standing there, Ty was sitting on the bench seat.

"Hi, there," he greeted her softly.

Jessica stood there dumbfounded, and almost put her hand to her tummy.

He patted the bench next to him. "Come here and have a seat. I've missed you."

Jessica walked over on legs that trembled and gratefully sat down.

"Feeling better?" he asked.

She nodded mutely.

"Good. I was worried."

"I'm sorry, Ty." Her heart hammered, and she lowered her gaze. She wanted to tell him and yet the words wouldn't come out of her mouth.

A moment later, Ty McKenna knelt down on one knee, and her heart just about beat out of her chest. "Jessica," he began, but she put a hand on his arm.

"Ty . . . no. There's something I have to tell you." Her words came out choked with emotion.

"That you're having my baby?"

Her eyes widened. "Did Aunt Myra tell you? Is that what this is all about?" She waved her hand in an arc.

"Ohmigod, so it's true? Jessica, are you pregnant?"

"Yes." When she nodded and put her palm over her tummy, she saw joy light up Ty's face.

"No, that isn't what this is all about. Listen. First of all, I bought this ring before I even suspected that you were pregnant. So this has nothing to do with you carrying my child. I love you, Jessica. And I want you to be my wife. The fact that you are carrying my baby is only icing on the cake."

"So . . . you're happy about it?" Her heart thudded and she peered at him closely. The joy remained shining in his eyes.

"Ecstatic! I couldn't be any happier."

"But we're . . . *old*!"

Ty chuckled. "We're ready. Besides, we have lots of help. This kid is going to be spoiled to death!"

Jessica laughed, but tears slid down her cheeks.

"Tears of joy?"

"Yes . . . oh yes!"

"Wait. Did you just say yes?"

Jessica nodded.

"I didn't even get to properly pop the question. Pretend you didn't say yes yet."

"Okay."

Ty cleared his throat. "Jessica Robinson, will you marry me?"

"Yes!" She shouted, and then raised a fist in the air before leaning down and giving him a long kiss. "I will marry you, Tyler McKenna."

"Oh, I almost forgot." He reached in his pocket and pulled out the ring box. His fingers trembled as he pulled it open.

Jessica sucked in a breath. "It's absolutely beautiful."

"You like it?" When she nodded, he took it from the box and slipped it on her finger. "Does it fit?"

"A perfect fit."

"Good. I guessed at the size."

"I wasn't talking about the ring." She put her hands to his cheeks and then leaned down and kissed him. "I am thrilled that you asked me to be your wife and to be having your baby, Ty."

He came up from his knee and sat down next to her. "I'm guessing you struggled at first."

She felt tears well up in her throat. "Yes."

"Jessica, this is your chance to go through the joy of it all. You are a great person and a wonderful mother. And you deserve happiness. I love you and I want to say those words to you in this gazebo when we're married."

"And I'm guessing Jason and Owen got this ready for your proposal?"

Ty nodded. "They worked their tails off."

"So who else knows about this?"

"Um . . . let's just say that I'm glad you said yes."

"Oh, boy."

"There might be a little celebration party over at Sully's."

"Might be?"

"Well, there is now that you said yes." He grinned, but then looked at her with serious eyes. "We don't have to go if you're not ready to tell the world."

"I'm ready."

"Good. Because Madison has been waiting for the go-ahead, she-said-yes text message. Can I send it?"

"Hit the SEND button," she answered with a laugh. "Do you want to walk?"

"Walk? You're pregnant. I'm going to carry you."

"You're kidding, right?"

"A little. But be ready to be pampered."

"Oh . . . Ty." She put her hand over her mouth.

"Did I say something wrong?"

Jessica shook her head. "You know, I was feeling all melancholy a few weeks ago when I was looking at brides' magazines on the night of my birthday party. It's every little girl's dream to have a flowing white dress with all the trimmings, and I knew my time for that was ticking away terribly fast."

"I'll give you any wedding that your heart desires."

Jessica smiled and slipped her hand in his. "I don't need the fairy-tale wedding."

"How about a fairy-tale life?"

"Now, that's an offer I can't refuse," she said. "And you know what?"

"What?"

She gazed up into his handsome face. "It was worth the wait."

"I couldn't agree more." Ty nodded, and they headed hand in hand over to Sully's. When they walked inside, they were met with a huge cheer. There was another gorgeous cake on the table where her birthday cake had been, but this one read: CONGRATULATIONS, TY AND JESSICA! And Jessica had to laugh when she looked up and saw that the original birthday banner now read LORDY, LORDY, JESSICA IS FORTY AND *GETTING MARRIED*!

Madison shrugged. "It was the best we could do on short notice." She leaned in and gave Jessica a hug, but then whispered in her ear. "And I hear that I'm going to have that brother or sister that I've always wanted."

"Who told you?"

"It finally hit me in a lightbulb moment, but I badgered Aunt Myra into confirming my suspicions."

"So how do you feel about it?"

"I'm absolutely thrilled. I couldn't be happier," Madison announced. "Although I must add that it's taken Santa a long time to deliver. I asked just about every year to bring me a baby brother or sister."

Jessica shook her head. "You did?"

"Yeah. Guess I was always on the naughty list."

"No doubt!" Jessica laughed, and then linked her arm through Madison's and stepped back to look at Ty. "While my life hasn't always gone exactly as I would have planned, every bump in the road has led me to right here and now. But one thing I know for sure." She paused to hug her daughter closer and smile up at Ty. "I wouldn't change a thing."

Read on for a sneak peek at the next book in LuAnn McLane's "delightful"* Cricket Creek series. Available in September 2012 from Signet Eclipse.

*Romantic Times, 4½ stars

"OH NO, NOT NOW!" MIA SCOWLED AT THE RED CHECK-engine light and gripped the steering wheel tighter. "Come on. I filled you with premium gas, you old clunker. What more do you want from me?" she grumbled, but when the light flickered and then went out, she managed a slight smile. "That's more like it." She patted the battered dashboard, making the miniature hula dancer swing her ample hips. "Okay, I take the 'old clunker' part back," Mia added in a soothing tone, and then settled back against the seat.

Having been an only child raised by a long string of un-interested au pairs, Mia Monroe was no stranger to talking to herself or to inanimate objects. Since she had often been left alone to entertain herself, Mia's possessions became treasured friends and admittedly were probably one of the reasons that as an adult she had become a shopaholic. "Dad just doesn't understand." She sighed and glanced over at her shiny black Prada purse that appeared ridiculously out of place perched on the worn cloth seat, which must have been red at one time but had faded to a dusty rose. The lack of credit cards inside her matching wallet made her shiver even though the battered Camry's air conditioner had failed her two states ago. Soon she might actually break a sweat. "Shopping is my therapy," she explained with a defensive pout, but the words sounded a bit hollow and she frowned. "Nothing wrong with that, right?" she added without as much conviction.

Mia flipped her long platinum blond hair over her shoulder, only to have the warm wind from the open window blow it right back across her face, momentarily blocking her view of the road. She swerved into the right lane, drawing the deep, angry honk of a massive truck.

"Sorry!" Mia winced as she jerked the car back into her own lane. The hula dancer's hips wiggled like crazy and Mia giggled in spite of her dire circumstances. She decided that when she purchased a new car, the happy hula chickie was coming with her. Oh and she would purchase a brand-new car with her very own hard-earned money. "And I'll pull up that circular drive and park it right at my father's front door!" she announced to the hula dancer, who bobbed her head as if in disagreement. "Oh, don't go shaking that head of yours. I will do it if it's the last thing I ever do!" Of course Mia didn't have anything ironed out—like where she would live or a really super job or anything of that nature. Minor details, she thought with a small shrug, but then frowned when she recalled her last conversation with her dad. "'You'll be back by the end of the summer,'" Mia mocked in her father's deep tone of voice. "Labor Day," he had added. "Something you've never had to do."

"Ha!" Mia said and smacked the steering wheel hard enough to make her hand smart. "I have . . . skills! And just who does he think is going to plan his lavish parties at the house? Huh? Entertain his clients?" She flipped one hand in the air and swerved again. "And just who will find impossible-to-get Cubs and Bulls tickets to seal the deal?" She tossed her hair again, only to have it fly back across her face once more. She gave it an impatient swipe, but several strands clung to her lip gloss. "I was his personal assistant and did it for free!" she grumbled. "He'll never be able to replace me. I have connections all over Chicago." She glanced at the hula dancer. "So what if I ran up a few credit cards? Bought a few things here and there and well . . . everywhere? I'm helping the economy, right? It's my civic duty or whatever that's called." She waved her French-tipped fingers back and forth and the sunshine glinted off her diamond tennis bracelet.

When the hula dancer stared back at her with accusing brown eyes, Mia sighed. "O-kaaaay, so I abused the credit cards a tiny bit. Traveled a little too much in the company jet." She lifted one slim shoulder. "But that jab about me never having had a real job was uncalled for. And my fine arts degree is not worthless! I worked hard for my father. He just didn't appreciate my efforts." She pressed her lips together in an effort not to cry. "I should have been on the official payroll!" she sputtered, but it wasn't the tired old argument about her working that had driven Mia away from her home and out into the cold, cruel world without credit cards or her baby blue Mercedes coupe. It was overhearing her father negotiating a ruthless business deal that had turned her blood cold. When Mia called him out on the hostile takeover of Hanover Candy, a family-owned Chicago-based company, she had been furious. She had grown up and gone to school with Hailey Hanover and couldn't imagine that her father would take advantage of tough times for the locally owned company, which made various flavors of hard-candy sticks that Mia often got to sample before the general public. She had suggested and was responsible for tasty flavors like cotton candy and cherry cheesecake. How could he go after her friends?

When her father had calmly explained that deals like these had paid for Mia's lavish lifestyle, she hotly declared that she no longer wanted his money and would fend for herself from this day forward!

There was only one problem. She didn't exactly have a plan in place when she stuffed her Louis Vuitton suitcase full of random clothes and stormed out of her father's estate. "Oh well, this will be an adventure!" she declared with much more moxie than she was actually feeling. She was suddenly a little light-headed. "Low blood sugar," she mumbled, refusing to believe it was nerves. She decided to find a nice restaurant to eat a little lunch, perhaps a Cobb salad or, then again, a panini would do nicely.

"Okay," Mia said firmly, but then sighed. So here she was in . . . Where was she again? Oh yeah, in Kentucky driving down the interstate in an old Toyota Camry that she had bought off of Manny Perez, their gardener. When Mia had offered to purchase Manny's car, he had rattled off something in Spanish about gas and oil while shaking his head and making hand gestures, little of which Mia had understood. But Mia's polite insistence and a cool thousand bucks had sealed the deal. One of the many things she had learned from her father was that money talks, and when all else fails, use leverage. So she had flashed cash and a pretty-please smile at Manny and he had handed over the battered vehicle without further protest.

When Mia's stomach grumbled she looked at the passing signs for something to capture the interest of her taste buds. She wasn't very familiar with fast food but Cracker Barrel sounded interesting. Mia had seen plenty of signs for the rustic restaurants along her aimless journey and there was the added enticement of shopping right there in the establishment. "Someone sure was thinking!" she said and was about to pull off at the next exit when she noticed a billboard advertising the Cricket Creek Cougars baseball stadium located five miles down the road.

"Hmmm . . . Why does that sound familiar?" Mia tapped

her cheek, then suddenly remembered that her father had attended opening day last summer. She also thought he might have some other business connection in Cricket Creek, but she couldn't put her finger on it. She didn't always pay close attention when her father rambled on about his business dealings, but she knew that he had also traveled to Cricket Creek quite a few times over the past few months. She did recall that he had mentioned that the head chef from Chicago Blue Bistro had moved there to run a restaurant and that the food was excellent.

"Aha!" Mia smiled when she spotted a billboard for Wine and Diner. "I do believe that was the very cute and clever name." She nodded slowly and then mustered up another smile. "Well, Wine and Diner, here I come!" When her stomach rumbled in anticipation she pressed on the gas pedal, but her smile faded when the car gave a funny little lurch and the check-engine light flickered and then came back on. "Oh no, you don't!" she pleaded, but this time the red light stubbornly remained lit. Luckily the Cricket Creek exit was only a mile down the road.

Mia eased her chunky sandal from the gas pedal and gingerly steered off the exit. She spotted the sign pointing to several restaurants and turned left toward town. "How quaint!" she said as the Camry chugged down Main Street. Colorful mid-May flowers spilled over the tops of large terracotta planters lining the sidewalk. An old-fashioned bakery named Grammars caught her eye, along with several antiques shops. When she spotted a vintage-clothing store with a sale rack out front, her shopping addiction kicked into high gear, but she lifted her chin in steely determination and kept on driving.

When Mia stopped for a red light, she watched people meander down the sidewalk and wander in and out of the shops. The town had a warm, welcoming feel to it and the chatter of shoppers sounded cheerful. Mia was used to the hustle and bustle of Chicago, and while she loved the energy of a big city, this slower pace had an instant calming effect on her frazzled nerves. After she inhaled deeply, the sweet scent of spring filled her head, making her sigh with pleasure.

Laughter brought Mia's attention to her open window and she smiled softly when she spotted children playing in the city park. Young mothers watched over the frolic and fun, bringing a pang of sadness to Mia's chest. When her father's first business had failed, Mia's mother left Mitch Monroe for a man with more wealth. Heartbroken, he had sued for full custody of Mia and had won, but his obsession with financial success kept him from spending much time with his two-year-old daughter—and thus began Mia's long string of au pairs. Just when she would become emotionally bonded to her caregiver, they would move on, leaving Mia feeling sad and making it much safer to find happiness in material things rather than people.

As an adult and no stranger to therapy, Mia realized that her father's intense drive to succeed was a direct result of his wife's desertion. But that didn't change the fact that Mia had been a lonely little girl longing for her father's attention and her mother's acceptance.

Oh, Mia had visited her mother but had always felt like an outsider in her mother's new life. Over the years her visits had become few and far between and sadly she believed that her mother had been mostly relieved.

A honking horn startled Mia out of her musing. "Oh, just hush!" she grumbled as she eased the car forward, but her mood lightened when she spotted Wine and Diner on the corner. The brick building with the cute red awning looked inviting, but it was the aroma of grilled food wafting through her open window that had her hurrying to locate a spot in the parking lot. "Well!" Mia had to circle twice before sliding into a vacant space, indicating that Wine and Diner was a popular place to eat. "Finally!"

After she turned the key, the engine coughed and sputtered as if in distress or, perhaps, relief. "Oh, please start when I get finished eating," Mia pleaded and gave the dash a quick pat. The door opened with a tired-sounding squeak and she gently closed it before hurrying toward the entrance of the restaurant.

# Also available in the Cricket Creek series

# LuAnn McLane

## *Playing for Keeps*

Olivia Lawson is peeved when ex-ace pitcher turned soap opera star Noah Falcon roars back into Cricket Creek, Kentucky, after all these years, to take the lead opposite her in the community theater's summer play. Noah's beloved hometown is having major financial woes and needs his status to turn this small-town play into a big-time hit. But Noah has bigger plans for this small town. And this time he's determined to show Olivia he's not just playing around—he's playing for keeps.

**Available wherever books are sold or at penguin.com**

# Also available from
# LuAnn McLane

## *He's No Prince Charming*

At sixteen, Dakota Dunn was America's Pop Princess. Now twenty-five, she's all grown up—and definitely feeling washed up. She decides to head to her family's lakefront retreat in Tennessee, planning to write songs and transform her image from squeaky clean to kickin' country.

Turns out there's a new manager at the marina, a sexy, if cranky, cowboy named Trace Coleman—a former bull riding champion benched by injuries. He's none too happy about Dakota's arrival—and makes no secret of it. But though Trace is rough around the edges, Dakota feels a pull of attraction she can't quite shake. For all his brooding, Trace has an animal magnetism that may just lead Dakota to dig in her heels and hold on tight...

**Available wherever books are sold or at penguin.com**

# LuAnn McLane

writes
"endearing and sexy romances that
sparkle with Southern charm."
—*New York Times* bestselling author
Julia London

## *Redneck Cinderella*

Raised by her widowed father, Jolie Russell could keep up
with any man—that is, until wealthy and sexy land
developer Cody Dean struts into her life.

Cody buys the Russell farm with an impossible-to-refuse
multimillion-dollar offer, then relocates Jolie and her dad
to the Copper Creek Estates. But the country club
atmosphere isn't ready for Jolie's kind of country. As
her two worlds collide, Jolie wonders how she can ever
hope to capture Cody's heart without giving up her grits.

**Available wherever books are sold or at
penguin.com**

## Penguin Group (USA) Online

### *What will you be reading tomorrow?*

Tom Clancy, Patricia Cornwell, W.E.B. Griffin,
Nora Roberts, William Gibson, Catherine Coulter,
Stephen King, Dean Koontz, Ken Follett, Nick Hornby,
Khaled Hosseini, Kathryn Stockett, Clive Cussler,
John Sandford, Terry McMillan, Sue Monk Kidd,
Amy Tan, J. R. Ward, Laurell K. Hamilton,
Charlaine Harris, Christine Feehan...

You'll find them all at
**penguin.com**
**facebook.com/PenguinGroupUSA**
**twitter.com/PenguinUSA**

*Read excerpts and newsletters, find tour schedules
and reading group guides, and enter contests.*

Subscribe to Penguin Group (USA) newsletters
and get an exclusive inside look
at exciting new titles and the authors you love
long before everyone else does.

## PENGUIN GROUP (USA)
us.penguingroup.com

S0151